THE FIRST TENET

Also by Mario Molinari:

SNAP

Acclaim for ***Snap***

"Snap is an exciting sci-fi thriller full of action."

—Cat Jones, TOP 500 Reviewer

Amazon.com 5/5 stars

"Engaging and fast paced!"

—Brenda McCreight, Author

"The pacing is fast and the action is high, so it's easy to just get swept along with the fun."

—Kris James, Red Adept Reviews

Coming soon by Mario Molinari:

THE FINAL TENET

Launch - Spring 2015

TO CATCH CARL

Launch - Christmas 2015

TANGENT

Launch - TBD

Lightning Source Inc.
Ingram Content Group Company
1246 Heil Quaker Blvd.
La Vergne, TN USA 37086

ISBN 978-0-9867002-3-1

All of the characters, events and locales in this book are fictitious, and a product of the author's imagination. Any resemblance to actual persons, living or dead, is purely coincidental.

Printed in the United States of America

ACKNOWLEDGMENTS

Mark Lavorato, author and poet, for starting me in the right direction with *The First Tenet.*

Lynn McNamee, owner Red Adept Publishing, for her services, support and encouragement. And to her wonderful editing staff, especially Misty Wolanski.

Max Losk, Graphic Artist, MLNY, New York, NY. For incredible cover and jacket design—again.

"D.G." retired security intelligence agent. For expert consultation on the book and long-term friendship.

Lindsey Molinari, D.I.L. and avid reader, for priceless advice on this book and for marrying our son.

For Linda.

The breath in that allows
me the breath out.

THE FIRST
TENET

A novel

MARIO
MOLINARI

tenet: a religious doctrine that is proclaimed as true without proof.

—thefreedictionary.com

1

Friday Night

"A man walks into a bar," Adam said softly, his finger tapping the steering wheel. "Damn. No turning back now."

He sighed then pulled his smart phone out of his jacket pocket. He clicked a shortcut icon on the screen that opened a folder on the cloud. He opened a photo file named *family*. He looked at the photo of his wife and children that had been merged to his memory. Their smiles, squinting eyes and two-week tans brought him back to that day on the beach in Greece. He could almost smell the sea and hear the children giggling.

He hesitated, closed the file then deleted the link and wiped his history. Adam slid the phone back into his pocket. *Will today help dull the grief, the pain?* Maybe not, but one thing was certain: the arduous wait for the perfect time was over. Everything was in line.

Adam closed his eyes, slowed his breathing, and focused on the sporadic rhythm of the light rain beading off his grey BMW. Time seemed to pause briefly. His placid thoughts abruptly slipped to the day his family was slaughtered. It had rained that day, as well.

He quickly shook the scarring image from his mind and opened his eyes, heart fluttering. The sun appeared, sneaking through cracks in the gravel grey clouds while the rain persisted.

He focused on the blue neon Roxy's Bar sign as he sat parked in front of the establishment in New Hyde Park.

He clenched the steering wheel hard with both hands. *Focus. Don't let those feelings distract you. There is still much work to be done.* Those first seven days would be crucial to his success.

Adam turned his wipers on then off, and he looked at his watch for the third time in the past two minutes. He pulled a tissue from his console and dabbed his brow.

It was finally five forty-five p.m. His heart raced.

Adam got out of his car and strolled through the light drizzle up to the castle-style wooden front doors of Roxy's. As he walked, his legs felt weak with the anticipation that everything would go off perfectly.

He grabbed the door handle and read the posted sign. *'Roxy's will be closed for major renovations Sat. to Mon. Re-opening Tuesday. Thanks for your patronage.'*

"Good thing I chose Friday. And happy hour—they're going to need a few extra shots."

He chuckled nervously, took a deep breath, and entered the bar.

Paraphernalia from various decades adorned the walls: movie posters, celebrity photos, sports memorabilia, and odd antiques like dentist tools and first-generation brick-sized cell phones. An eclectic collection, representing a snapshot of what the world had been up to that point.

Patrons displayed the local mix of genders, classes, and ethnicity in the New York City commuter town of New Hyde Park: blue-collar, white-collar, and pink-collar workers, even some middle-aged housewives winding down from an afternoon of boredom shopping. *All perfect targets.*

There was a short lull in the music between songs, and a few people looked at him as he crossed the empty dance floor. Adam smiled and nodded. His brother, dressed in a short-sleeved mechanics shirt and with an aqua blue dove tattooed on his forearm, winked at him. Adam winked back.

Adam stepped up onto the unlit stage and stared out at Roxy's Friday night patrons. The years of waiting and meticulous preparing made him want to slow down, to relish every second, to absorb the intense feeling.

He took a big breath and stood calmly as more people began to notice him on the stage in his casual Friday clothes. Black slacks, blue denim shirt with button-down collar, and a black golf jacket with a discreet Conestry Technology logo. His tidy, collar-length hair was a subtle blend of black and silver-grey, the kind that made some women feel old but made men look distinguished.

Adam wondered if the plan would work. *Will everyone here do their parts, as planned and paid for?* He rubbed his five-o'clock stubble with one hand.

He smiled and discreetly nodded to the bar owner, Darnell Williams.

Darnell returned the nod then dashed over to Adam. "Excuse me, can I help you? Open mic is Sundays." He smiled.

"I'm Adam Johl, could you please turn the music down?" he shouted.

Customers sitting at tables surrounding the dance floor continued to chat, keeping curious eyes on the stage. Adam heard a glass break behind the bar, followed by a few people clapping.

Darnell put his hands on his hips. "The music *down*? Why?"

"I need to everyone to hear me." He indicated the crowd.

"Hear what? Selling something? If you are, this isn't the way to go about it, bud."

"I guess you could say I'm selling something."

Darnell nodded. "Let's talk about it. Come down, please. We have a local community paper you could buy an ad in to reach my customers. They're mostly locals in here."

"I'm not coming down until I've done what I came here to do."

More people were making eye contact with Adam, obviously tuning in to the exchange.

"Okay, I've been patient enough. Please come down from there. If you want to speak to my customers, buy a radio ad," Darnell said, loud enough for most to hear.

"This'll have much more impact than radio. Trust me."

The crowd hushed.

"You leave me no option. I'm going to force you down from there."

Adam raised his right hand and motioned as if turning a knob. The music lowered in perfect synchronization with his movement.

Darnell stood still, blinking as if he was trying to process what just happened. The patrons looked over at the DJ booth. No one manned the controls. Most probably thought it was just the song ending.

"No, that was me," Adam said calmly, then bellowed, "Now, can I please have everyone's attention?"

Darnell made a motion to jump up onto the stage but stopped instantly when Adam raised his hand, palm out.

The thirty-year-old, six-foot-two owner of Roxy's went completely silent and stood frozen, like a silver-painted busker.

That definitely piqued the viewers' interest. Adam noticed a few people trying to use their phones to capture the action on video. Their expressions of confusion were good. That probably meant his jammer was working and their phones and cameras weren't.

All the lights in the establishment went off and on. *Once... Twice...*

After the third time they went off, only one light came back on: a vibrant lime-green spotlight, centered on Adam. The color made him think of the three thousand-year-old emerald tablet—the extremely rare and holy artifact that had funded his whole plan. He smiled again. *This is really happening.*

The crowd noise settled down to a curious murmur. A man in his twenties came running out of the back room, followed by a waitress tucking in her blouse. He made his way across the dance floor, where he witnessed Darnell standing still like a mime. "Hey, boss, what the hell is going on here? *Darnell*? You all right, man?"

Darnell didn't reply or move. His eyes were glazed over, and he stared into space.

The man shook Darnell by the shoulders; he didn't respond. The man turned to Adam. "What'd you do to him?"

"I have a message," Adam said clearly.

"I'm the assistant manager, and I'm asking you to leave. Now!"

Adam looked at the man's name badge. "Well, Assistant Manager Todd. I'll be out of here shortly, so I'll kindly ask you to give me a few minutes. It would be much appreciated."

"On with it, so we can finish our pints," an elderly man blurted. "Go on, sell us your promotion... You have our attention—and it better be damn good."

Todd, with his mouth open, stood at Darnell's side while trying to keep an eye on Adam. He poked Darnell then pinched him. He looked back at the bartender for some kind of direction. The bartender shrugged.

Many people returned to their conversations and drinks.

"I have a message from God." Adam's words resonated as if he were speaking through a multi-channel surround-sound theatre system, with a vibration that lingered.

Everyone fell silent; the only sound was the hum from the ventilation fan.

Then a few younger construction workers swilled their beers and laughed. The laughter cut the tension and spread through the entire crowd like an intoxicating virus.

Adam raised his right arm, palm up. With that single motion, the doors locked, and all the dark mahogany Venetian blinds snapped shut.

Small trickles of daylight streamed around the edges of the blinds; otherwise the room was dark, with the exception of the green glow on Adam, the master of ceremonies, centered on the small stage.

The laughter halted. The ventilation fan tinkled faintly as it hummed.

"Good. I have your attention." Adam lowered his arm. "Please, listen very carefully and take this with the utmost seriousness. Let there be no doubt, this is a message from God. After I deliver it, I will be on my way." He rubbed his sweaty palms on his pants.

Adam could see the crowd fidgeting, stirring. Some were probably thinking of Columbine, Jonestown, Aurora, and other fanatic scenarios. Rightfully so, Adam thought. New Yorkers had a right to be paranoid after 9/11. He wondered when someone would try to be the hero and attack him on the stage.

He noticed a pretty woman he recognized, sitting at a table with two men wearing KCOD TV jackets, take out what looked like a voice recorder and slide it across the table, closer to him. A little red light went on.

"Samantha Cott? Reporter for KCOD, right?" he asked. "Wanna great story?"

She nodded slowly. "Sam, I am," she said, then calmly took a sip of her wine. "Always looking for the scoop."

Her soft tone seemed to be trying to calm the situation. Maybe intentionally. That was good.

"What the hell's the message already?" a man slurred.

Adam had studied bios and pictures of all the regulars. Darnell had supplied him with security videotape and as much detail as he personally knew on his customers, and Adam had used his own computer skills to dig up as much as he could on top of that, so his act would be convincing. "Marty Graham, car salesman. You really should go easy on the drinking—and watch your language. You spend too much time here. Your lovely wife, Tina, and two children really need you. Sober."

Marty, expression stunned, shouted back, "You know her? Sorry about that." Then he took a wholesale gulp of his Jack Daniels and Coke while many people laughed.

His brother, in character, got up and made for the door. Two girls who had been sitting at the bar with him followed. "This is bullshit, asshole! You're spoilin' good food and a good time. Let's go, girls."

"Mr. Nat Fossano—or should I call you by your nickname, Dove? Like the bird tattoo on your forearm. And the large one on your back."

Dove looked at his arm and rubbed the tattoo.

"And what a foul mouth, and in front of women." Adam made a circular motion above his head with his hand.

Dove stopped in the middle of the crowd, halfway to the door, and placed his hands over his mouth. He slowly turned around and faced the crowd. He opened his mouth wide, and dozens of bees escaped into the darkened room.

Those who witnessed it screamed and dropped to take cover under their tables. People at the back of the room asked, "What happened?"

"Bees!" yelled the two girls that followed him. "Oh my God!"

"What the hell is going on here!" someone else bellowed.

Dove dropped to his knees, holding his face and shaking his head. "Damn! One bit me!"

Patrons fled in all directions from where they each thought the bees were, questioning each other on what they had seen and heard so far.

Darnell snapped out of his frozen state and went behind the bar to calm down the staff.

Adam continued, "Each and every one of the one hundred seventy-seven people in this establishment today has a distinct responsibility to *save the world*. You have been given the task of convincing the people, politicians, and entire countries that they need to repent and truly accept God into their hearts. To do whatever it takes to make this happen around the globe." He rubbed his hands on his pants again.

"Who are you?" Sam shouted, holding up the recorder. "And what exactly are you talking about? This has to be some kind of joke or hype for a movie."

"How do you know how many people are here?" someone else piped up.

"Cheap tricks! A big joke! Where's the cameras? We're on one of those TV hoax shows."

"You should be locked up! There is no God!" someone yelled from the back while someone else threw a coaster at Adam. "Bible-thumper!"

"We sure have our work cut out for us. I'm Adam Johl, and I am talking about our one last chance before it ends."

"Before what ends? Your magic act? Get the hell out of here!"

The crowd became loud, congregating in larger groups, milling about. Someone would soon try to get him out of there.

Adam scanned the crowd in an authoritative manner and slowly said resonating words that again rocked the crowd and rattled anything that wasn't fastened down: "*The world.*"

2

After his profound statement that the world would end, Adam expected skepticism, and that's what he got.

After a few chuckles and more concerned murmuring, one of the patrons spoke up. "Come on. You've had your fun. You've really entertained us. Now tell us what you're selling so we can get on with our drinks. The media's already been hyping the latest end-of-world movie like it's the Super Bowl! Besides, it's Friday night. We're here to chill, not be sold some shit! It's like sitting through fifteen minutes of trailers!"

"Yeah!"

"Nice try!"

"Lame!"

A few more people clapped, and on schedule, Mark Little yelled, "Get on with it, or get out!"

"That's my point, Mark. You only have seven days before the end. So if you would like to get on with those last seven days and choose to ignore God, so be the fate of mankind."

"How do you know my name?" Little asked, sitting on the edge of his seat. "How do you know anyone's names?"

"I'm here for a last-minute plea bargain. The date everyone has been wondering about for thousands of years is next Friday, at seven p.m. That is when the world as you know it will end."

"Really? I mean, come on. You have to be a little more convincing than that 'The world's going to end, blah blah blah.' I'm going to call for a nice padded wagon to come pick you up." Little stood up then pulled out his cell phone.

"Detective Mark Little, help is not coming. Put your phones away. They won't work."

Sam tried to text, but Adam knew nobody in the building would get a signal. People quickly tried their devices, holding them up over their heads and waving like they were swatting for flies in search of a connection.

Little went for his sidearm and drew his weapon. "Okay! Show's over, Mr. Johl. Come down slowly and keep your hands where I can see them!"

People gasped.

"No." Adam crossed his arms. "I have no weapons and will harm no one here."

"No? We can do this two ways, willingly or—"

"Willingly. That's what I'm trying to do here, Detective Little. You and everyone else here—I need your free will. Now put your gun down, take a seat, and listen. It'll all be over in a few minutes." Adam raised and lowered his arm in a powerful gesture.

On that cue, Little's arm trembled as he slowly lowered his gun and holstered it. His body shook, and he fell back into the chair, shaking his head—a convincing performance, Adam was happy to see.

The crowd went silent but for a few more gasps.

One man went for the detective's gun, but Little had a vise grip on the weapon. The man slowly went back to his chair. Adam approached Little, easily took the gun from his hand, pointed it at the ceiling, and fired. People screamed, a few cried.

"It's dangerous." Adam ejected the magazine, put it in his pocket, and placed the unloaded gun on the table next to Little. "Now it's not. And I'm not. Please trust me for just a few more minutes. Then Roxy's will buy everyone some free drinks."

"I think we just need to hear this guy out. He's not going to hurt anyone. I'm sure it will be over soon, folks," Little tried reassuring the crowd. "It's just some kind of innocent prank, don't worry! I'll arrest him outside; I promise!"

"You're a cop! Do something now!" someone yelled.

"He's a twisted Bible-thumper!" Dove yelled. "Don't worry. I'll kick his ass in a minute, after I finish my beer."

"Hell, this guy is harmless! He gave me my gun back," Little said, reholstering his gun. "Carry on, Johl. I'll let you finish your little show! Make it fast! And there will be a charge for firing my gun."

Adam eyed the crowd. Were they buying into his message? *No, not yet.*

"We need proof!" the boldest of three housewives sitting in the corner yelled.

"You need proof, Claire, and God needs faith," Adam responded.

Claire's eyes widened. "Give us real proof, and you'll have real faith."

"You have a great soul, Claire Nadeau. What kind of proof would you like?"

"Why don't you fly or disappear or something," Dove piped up. "Give us our money's worth."

"You're quite the mouthpiece, Dove," Adam said, pacing slowly on the stage. "Thought the bees got your tongue."

"Yeah maybe, but shouldn't God be able to make you fly? Walk on water? Permanently disappear?"

"Yeah, fly the hell out of here!" someone shouted.

A few people broke out in light laughter, but most had had enough of the charade. Several people stormed the exits and front doors, pounding on them. A woman cried on a man's shoulder. It was like everyone was waiting for a hero to put a stop to this.

"Here it is. If you can't fly, me and a hundred and seventy-something people are going to rush the stage and beat the shit out of you, no matter what the cop says. Enough's enough! You're going to be a dead Bible-thumper," Dove declared.

People clapped and cheered. A few men stood up in preparation, and those pounding on the exit doors stopped, turned, and took a few steps in the direction of the stage.

Adam looked around the darkened room. "Fly it is."

The crowd went silent in anticipation.

Adam closed his eyes and raised his arms to shoulder height, then levitated about two feet off of the stage.

Claire gasped, spitting out a bit of her drink. "Damn! Will you look at that!"

Adam floated forward in seamless, fluid motion, and gently alighted onto the dance floor.

The people who were close to the exit doors tried again to evacuate.

"Where are the wires?" Sam shouted above the other voices.

"My kid could do that!" someone shouted. "Seen it a million times in Vegas!"

"Sit down, please. I'm not done," Adam said, grinned, then raised both of his arms with his fingers spread out and his palms facing upward. All the chairs in the establishment—even the empty ones—rose about six inches off the floor and wobbled slightly as they hovered in midair. People's feet hung just above the wood floor. Men and women waved their hands above and around their heads in search of wires. The hysteria continued through the crowd as everyone's chairs suddenly dropped to the ground just as quickly as they'd risen.

"I ask you... Where are *your* wires?" Adam made a circular motion above his head, and a violent, noisy wind stirred up everything lighter than a glass and spun it around the room. People guarded their faces as straws, napkins, hats, and fruit garnishes took flight. All the debris collected in a mini tornado funnel and made its way to the dance floor, toward Adam.

He snapped his fingers, and the debris floated up and disappeared through a camouflaged hole in the ceiling.

The room settled down slightly, and Adam spoke up again. "As I was saying, you have seven days in which to change the world!"

Darnell came out from behind the bar and charged Adam. Adam raised his hand to indicate *Halt!* Darnell stopped, fell backward, and hit the floor. Adam shook his head. He hoped Darnell would get the hint and stop 'helping.' His charging the stage was not scripted. Dove charged the stage, stopped, and fell backward. That was scripted and believable.

The patrons looked at each other, puzzled and frightened. No one else made a move to attack Adam.

"Stay calm, everyone, please!" Little shouted, raising his badge in his hand. "I've got things under control here!"

Adam witnessed a few people rolling their eyes.

Darnell sat where he'd fallen, shaking his head. "What the fuck is going on? Change the world... how?" were the first words spoken by the bar manager since he'd first tried to get Adam off the stage.

Dove got up and sat in a chair.

"Finally. A great question, Mr. Darnell. Although we could do without the profanity."

The room quieted, some patrons sitting at the edge of their seats, others standing up and pushing their chairs aside as if they were contaminated.

He heard a woman sobbing, calling out for help.

"Your answer is twofold. First, you must convince the world to have faith in the fact that God really did speak through me here today. Then, you must use that faith to influence the seven billion people on this planet to completely change their ways."

"Who're you kidding? Change the world? We can't even get the city to agree on a recycling program, forget the world!"

Adam said, "Let me help you understand—"

"It's about time!" someone from the back of the room yelled.

A waitress cried softly as she hugged the bartender.

Someone could be heard pounding on an exit door in the kitchen.

Adam felt that he was in control, that it was *working*. His palms were dry; his breathing had slowed to normal again. The crowd knew he wasn't there to hurt anyone. He hoped he wouldn't have any unscripted trouble from them. "This was tried before, a few thousand years ago. But God has decided to give mankind another chance. That second chance has come and gone, the deadline was today, and now we've been given the final seven-day warning. Only one hundred sixty-eight hours to prove the Son of God, Jesus, didn't die in vain and that mankind can fully repent and is worthy to be saved."

Marty, the salesman, jumped in again. He seemed to have sobered up to the dire situation. "Seriously, how are we going to convince seven billion people. Seven *billion*?"

"You are my witnesses. Good people. One hundred seventy-seven people from all walks of life, races, and ages, who through a chance meeting in a public house have all been witness to some miracles to make you believe. You have CNN, Internet, newspapers... *60 Minutes*. Look on the bright side—if you fail, God has actually chosen millions that are pure of heart to carry on. Maybe you're one of them?"

"Listen, that entire crowd floating, bees, wind, and other parlor tricks were great, real good stuff, but not enough to convince the world," Sam said. "Why don't you just show up at the World Cup or Super Bowl and float the whole crowd? Then you've got something, and the whole world will buy in to a miracle on live television in seconds."

"He"—Adam pointed upward—"is making it much tougher on us this time. He knows it would be too easy to part the Red Sea again and broadcast it. People would be forced to change out of fear and not change of their own free wills. Evil would just hibernate. It's all about faith now. Does the world have enough without definitive proof?"

"No one knows when the world will end. It says so in the Bible!" Claire shouted. "Only God knows of the day and hour!"

"Exactly, Claire," Adam said, pointing at her. "And He's speaking through me right now, telling you it will all end in a week."

"Show us something substantial that it will end!" Little said. "We've all had enough—and your time is up!"

"Fine. With the help of modern technology, why don't we just check it out? Let's see what'll be on the tube, a week from now."

All twelve seventy-inch plasma TVs that were suspended from the ceiling came alive to a haze of gray static. Slowly the picture of a major network news broadcast came into focus. The time and date were stamped on the left side of the screen, along with the weather and miscellaneous scrolling news headlines. It was May 9th, 7:07 p.m.—one week from the current day. Paul Mansfield, a well-known and trusted network anchor, spoke.

Sam's face went pale. "Damn... I work with him."

Mansfield's distinctive deep voice slowly crackled into clarity. "I'm sorry about that brief interruption to our broadcast, but we will continue to broadcast from our makeshift bunker for as long as possible and as long as our generators hold out." He shuffled some papers on his desk, then continued. "After one week of mounting catastrophes around the globe, it would seem to many believers that the Adam Johl Prophecy delivered at Roxy's has commenced this evening as predicted. At precisely seven p.m., major earthquakes hit large cities around the world, including New York, Los Angeles, London, Beijing, Toronto, and many other smaller cities, after the tremors that have been building all week. These unbelievable catastrophic events were triggered by a massive slipping of the tectonic plates around the world. Experts are saying it could be the result of the polarity shift that had been moving from twenty to forty kilometers per year, shifting from Canada toward Siberia.

Damage is estimated in the trillions, and loss of life, catastrophic. Explosions, fires, and pandemonium have broken out everywhere, sparking martial law in some countries. Nuclear power plants around the globe are at risk of meltdown."

Pictures of burning buildings filled the screen, sirens blaring, people screaming. "Oh, sorry, this just in." Mansfield held his earpiece, then continued. "Major tsunamis have been picked up from ocean monitors off the coasts of New York, Florida, Western Europe, South Africa, Australia, and practically everywhere there is ocean water." Satellite images filled the screen. "*God help us all.*"

The TV screen crackled to grey static and faded to black. All twelve TVs had whisps of smoke trailing from the back of them, followed by a few static pops and snaps, as if they were electronically fried.

The crowds' eyes were glazed over—some with tears—and mouths hung open like dumbstruck school kids'.

"Wonder how they'll follow that lead story?" Adam asked with a somber smile. He surveyed the room with his head tilted down and intense eyes. "Next, social meltdown, war, nukes... I think you get the picture."

Some of the confused patrons got up from their chairs and looked around, as if seeking someone to take action. A few tried the doors again, which remained as if nailed shut.

"Please sit down. I'll let you all out in a minute. I promise no one in this room will be hurt."

"What is it, exactly, that we need to accomplish to save the world?" Sam challenged.

"It's straightforward, Samantha. He wants everyone to be good. Do good. No more war. No more hate." Adam paused. "He wants people to open their eyes and respect this beautiful gift of a planet He endowed to us, to really love and respect one another. And He will know when and if this happens."

Some people trembled as they shook their heads in disbelief.

"Stay tuned. All will be revealed soon," Adam said.

"Time to start over with Adam and Eve," someone piped up. "Hide the apple tree this time. Kill the snake!"

"I sense your skepticism and lack of hope, but if you have any doubt, we've already failed," Adam preached.

"*Skepticism*? No disrespect, but are you nuts? Not only is this entire situation totally unbelievable, but it ties in too coincidently to the launch of the movie premiere. Besides, what you're asking is impossible, can't be done, even in seven *years*," Sam said.

Adam clasped his hands in front of him. "You can put a man on the moon; you can make a computer chip the size of a pea that holds as much knowledge as all humans have combined. I'm sure these things seemed impossible, too."

"In seven days and to seven billion—who's gonna believe us? I'd need a government-sized promotional budget, an army of lobbyists, and Super Bowl TV ads to sell this."

Adam looked into the confused eyes of the people in front of him. He had delivered his message and performed miracles in front of the half-inebriated patrons. *Just one last thing to do.*

He said quickly, hardly taking a breath, "Yes, Claire Nadeau, you will see Brenda, your daughter in Australia, again. You will. Soon she will come to you."

Claire looked shocked.

Adam continued, "Marty Graham, you received a job offer today, but you are unsure about the company. You did sign the offer at two p.m. and spilled coffee on your new boss's desk. You took a drink from a flask in your car before entering the bar."

Marty turned red.

"Daisy Beech, you came here to meet a man that you connected with on an online dating site. You lied about your age, and he didn't show. He's two hours late. You called your daughter, Mary, to come share a drink with you. You still love the second of your four husbands. You creeped his Facebook page last night."

The dark-skinned Daisy teared up and nodded. "I just figured out that Facebook last night..." she said in her Caribbean accent, then made the sign of the Cross.

"Nat Fossano—Dove. When you were ten, you broke your mother's favorite teacup. One handed down for three generations. She thought it was the cat."

"I never told a soul! Swear!"

"Samantha. You are wondering about your daughter. Don't worry; you're doing the best job possible. Don't feel guilty. Just spend more quality time with her." Adam smiled at her. "I'm very sorry about your husband."

Sam teared up.

"Darnell Williams keeps a picture of his first love, Shanice Johnstone, at the bottom of a baseball card box. He looks at it whenever he feels lonely. He's sorry for how he treated her." Adam took a breath.

"How do you know that—"

He continued over Darnell. "And our detective, Mark Little. So many secrets. You keep booze in your locker. Vodka. It's in a water bottle. And a bottle in the garage—bottom drawer, tool chest, behind the WD-40 can. And you've cheated on your last two wives."

Little put his head down and rubbed his forehead.

People seemed stunned by Adam's rapid-fire statements.

"I could go on about everyone in here, but I must leave, so I ask everyone to raise their glasses, and toast what will hopefully be a beautiful new world." Adam went to the table closest to him and picked up a glass of water.

A few people raised their drinks, looking around to see who would follow. Several more joined in.

Adam panned the room. His show was over, and the question to himself before he entered Roxy's—*Will today help dull the grief, the pain?*—was answered. No, it didn't.

He held his glass up in front of him, and the water turned red. "Cheers." He took a sip, threw his glass in the air, and it disappeared. He floated out above the crowd, arms spread up, and all the chairs levitated once again. A blinding white light filled the room, as if the sun was born on the dance floor. Glasses and bottles rattled; some smashed to the floor. The window blinds and light fixtures swayed. A brilliant, golden, ghostly orb flew slowly around the room, then engulfed Adam.

Adam Johl, wrapped by the orb, then rocketed toward the twenty-foot high ceiling and disappeared as everyone's chairs went crashing to the floor.

There was a rash of gasps and a few screams, then dead silence.

The establishment on Jericho Turnpike in New Hyde Park would never be just a neighborhood bar again.

The patrons sat with mouths wide open in disbelief, shaking and seeing spots.

The blinds snapped open, the doors unlocked, and the lights came back on along with the music. The song "It's the End of the World as We Know it (And I Feel Fine)," by R.E.M., continued exactly where it had left off.

"*Ohhh, dear Lord,* I need a shooter," Daisy shouted before chugging the rest of her beer.

A plump older woman lit up a cigarette, not caring that it was against the law to light up in bars, and shook her head. She inspected her glass of water then looked down at the chair legs. She lifted the chair and inspected the bottom. She shrugged then dropped the chair.

Sam thought of her daughter, and a solitary tear clung to the corner of her eye.

3

Dove strolled slowly around the bar, assessing the patrons and their emotions, wondering if they'd bought it.

A middle-aged man took a few hits from his asthma inhaler. The bartender still hugged a waitress, who constantly dabbed her tears. A number of people were on their phones. People congregated in small groups, talking in hushed voices.

A few men entered the bar.

"Hey, Darnell!" Dove shouted. "I think we should lock the doors until we figure out what we're doing here. If everyone's okay with that?"

No one objected.

Dove watched Darnell usher the new customers out of the bar and lock the doors.

A slightly shaky and timid voice piped up from the back of the room. "Let's do it!" Daisy said. "I'll do it!"

"You?" Dove asked.

"Yes, me. Daisy Beech. I'm seventy-nine, and I'm not afraid to get out there and spread the good Lord's message!" She looked at her daughter, who still sat, shaking her head.

"Mom, please sit down."

"Hush, Mary! I know what I'm doing!" Daisy insisted as she walked toward Dove.

The crowd stared at Daisy, who walked with a slight limp.

"I think you are doing a great job organizing the troops here, too," Daisy said, smiling. She touched Dove's arm, then quickly pulled away as if it had bit her. She looked into his eyes and slowly backed away. Goose bumps were visible on her bare arms.

"What's wrong, mother—I've seen that look before," Mary asked.

"Spread the Lord's message? Are you kidding me? I can see this magic shit any day. Blaine, Angel, Cosentino. It's all been done! This guy's a certified nutjob," a man in a crisp blue suit said as he stood with feet pointed to the door. "He has some kind of twisted motive. I don't even believe in God or any of that bullshit."

"How did he fabricate the TV thing? That looked awfully real," Darnell said, doing his part in helping to get people to believe.

"Do you believe everything you see on TV? On YouTube?" the man in the suit replied. "Come on. This was nothing more than a very good magic act."

"This wasn't on YouTube! This was in our face, and it seemed damn real to me!" a woman blurted.

"Me, too," a few people said.

People started to shout over each other. The room filled with confusion.

"Hold on!" Little shouted twice.

The crowd noise eased up.

"We need a moderator, a leader, just to stay organized here so we don't rip each other's heads off. Any volunteers?"

"You're a cop? Right?" Dove said to Little. "You should take charge."

"No, thanks. I'll help, but I'm no leader. Any volunteers?"

Claire made her way to Dove and gently grabbed his arm. She looked at the tattoo. "I nominate you, young man. You're already in charge. People listen to you." She smiled and stroked his tattoo. "Our dove of peace."

"You're gonna make me blush," he said as he teetered on the chair. "What the hell. I'll do it. Shouldn't be too hard." *Excellent,* he thought. *I don't have to volunteer.* Getting asked to lead the group made him more anonymous. He grinned.

Daisy looked upset and shook her head. She gulped her beer as her daughter rubbed her back. Dove smirked at them.

"Great," several people mumbled as they stared at Dove.

"Kinda young to take big responsibility," an oriental woman said. "But you good-looking for sure. Yum."

Dove winked at her. "Thanks, but I'm twenty-eight, practically ancient. And I had to grow up very young." Some in the crowd gave not-so-subtle groans, and Dove stopped. "Wait. I don't really need to do this. If anyone else wants to step up, by all means, do it now." He gave a charismatic grin and pose that belonged on the campaign trail. "Speak up!"

No one volunteered.

A few people on the dance floor looked up at the ceiling again, where Adam had disappeared.

One man pointed up. "Look at that—no holes! How did he do it? That was crazy."

Dove went out to the middle of the floor, then looked up at the ceiling as well. "Okay, I guess we need to do a vote or something. See if we think this guy is a whack job or legit." He pointed up. "Damn, he's right. No hole."

A sixty-something woman the shape of a large tree stump marched up to the front of the group with her shopping bags. She took a drag of her cigarette then said, "I'll tell you what he is. He was a magician—a damn good one—and this is all hocus pocus crap, no damn miracle. The only miracle is that you all bought into this bullshit. I'm agreeing with the suit over there." She pointed to the man who'd spoken up and didn't believe in God. "I can watch these tricks any night of the week on TV. Or on a street corner, to boot!"

"Okay, and you are?" Dove asked.

"I'm Bett, and you Kool-Aid drinkers are stupid to believe in this. Really."

"So you know how he did all of this, Bett?" Dove asked. "Please fill us in."

"I don't need to know. I say bullshit, and I'm leaving—and if any of you had any sense, you'd leave too." The sour-faced Bett took another drag from the cigarette that precariously clung to her bottom lip, grabbed her two plastic shopping bags, and stomped to the front doors. "Hell, I know just about everything about everyone in here, too. Idiots," she said, as she opened the doors. "Wait until I tell my Peter what fools you are!"

Slowly, another couple got up and left, shaking their heads. A group of five men in suits followed, one of them the atheist who had spoken up earlier. One couple that argued got up; the woman apologized to their friends as her husband pulled her by the hand, and they left.

"Am I assuming everyone else here believes in what happened?" Dove asked.

"Do you believe in what happened here?" Darnell asked.

Dove looked around the room. People seemed to be waiting for his response, as if he had influence. *Exactly what we wanted.* He smiled. "Hell, yeah! I think this guy was legit. I had live bees come out of my damn mouth, and I know for sure I didn't eat them this summer and all of a sudden belch them up with my beer!" Dove pulled his lip down to show the stings.

"Maybe you're in on the act?" a man standing at the back of the room suggested.

"It's all about faith, friend," Dove said. "And at this moment, I have it, and maybe you don't."

"You're right, I don't think I have enough, and I do believe in God. But this is way out there. Kind of scary." The man got up, and two others followed him out the door.

"You're not breaking my heart, man. That it? Anyone else?" Dove shouted.

People murmured.

"Good. Last thing we want is a non-believer. Hard to sell something if you don't believe." Dove looked around the room. "If Adam's count was right, we're at... one hundred sixty-four-ish?"

"I'm Sam, a reporter, and reporters should remain objective. But I'm having trouble being objective here. I saw what happened, and it was truly believable," she said, walking onto the dance floor. "I was pulled into what was happening. But my common sense says, really? God is going to speak through a bunch of people in a bar who have been drinking?"

"I hear you," Dove said.

"But I can't see any harm in spreading the good word, just in case. What harm could it do? By next Friday, maybe the world will be a little better place, even if it isn't all going to hell," Sam said, then sipped her wine. "This whole thing could be what the world needs right now. Spreading acts of kindness and love?"

People nodded, some saying "Yes" and "Right."

"I was here with all of you, too, and I've never seen anything like this. You can say it's magic, but wow." Marty took a big drink. "Maybe he can get my teenagers to act normal."

No one laughed. People spoke softly.

"I'm guessing we can move forward? Anyone else want to say something?" Dove asked. The show had been a success.

The crowd mumbled.

"We should to do a live interview, get the ball rolling," someone piped up.

"I can get this on the eleven p.m. news tonight. Let me call my boss." Sam held her phone to one ear, the call already in progress.

"Yeah, great! You'll have the first exclusive," Dove said.

The crowd murmured as Sam explained the situation to her boss. After several minutes, she announced that the KCOD crew would be at Roxy's within the hour. She would do the live report.

"Time for one more drink," Marty yelled.

"And some music. Put something inspirational on. And loud," Dove said. "I love music. It inspires me."

The crowd let out a moderate cheer as waitresses took drink orders, and people mingled, getting to know each other.

Sam's smartphone vibrated and beeped a few times. She looked at the display. *Sunshine*—it was her seven-year-old daughter, Lucy. "Hi, sweetie, anything wrong?"

"Benita's having trouble setting me up on YouTube, and I got to start my school project. She tried, but I don't think she's good with the computer stuff—but she made me a super lunch—it was those special crusty—" Lucy rambled in one long breath.

"Honey, Mommy's extremely busy, working. I promise I'll help you make a fantastic YouTube video when I get home. It'll be the best one in your class." She paused. "I've got a great story for you to spread."

"You always promise," she said, sounding dejected, followed by a sigh.

"I mean it this time."

"You always mean it."

"Trust me."

"I do. I love you, even if you lie to me."

"Love you too, Sunshine," Sam said then disconnected. She felt as if she had been overusing *Trust me* lately. Maybe she needed to start saving it for when she was ninety percent positive she wouldn't let Lucy down.

4

At KCOD, the news department team was collected around a boardroom table filled with papers, laptops, and beverages as they rushed to make the evening news deadline.

When Samantha Cott said, *Come to Roxy's to find God*, her boss, Barry Fielding, didn't question her. She had a killer intuition for a good story that had won her many journalistic awards over the past five years. The same intuition had gotten her foot in the door at KCOD as a video editor, using a diploma she'd received as a back-up plan if she was unsuccessful at realizing her dream job: TV reporter.

She had never felt her looks were good enough to be in front of the camera, although her husband always told her how beautiful she was. She was physically fit, trim, and five-foot-seven, but she had a larger nose, slightly bony jawline, and what she considered large ears. She even styled her hair over her ears to hide them.

But despite her self-perceived shortcomings in the beauty department, she got a lucky break. From there, she'd worked extremely hard, taking all the small and local assignments and tackling them with the same vigor as the reporters on the sensational, international stories. Her husband always told her "The harder you work, the luckier you get," and that's what happened to Sam. She worked hard, all the way up to lead reporter, finally utilizing her degree in journalism and realizing her dream.

"Adam Johl. Single. Age thirty-six!" Fielding barked. "That's the name of the 'chosen one' we need to talk to before anyone else does. Find out where he lives, send a crew—yesterday! Baxter, I want you to do the interview."

"Excellent. I'll crucify him," Tom Baxter replied, smirking.

"Just get the facts. Let the viewers decide on crucifixion," Fielding shot back. "Then hit up some of the more outspoken patrons. Pick the colorful characters."

Baxter saluted.

"We're going to lead with this at eleven, so polish it. This could be a big one. Jody, what do you have for a lead?"

"Well... Seven Days to Armageddon?" Jody, the young copywriter, asked.

"No, something that snaps."

"Magic or Mystic, Are We All Going to Hell?"

"You're kidding," Fielding said. "A monkey with a pencil and pad could do better."

The copywriter turned red then scribbled on her pad with her pencil.

Fielding added, "Give it some *real* thought. Don't make me phone my pet monkey."

One of the drivers poked his head into the boardroom. "Vans are waiting. Let's roll."

"A man walks into a bar!" the copywriter blurted out.

Everyone looked at Fielding.

"Good start," Fielding responded.

An hour after Sam placed her call to her boss, the KCOD vans rolled up to Roxy's Bar and Adam Johl's house. Each vehicle had a reporter, key grip, cameraman, and lighting technician.

"Freaky," Baxter said, looking up at the bungalow in the corner of the cul-de-sac.

"What?" the cameraman asked.

"The brief said one hundred seventy-seven people were in the bar."

"So?"

"Adam Johl's address is 177 Lark Court."

"It's a lark, all right," the lighting tech said. "So many whack jobs out there."

They sat staring at the 1970s-style home with white stucco siding, and lawn split down the middle by a walking path, with a majestic elm tree to the right side.

They gathered their equipment and walked up the narrow, weather-pitted concrete walk to the front door.

Adam answered promptly, as if he were expecting them. "Good evening, Mr. Baxter." Adam nodded to the other three men from his crew.

"Right. I'm Tom Baxter from KCOD, and this is my film team. You've probably seen me on TV. Been there for fourteen years." Adam looked nothing like what Tom had expected. Not that he was sure what God's messenger should look like, but Adam looked more like the kind of guy Baxter would date than a prophet. Fine yet rugged features. *Like a modern-day Lawrence Oliver.*

"That long, huh? No, I can't say I have, but please come in. You look like the real thing—plastic hair, perfect white teeth, square jaw."

Baxter's hopes of flirting were dashed. Adam was either straight or not attracted to him. Either was a waste of a hunk of a man. He ushered his team into the house, and they made their way into the living room. *Screw Fielding. I'm going for the crucifixion.*

The room had bare, lily-white walls. The furniture had a Moroccan or Middle Eastern feel, with a modern flair. The large print above the sofa featured an olive grove in a Mediterranean-looking setting.

"I have a pot of coffee," Adam said cordially.

"Coffee would be great," Baxter answered. "For my crew, too."

Adam filled cups that were laid out on the intricately carved mahogany coffee table.

The lighting tech turned on the light-tree, and the white-walled room brightened up as if it was under full sunlight.

"If you don't mind, we'll get right to it," Baxter said.

The cameraman pointed his camera at Baxter, and the red record light lit up on the front.

Adam nodded. "No problem."

Baxter started immediately. "I'm here at the home of Adam Johl, the man who claims to have delivered a profound message from God this evening at six p.m. He delivered it in front of one hundred seventy-seven patrons at Roxy's Bar and performed several miracles to validate his claim." Baxter took a quick breath. "Do you think you're God, Mr. Johl? Or a supreme being?"

"No," he answered, crossing his legs.

"Who are you, exactly?"

"I'm Adam Johl, a thirty-six-year-old computer programmer, and you are here because I delivered a dire message from God."

"Why did God choose you? A computer programmer?"

"Good question."

"Why wouldn't God talk to the Pope? Or the Reverend Jesse Jackson, the Dalai Lama—or any preacher, minister, or deacon instead of you, a regular guy? A computer programmer?"

"There are plenty of examples in Scripture of God appearing to the lowly, if that is what you are saying I am. But if I see him, I'll ask why he picked just a *computer programmer*."

"That's not really what I meant, just that well-known people would have an immediate following or believability."

Adam raised his eyebrows.

"And the message—what was the message?"

The bright lights appeared to bother Adam, and he looked away from them. "The message, it was very clear."

Baxter and his crew leaned forward.

"And if you want to hear it, you should talk to one of the one hundred seventy-seven patrons that witnessed it at Roxy's tonight. It is ultimately their task to spread the word and convince the world."

"We know what the message is. We just want to hear it from its originator. You."

"Tom, I've said all I'm going to say. You may finish your coffee. We can discuss football, baseball, but not religion or politics. Then you can leave."

"You profess to be a messenger from God, yet you don't want to deliver the message to millions of viewers? Why don't you give us a little miracle, something to help prove to us you are really the chosen one?"

"I'm done."

"How can you be done? You let us into your home and say virtually nothing, then ask us to leave? What kind of game are you playing here?"

"It is no game, Tom. You will all find out soon how serious this all is." Adam stood up.

"Are you personally threatening the United States of America? The world? Are *you* going to do something if the world doesn't repent? You're supposed to be speaking for God, not acting like a terrorist."

Adam clenched his jaw. "The fate of mankind must be left up to faith. Pure faith from the Roxy's disciples, and I've said too much already. You can finish your coffee." He bowed slightly and left the room.

***

Roxy's supplied an assortment of complimentary appetizers, as well as the first round of drinks, to feed the hungry mob waiting for KCOD to start the broadcast.

All eyes focused on Sam as she sat on a stool center stage, getting prepped with makeup. She self-consciously looked in the handheld mirror. Her close friends told her she looked fresh, unusually attractive, with her mocha-brunette wavy hair and trademark nose that had that Streisand—or Jennifer Grey–before–the–nose job—sex appeal. She turned her head to view her profile, then remembered her husband telling her, "Stop being so vain; you're beautiful as is." She dropped the mirror onto her lap.

They finished the makeup and hair touch-up, Sam stood up, and they removed the stool.

"On five, four..." The production manager finished the count of three-two-one with his fingers.

"Good evening, I am Samantha Cott, and I am here at Roxy's Bar on Jericho Turnpike in New Hyde Park. We're here tonight because one hundred seventy-seven patrons, including myself, witnessed a man earlier today, at this popular spot, who claimed to be delivering a message directly from God. And to prove he was a messenger from God, he performed unbelievable miracles."

The second cameraman zoomed in on Dove.

"Mr. Fossano—" Sam started.

"Call me Dove. Like the bird, or dove of peace," he said, smiling and pointing at Claire, who smiled.

"Okay, Mr. Dove—"

"Just Dove, like the bird. No 'mister.'"

"Great. Dove, like the bird. Could you please explain to our viewing audience what exactly happened here this evening?"

"This complete stranger, Adam Johl, shows up and tells us he's delivering a message from God."

"Did you believe him?" Sam asked.

"Hell, yeah. He was very convincing. Didn't you?"

"Please just answer the questions as if I wasn't here when it happened." Sam took a breath. "Why do you believe?"

"First, he knew things about me, and other people, that was very personal."

"Things that no one knew?"

"Yeah."

"So no one on the planet knew these facts?"

"I—I'm not sure about the other people, but for me, absolutely. As soon as he revealed my secret, I knew he was the real thing. I instantly believed."

"Why else do you believe he was a messenger from God?"

"The miracles. And there were one hundred seventy-seven people here from all walks of life that all witnessed the same shit... Can I say *shit* on TV?"

"You did. Please explain what you saw and heard tonight, and what the message was."

"He floated around. He made every chair in the room float—bees come out of my mouth." Dove showed his lip. "Stung me right here. Showed a newscast from a week down the road on the TVs—that was insane—lots of earthquakes and stuff coming next week. He created a mini tornado in the bar, turned water into wine, floated up on some bright yellow ball of light, and disappeared into thin air right in front of us. Just like that." He snapped his fingers. "It was something from another world, let me tell you."

"What was the message, Dove?" Sam asked quickly.

"We have just seven days to redeem the world. Seven days for everyone to repent all that's bad and have a pure change of heart and soul."

"I wonder why seven days? It's a tight time-line for such an incredible project. And what will happen after the deadline should we fail to repent?"

"Not sure why seven—maybe because the world was supposedly created in seven days? Actually six. Anyway, seven is all he could negotiate, and the end of the world will happen, sure as shit." He smiled. "Yeah, I guess that's when the end is slated for. Fire and brimstone for all—except for several million good people. According to Adam."

The crowd of new disciples all nodded, concurring with Dove. The second camera panned the crowd to capture reactions. Daisy Beech's watery eyes and weathered face showed up on the large monitor.

"Do we know who these lucky several mil-lions are?"

"He didn't tell us... as you know. Only God has that file."

The crowd let out some *oohs* and a few claps.

"Can you give us a little more detail on these so-called miracles Adam Johl performed that were so convincing to you and these one hundred seventy-seven people?"

"Actually, there's only one hundred sixty-four left. A few didn't quite believe, or were chicken shit, or maybe were in the bar with someone they weren't supposed to be with."

"Right. One hundred sixty-four people here now," Sam corrected.

Speaking into the camera, Dove detailed the acts that had convinced the patrons on the origin of the message as the crowd edged closer. By the end of his monologue, they had surrounded him, some putting their hands on his shoulders. When he was done, someone handed him a tissue, and he wiped a tear from his eye.

Sam then interviewed the bar owner and a few select people who stepped up. Marty Graham used a selling cars analogy that made no sense, and he kept repeating himself. Mark Little reported the facts coldly and straight-faced, as if he were speaking to a judge. Claire Nadeau cried when she described her chair floating and couldn't finish her accounting of the events. Daisy Beech told everyone she felt Revelations was upon them and that Satan hid somewhere on earth—maybe closer than they knew, she added, staring at Dove.

The tone of the segment had shifted from a *National Enquirer* headline to a heartfelt documentary. *This is a good story,* Sam thought. *An award-winning story*. One that may propel her to the next pay grade.

After the KCOD film crew left, Dove brainstormed with the believers for next steps and whom they should contact to get the story out. He asked everyone to exchange phone numbers and email addresses.

At the end of the evening, there was an air of brittle optimism that they just might be able to get the word out to every corner of the planet by Monday, using all available mediums. Whether every corner of the planet would believe it or not—that was another issue.

As Dove left the bar, Darnell yelled, "Thanks! Nice work."

Dove looked back, smiled, and gave a sloppy two-finger salute from his forehead.

As the sign on the front door of Roxy's had stated, renovations were still going ahead, despite the fact that God might have spoken through Adam Johl and that some people might've thought it should've remained exactly as it was, blessed and a shrine.

At five past midnight, semis rolled onto the Jericho Turnpike in New Hyde Park and stopped in front of Roxy's Bar. The two large fifty-three-foot trailers held dozens of hired hands. One trailer would load all the old chattels and fixtures, and the other would unload all the new ones. The renovations had to be completed by Monday afternoon, as promised to the patrons.

Sam raced straight home to see her daughter before the nanny put her to bed. She helped Lucy set up her YouTube message as promised, despite it being hours past her bedtime. Lucy's project was to create a positive message that would help people in any way. In her message, Lucy spoke about being good to people and animals, "especially hamsters." Sam produced the clip as if it were made for a TV broadcast.

That should help Lucy get the most hits in the classroom, she thought, *and make up for some broken promises.* Her husband, Brad, had helped Lucy with school projects and homework, giving Sam breathing room for her career. She had never missed a deadline or assignment at work, but she constantly missed them with her daughter. His accidental death left an immeasurable void in their lives and hearts. Sam felt guilty that she was overworking, but part of the reason was to keep her mind busy and off Brad. When she was with Lucy, all she could see were Brad's eyes and smile. She needed to deal with that.

Sam went to bed before her Roxy's piece aired. She let Lucy snuggle in with her as a special treat for both of them, and they fell asleep within minutes.

KCOD broke their Friday eleven p.m. news with the incredulous story of Adam Johl and his "Warning from God?" The phone lines at the station lit up like a contest for Elton John's final tour tickets, all listeners wondering if it was an elaborate hoax.

CNN and the major networks struck an immediate deal with Barry Fielding, as well, to start airing KCOD's segments.

Adam's home and cell phone rang continuously. Coworkers, acquaintances, curiosity seekers, and every possible news and entertainment medium all wanted to talk to him.

After midnight—and a marathon of intense pounding away at his computer, setting in motion the false seismic reports for the next stage of his plan—Adam unplugged his phone and went to bed.

He let out a tired sigh, rolled onto his side, and looked at his alarm clock wondering if he would still be looking at it at seven a.m.

His mind would not shut down.

As he did many nights, Adam tried to envision the faces of his wife and children to try to help him fall asleep. As time passed, it got harder to get a crisp memory of them. He recalled the nightly rituals his wife did before coming to bed. He imagined giving each of them a kiss good night and tried to sense that comfort he'd received from doing that, even if the feeling lasted for only a brief moment.

Adam opened his eyes and stared at the shadows on the wall from the streetlight streaming through the cracks of his blinds.

He was not sleeping that night.

5

The dank, musty odor was augmented by the stench of stale death and cigarettes as the two FBI agents made their way through the narrow vestibule into the old Brooklyn suite. They had received the brief on the situation, the preliminary forensic report, and were expecting a gruesome sight.

Breno Lobato had been in the field for two months, and it was his introduction to the smell of a four-day-old corpse. His partner, Cassia Arena, had been with the Bureau for six years and gave him some Vick's gel to dab beneath his nostrils.

A crime scene photographer and two forensic people worked quietly in the room.

The older male's eyes were swollen shut, and his face, the color of an almost ripe plum, looked as if it would burst if you poked it with a pin. The rigid body was slumped over in a well-worn, plaid recliner, a chair that he undoubtedly passed out in night after night while his TV faded to fuzz.

His right arm hung over the side of the chair, and his cigarette had dropped to the linoleum tile floor, burning another brownish-yellow mark right next to his empty sherry bottle.

There were two clean entry points right at his heart, with dried trickles of blood on his soiled white muscle shirt. There was also one shot to the forehead.

"Same killer, for sure," Lobato mumbled.

"What's that?"

"Just thinking out loud."

"You need to stop that." Arena poked her pen through the small bullet hole in the wall where one of the heart shots had passed through the body.

"It's to help you out. It's good to know what your partner's thinking... it's called brain-storming."

"Just *storming*, in your case."

"I'll take that as a compliment, I guess," Lobato said, looking her way for something to distract him from the corpse.

Arena continued speaking her assessment of the situation into her mini recorder. "We have a seventy-two-year-old male, executed in his sleep, money still in his wallet, suite ransacked."

"It's a rat's nest." He picked up a pile of bills and papers from the coffee table and flipped through them. He put them back then examined a pile of empty beer cans in the corner of the living room. Most of the cans were Rolling Rock brand and had been crushed slightly. Probably tossed there from Rutherford's recliner.

"Phil Rutherford. Retired, full-time boozer. Dead for approximately ninety-six hours, according to forensics," she continued.

"Must've seen or heard something he wasn't supposed to. He was connected to the Queens shooting somehow. Ballistics was a match."

"What they were looking for was probably in his mind. I wonder if they got it," Arena said quietly.

"Or they were looking for something that disclosed the terrorist sleeper cell. Some kind of evidence that he possessed. Based on this mess, he could have some kind of information lying around."

Arena was pensive.

"What're you thinking, Cass?" Lobato asked as they noticed Mark Little quietly enter the room.

Arena glanced at Little—his gut protruding over his belt, his almost triple chin, and his arrogant smirk. She looked back at the corpse.

"What *are* you thinking?" Little asked.

"That I'd rather stare at this corpse than your face."

Little was expressionless, as if he were used to people slamming him.

A crime scene photographer snapped off a couple more pictures of the bullet hole in the wall just behind the victim's head, momentarily blinding Arena as she looked up.

"You're supposed to check in with me, my collaborating friends," he said arrogantly. "We're supposed to escort you in these situations."

"We couldn't wait another two hours for you to get out of someone's bed like we did at the Queens high-rise murder," Arena said. "Why don't you go have another beer?"

"Maybe with you?" Little smiled.

Arena shot Little an exaggerated stink-eye stare.

"Why are FBI counterterrorism special agents meddling in yet another basic homicide investigation?"

"If it were basic, we'd leave it up to you," Arena responded, batting her eyelashes.

"Seems like it's right where we left off last time—why is such a pretty redhead so damn nasty?" Little asked, as he looked her up and down, focusing on the down. "Does the FBI on your jacket stand for Fully Bitch Injected?"

Arena's jaw tightened. "Why is such an ugly thing so... Did I load my weapon this morning? Breno?" she asked, as she drew her weapon halfway from the holster, then reholstered it, all while maintaining eye contact with Little.

"Easy, tiger," Lobato said. "The execution-style murder in Queens we met you at? The one you were two hours late for the meeting? Ballistics confirmed the match to that, and we're on a call list. And we're religious-slash-terrorist specialists—"

"I'm happy for you. Your point?"

"The Queens victim was a terrorist and a forger, as you know, part of an extreme Islamic sleeper cell we'd been watching."

"If you were watching him, why's he dead?"

Lobato ground his jaw.

"Actually, we made a mistake," Arena said.

"I see that," Little said.

"Yeah, we asked for your department's help watching him..."

Detective Little stared blankly and yawned without covering his mouth. He picked at his teeth. "So you think they're planning something, huh? Any idea what?"

"When we've found out what, you'll be the first person I call. Right after everyone else in the New York directory."

"Easy. Sorry about that crack. We're protective of our turf here. New York pride."

"If there's nothing else, we've got to get on with *our* investigation," Lobato said.

"No, that's it. If you need our help, we're here for you. All you have to do is call."

"We won't be needing you. We're fine," Arena responded.

"Yes, you are," Little muttered, then continued. "I'll leave one of our finest here, just to follow protocol. And send me a copy of your report."

Arena gave him a blank stare. "You bet, Detective *Little*." Then she said under her breath, "*dick*."

He shook his head, turned, and walked to the door. He stopped at the doorway and turned around. "Say. Did you happen to catch what happened at Roxy's tonight?" He checked his watch. "Well, actually, last night."

"We're kind of busy working," Arena said. "While you're drinking."

"Too bad. Guess you can read about it in the morning. Nothing special, just possibly the second coming of Christ."

Arena and Lobato stared at each other.

Little quickly left the old Brooklyn hotel and called Dove on his cell phone. He tapped a cigarette out of the pack and lit up as he leaned on his car. "It's me, Mark. They won't really cooperate with us. I have no idea why they have such a hate on. I'm so likable."

Little paused. "Yeah, well, they won't piece shit together. Nothing to piece here. We've made sure this loose end is ended."

Little listened then disconnected. Would he soon be a loose end?

He got into his car and went to his favorite greasy spoon breakfast spot, where he would plan his loose-end protection policy.

"Protocol, my ass," Arena continued after the photographer went into the kitchen. "That fat, rude freak. I'd like to kick him in his little package. And FBI doesn't wait for anyone—"

"Easy. What's that?" Lobato interrupted.

"What's what?"

"Under his big protocol ass."

Arena used the tip of her pen to grab a small piece of a blue cord from just under the corpse's upper thigh. She pulled it out a ways, then grabbed the cord with her hand, tugged it out, and dangled it from her pen. "A security pass for KCOD, NYC TV studio. Says 'janitor.'"

"That didn't show up on his profile. Maybe they paid him cash, no records."

"A big outfit like KCOD paying someone cash? And what about the union? Nah. It's forged."

"We may have just found what they were looking for," Lobato said.

"Nice work, rookie."

"And it only took"—Lobato looked at his sports watch—"fifty-three minutes. We deserve a reward."

"I'm just waiting for it." Arena closed one eye.

"Breakfast. I know a great diner in Brooklyn."

"I'm beat, and it's after two a.m."

"I'll pay."

Arena sighed. "My stomach is growling. Okay, quick one."

"Well, Miss Cassia Arena, it's my lucky day."

"It's eggs, not a date."

"That's what you think," Lobato responded with a hopeful wink. "Baby steps, Cass, that's what partnerships are all about."

"I can see it's going to be a long meal."

"And you are going to love every bite, Cass."

"Why did I say yes—"

"Because—"

"Stop right there," she said.

Lobato smiled and followed Arena out of the room.

"You like my ass that much?" she asked.

Lobato blushed and focused on the back of her red hair.

6
Saturday – Day 1

Adam sat on his sofa, sipped coffee, and gazed out the window down the tree-lined street in Woodmere as the morning sun outlined the trees with an orange halo. A long string of communication vans and reporters' vehicles could be seen for blocks. People walked down the street, carrying rolls of cable and wheeling carts with video equipment and lighting.

A similar circus of vehicles jammed all available parking spots in the busy commercial area where Roxy's was located. Dove also had a flock of reporters perched outside his condo, waiting to dive-bomb the spokesman of the Roxy's Apostles.

The media was void of a global viral story. It had all the makings for a rating sweep, if handled properly.

Adam made an appearance on his front door step at seven a.m. He took a breath of damp morning air, amidst dozens of reporters shouting questions. "Thank you for taking such zealous interest in the happenings at Roxy's last night! There is hope."

"Do you really think you're God?" a reporter spat out, ramming a microphone in Adam's face, hitting his chin. "Or some supernatural being?"

"Not at all," he said, rubbing his chin.

All the reporters rapid-fired questions.

"Please ask any of the people who witnessed the events. It's their task to convince the world that God spoke through me not mine!"

The reporters pushed closer. Adam backed against the door and opened it.

"Did you somehow brainwash these people?" a woman yelled from the back.

"Tell us how you did the miracles? Is this a hoax?" shouted another reporter.

"The TV news reports from next week! How did you do it?"

"Give us a sign!"

Adam had expected and prepared for this phase. He smiled and raised his arms as if he was about to part the Red Sea. The reporters stepped back a little.

Most of the vans and cars within sight on the street started.

The reporters and their crew looked out at the vehicles and asked each other, "Did you do that?" They all answered "No."

The vehicles clicked into forward gear and rolled down the street. They crashed like bumper cars, metal scraping and plastic cracking.

While the reporters stood momentarily stunned, then dashed for their vehicles, Adam slipped in through his slightly open door, waved good-bye, and closed it.

It all seems to be working.

Dove bounced out of his front door before the sun hit the horizon, grinning ear to ear. "Time is of the essence!" were Dove's first words to Tom Baxter, KCOD reporter, from the front steps of his Queens condo.

"What were you doing in the New Hyde Park bar on Friday night?" Baxter asked.

"Working on a construction project in New Hyde Park. Having a beer after work. What a bar to pick, hey?"

The following questions seemed just as trivial to Dove. Then, finally, a good question. Baxter asked about the Dove tattoo on his arm and his newly bestowed alias.

It was to remind him of his mother who had passed away. "She loved doves," Dove said, with teary eyes.

Baxter rubbed it a little too long, so Dove jerked his arm away and said, "Easy, cowboy."

Dove handed him a contact list of all one hundred sixty-four believers, and Baxter left abruptly.

Darnell gave an interview to Baxter just outside the front doors of Roxy's, since renovations were underway. "No, never met Adam until Friday night," he said.

"Was this a publicity stunt to drive your business? Pay for your renovations?" Baxter asked.

"I was doing just fine before the miracles. Packed every night and voted the number one neighborhood bar in New Hyde Park. Four years in a row! I even ran ads on your station, paid all my bills on time."

"I think I speak for the public when I say we are seriously skeptical. Why is it you all believe in what seems to be a few magic tricks?"

"If you tune into the latest news, I bet you a bunch of reporters that interviewed Adam this morning also believe. It seems most of the reporters' vehicles drove off on their own."

"More tricks, perhaps? I can start my car with my smartphone, and Adam Johl is a computer programmer."

"You can continue to say it's tricks, magic, but what will it take? For everyone on the planet to witness it themselves? Then there is no reason for faith, right? But isn't that what this is all about?"

"If you did not witness the miracles and were just watching the news, how would you feel?"

"With one hundred sixty-four people swearing it was true—and now a dozen reporters—I guess I would have to have a little faith," Darnell said. "What options do we have? And what harm could believing do?" He opened his front door to go back inside.

"Why are you renovating what could be a shrine to—"

"Thanks. Really gotta get back to work." Darnell went inside the bar, locking the door behind him.

Daisy Beech invited Baxter and his crew into her home, which was walking distance to Roxy's, for some home-baked Caribbean coffee flan.

"I've seen almost everything in my seventy-nine years on this earth!" she said with vigor. "But this, this is like starting from scratch. First you gotta believe, then you're reborn. That's how I feel—like a dancing newborn!"

"So you truly believe what happened was real? The miracles, the message?" Baxter asked.

"So much that I cried myself to sleep last night. Praise God!"

"Your daughter, Mary, was also there. Does she believe with the same conviction?"

"Yes. But she's not much of a talker, in person—shy, unlike her two sisters and three brothers." Daisy chuckled. "She's blogging and tweeting like mad though."

"Are you a regular in the bar, and did you know Adam before last night? Was he a regular?"

"Practically everyone there were regulars. Same faces—and yes, I tip a few back there, now and again. Keeps my heart runnin' smooth! But no, didn't know Adam, to answer your question."

Baxter laughed.

"Dove was no regular, either. Not sure where he came from."

"I interviewed him this morning. He was working on a construction project and stopped in for a beer."

"Whatever," Daisy said.

Baxter sat on the edge of his seat and took a piece of flan. The cameraman grabbed one too.

"What do you mean?" Baxter asked.

"I have this curse. I see things sometimes, and when I touched his arm, I saw some terrible things."

"Are you psychic?" he asked then took a bite of his flan.

"I don't like to call it that. Just say I'm intuitive, and sometimes, I see things. And I have some very vivid dreams that always seem to mean something. Sometimes I figure them out."

"What kind of terrible things did you see?"

"Fires. Bombs. People dying, drowning."

Baxter held his finger across his lips.

"But if we all do our part, no worries! I've had some visions that never materialized!" Daisy piped up with a big smile.

"What connection do you think Dove has with your visions?"

"I never really know. But something's not quite right."

"Not right, as in fraud?"

"Oh, I believe things are going to happen, but maybe not quite in the way we think they will, dearie," she said, reaching over and tapping Baxter's arm.

He glanced at his arm, then at Daisy.

The cameraman laughed.

Daisy laughed. "You're fine. No visions! Now finish up the flan and get out there and spread the good word. Quickly!"

"It is marvelous dessert, Daisy. You should give me the recipe," Baxter said.

Daisy winked and tapped his leg.

Marty Graham's hands shook as he stood in front of the liquor cabinet. He reached for the door, left his hand on the handle for a moment, then went to the kitchen to pour himself some extra-strong coffee. He was going to talk to the press sober.

He went to the front door, where Baxter waited. Marty joined Baxter outside on the porch. They sat on plastic lawn chairs. Marty's teenage son and daughter peeked out through the living room window while his wife stayed in the kitchen.

"Are you a religious man, Mr. Graham?"

"I've never believed in God or religion much. But I do believe in what was said and done at Roxy's. Call it divine intervention or whatever. It did happen. It was real, and you had to be there."

"I've interviewed a lot of people today, and you all seem so convinced it was a supernatural event—divine intervention, as you put it."

Marty nodded. "You really had to be there, man."

"We've all seen magic tricks that we can't figure out, that seem impossible. So what can you tell us that will help us believe what you saw and heard was real?" Baxter asked.

Marty thought for a moment. "Think of a secret about yourself, one that you didn't share with anyone. Now imagine that secret revealed in front of a bar full of people. Would that make you believe? Isn't that always what they do in those time-travel movies when the guy's trying to prove to the woman that he was someone she knew? That's what Adam did. And that's the one that cinched the deal for me. I hope the world gets it, because I think it will all end if we don't."

Baxter nodded and looked at his watch. He had seen tricks like this before. Apparent mind-reading tricks. Adam Johl was *real* good.

Claire Nadeau gave a convincing, heartfelt account of the events from the front steps of her large, empty home in New Hyde Park. She was meticulous with the details and descriptions, and she had a poetic flair to her vocabulary. Her years as editor for a major publisher of romance novels helped.

"I believe," she said to Baxter, her head high. "Not since I divorced my cheating-lying-son-of-bitch husband have I been more sure."

Baxter laughed. "*Men*."

After Baxter left, she poured herself a neat twenty-year-old scotch and cried. She wasn't sure why she cried. She wiped her tears, took a large gulp of her drink, then took her journal out of her antique writing desk. She hadn't written in it for over a year. She flipped the page open to her last entry. It was about her husband. She flipped to a blank page so she didn't have to read it.

She grabbed her pen and wrote, "Today, I have a new purpose in life. Or should I say, I have *a* purpose in life, one that I pray lasts for more than seven days. One that I hope changes the world. Am I up to the challenge? How will this change me? For the better, I hope. For the better, I pray."

Fielding sat back in his chair, reviewing the interviews and news from the day. The eight TV monitors on his wall cycled all the major news channels. The news and interviews of the event were running continuously, with special broadcasts advertised for tomorrow morning during the Sunday morning features. Newspapers advertised multi-page exposés on the entire event and the "Roxy's Apostles," as the media had tagged them.

The story had gone global in twelve hours. Viewers were watching, listening, and reading about it in almost every country and language, and Fielding's station received a royalty every time the initial interviews ran.

He got up, closed his door, turned an exhaust fan on, and lit a Cuban cigar.

Sam quickly organized a town hall forum, inviting all of the "Roxy's Apostles" (including Adam Johl), select members of various religious communities, and a respected theologian from New York University. Benita agreed to spend the weekend with Lucy at double time. Lucy had cried when she found out her mother cancelled their Saturday night movie night, again. Sam was obsessed with another story that hurt her daughter, and she was disappointed with herself. It gave her a pain in her gut.

With speed and experience, Sam teed up a "Live Special Broadcast" following the six p.m. Saturday evening news. She hoped that that would propel the story and give it the legs it needed to do one of two things: last for seven days of great ratings, or actually influence change in the world. Either way, she would be a winner with her boss, but not her daughter. Could she handle that?

7

The news of the Saturday night town hall meeting spread through the social network faster than the word of a high school house party. And thanks to that viral networking, Adam watched hundreds of assorted worshippers make the pilgrimage down the street to his home from the comfort of his living room.

A shrine of crosses, candles, religious icons, and flowers collected at the base of the large elm tree in his front yard. Dozens of five-decade rosaries hung from low branches.

Adam adjusted the venetian blind to gaze out onto the street. A group of Hare Krishnas sat in the middle of his lawn with signs that read "Getting Faith!"

He looked down the street. A Jehovah's Witness school bus unloaded people carrying lawn chairs and coolers. Behind the bus was a white van with a banner draped across the side that read, "Don't waste your time talking about it! There is no God!" And the logo on the door of the van read, "Atheist Alliance of America."

Across the street, FBI agents Cassia Arena and Breno Lobato had discreetly set up shop in a TV network van. They were thirty minutes behind schedule because they had stopped to have coffee on the comfy leather chairs of the coffee shop instead of in the white van that smelled as though men had slept in it for a week without showering.

Arena had read through Adam's file, which they had picked up at six a.m. from their office. The report deemed the events at Roxy's as possible psychological terrorism, targeting people's psychological well-being and state of mind. In addition, it stated that there was a threat of further actions in the way of actual attacks on American citizens.

"All this from a magic act?" Lobato asked, flipping through the pages in the file.

"For sure. I bet you, this morning the sales of generators and water bottles went up. If people think that any of this is true, watch out. It will get crazy."

"We really explore all threats, don't we?"

"These days, toothpaste or diapers in an airport is a threat."

Lobato nodded as he looked at all the people congregating on the street and sidewalk.

"If nothing further develops over the next two or three days, this will all blow over as a hoax. But we need to keep a close watch on Johl and possibly others from Roxy's who may be connected. He didn't do this alone," Arena said as she used binoculars to zoom into Johl's living room.

"I think the bar owner is in this, for sure."

"And the report says possible connections for Johl to the shootings, if this Roxy's thing is a terrorist plot." She put the binoculars down.

"Johl had the janitor whacked?" Lobato asked.

"Wasn't the fake broadcast at Roxy's from a KCOD anchor? The janitor had a KCOD ID tag. Too many coincidences, and Johl went through a lot of planning and thought to pull this off."

"You're right, of course."

"One thing is certain, however. He threatened the world—and more importantly, he threatened the safety of the US. If the world doesn't repent, the world will end. What does that mean? Dirty bombs? Biologicals? Regardless, he's listed as a possible terrorist now. And it's too much coincidence, with the recent deaths and chatter that's been going on in the area."

"What do the files say on that?"

"Right now, not much. And only seven years of history on Johl. I guess there will be more to come. He's been quite the loner. Not a good sign."

"Can't wait." Lobato stuck his head out the window and peered down the vehicle-lined street. He took in a big breath of fresh, cool air. “The news has really spread fast.”

“It brings all kinds out of the sewers and shopping malls.”

Lobato chuckled. “With all your theological expertise, can this guy even remotely be real? Or does he just believe he is?” He coughed. “Or is he a clever terrorist dressed like a computer programmer?”

“In the six years I’ve been with the Bureau, I’ve seen a lot of things I never thought possible. Complete opposite profiling of terrorists, ones we couldn’t believe fit the mold. I’ve seen terrorist plots so intricate, you would need a supercomputer to plan them.”

“Straight answer—what’s your best guess: freak or genius?”

“I think he’s either a genius or supreme nut job. The real question is why. Why is he doing this, and who is he really?”

“What’s in the file that helps us connect the dots with the janitor? That would be a good place to start.” Lobato finished his coffee and tossed the empty cup in a cardboard box filled with other stakeout garbage.

“The KCOD badge. Mansfield works there, a reporter that was at Roxy’s works there, and the dead janitor was there at some time. Maybe he was involved or saw something to do with the future news broadcast at Roxy’s. It had to be recorded. Maybe all three of these KCOD people are in on it.”

They gazed up at Adam Johl's house. It was as average as Joe.

"I agree," Lobato said. "I don't really buy it. I mean there are so many unanswered questions. I'm a good Catholic and all, but I still believe in dinosaurs, Darwin, and Democrats. And I can't even get my car repaired in seven days, forget building a planet."

Arena checked her side-view mirror, then went into the back to sit in front of controls for listening devices.

"I've done some studies, too, Cass. Both sides of the argument."

"I don't think all the studying in the world could prepare you for this. There is nothing that can prove the validity of God, really."

"You're the one with the religious degree. Enlighten me."

"First thing is to keep an unbiased open mind, and listen to all viewpoints," she said as she booted up the computer. "But again, it really is all about faith."

Lobato nodded.

"And as for you believing that the world was built in six—*not* seven—days, there are many viewpoints. Again, listen to all, keep an open mind, and form your own opinion."

"How about as I have questions, you answer them."

"Okay," Arena said. "Let's start with *yộm*."

"Yum?"

"*Yộm*. One viewpoint is that the world created in six *yộm*. In Genesis, the word is translated into English as day, six days, rested on the seventh. But Hebrew actually allows for four meanings of the word, one of which is a long but finite period of time—could be six billion, or six hundred million. And most interesting is that biblical Hebrew has no other word for a finite era or epoch, and they chose to use it in Genesis. Besides, ancients would never be able to comprehend six billion years. This is a controversial view. Some people, religious and not, will say blasphemy, have faith, it was actually six days."

"Now you're just flexing your religious muscle." Lobato smiled.

"Why are you smiling?"

"Because I'm learning more from you than I learned in all those damn textbooks at the academy. It's been a great couple of months."

"You're welcome."

"And you're a hot teacher, to boot. In a smart, tough way. The women teaching at the academy were like mini Mussolinis."

"A crush will hinder your learning." Arena opened her notebook and jotted something down that she'd read on her laptop screen.

"Never."

Arena looked at her smartphone, which had vibrated for new mail. She opened it. "Just received the full-check on Johl."

Lobato checked his email, but he hadn't received a copy. He re-holstered his smartphone.

Arena opened the attached encrypted file. "Seven years. That's all we were able to go back on him. Fake name." She rubbed her chin. "Who are you, Adam…"

"Whose name did he take? Someone deceased?"

"Odd name. Johl. Not your average alias. I'll Google it," she said as she worked on her smartphone.

Lobato waited while she clicked and scrolled on her device.

"Interesting. It says, 'the unusual name is of medieval German origin, adopted from the Hebrew name "Yochanan," "Jehovah has favored (me with a son)," or "may Jehovah favor (this child)."'"

"The press will sensationalize that once they catch on. Now it makes sense why he chose it."

"Maybe." She thumbed down through the document as she sipped her coffee. "Odd."

"What?" Lobato asked, as he glanced up at Adam's house.

"His identity is too clean. It's as if someone just dropped him on the planet seven years ago. American citizen, born in Boise. But that's it. No school or family records. No prior addresses. He has a valid driver's license and passport."

"Great forger."

"He needs more than a great forger to pull this off. He needs someone inside law enforcement. Or... he's in WITSEC. Not sure why he'd expose himself like this, though, if he was in witness protection," Arena said. "And he doesn't look Caucasian."

"He's got light olive-colored skin. He could be Middle Eastern or European."

"Agreed. He's half and half of something."

"I think this guy is up to something big."

Arena looked at Lobato. "Let's hope we stop him before he gets to his *big* part." She put on a listening device and flipped switches and adjusted dials. "We need to get to work."

Lobato sat next to her at the workbench. "Kidding and constant sexual innuendos aside, I don't think I could have a better partner to break me in."

Arena turned and looked at Lobato as she pinched his ass. "Don't start getting all serious and shit. It's a sign of weakness and vulnerability."

"Oh, yeah." He nodded. "Does that mean I can grab your ass too?"

"If you like lead with your coffee, rookie."

8

The town hall meeting was held in the basement of St. John the Divine Cathedral—nicknamed St. John the Unfinished—in New York, one block east of Broadway.

Sam chose the location because it was one of the largest cathedrals in the world, with an awe-inspiring presence. Construction of the weathered and morose colossal stone structure had started in 1892, and it was the official ecclesiastical seat of the Bishop. It would be an idyllic and controversial backdrop for this epic religious challenge.

She walked up the wide steps leading up to three-ton bronze doors with five portals arching overhead. And high above the doors was the Great Rose Window, the largest stained-glass window in the United States, made of more than ten thousand pieces of colored glass.

Sam stopped with her hand on the door handle, looked up at the stone cross positioned in the middle of the stained glass masterpiece, and wondered how the night would unfold.

She entered. As she walked through the church, with her heels echoing toward the 124-foot-high nave ceiling, she passed the artist's exhibition of the Stations of the Cross. She stopped in front of a contemporary depiction of the seventh stage of the cross. It was a distinct contradiction to the gothic architecture and aura of the building—almost sacrilegious, she thought.

Gazing at the blue, grey, and black paintings, she couldn't help wondering *What if—?* What if what was happening was real? She looked at the long row of unusual paintings on the wall and said out loud, "No way."

The words echoed. She looked over her shoulder.

Remain neutral. Professional, she thought. *Don't let your beliefs sway your journalistic professionalism.* "Forgive me," she said, looking up at Jesus nailed to the gold cross positioned above the high altar.

Sam continued on her way to the basement hall where the church often fed the underprivileged and homeless. It had a musty food odor. She gathered her crew, and they reviewed and planned for the show.

At five forty-five p.m., the hall was filled to standing room only. All the networks that Fielding had struck a deal with were set up and ready, and Sam would host and moderate the event. As she reviewed the list of attendees who had signed in, including Adam Johl and the panel of experts, a man and woman approached her.

"Hello, Ms. Cott. I'm Cassia Arena, and this is Breno Lobato. We're with the FBI."

"Hello. Why is the FBI here?" Sam asked quietly.

"The events that happened at Roxy's are perceived as a potential threat to the safety of the United States."

"What? And how is a message from God a threat?"

"It's not the message," Arena said. "It's the threat of the world ending. That's a threat. Not to mention Johl did keep one hundred seventy-seven people hostage for almost an hour. They couldn't leave the establishment until he allowed them."

One of crew tried to get Sam's attention. She glanced at her watch. "Okay, please try to stay in the background. I don't want to cast a shadow over what could be an inspiring story."

Sam's phone went off; it was Fielding. "Excuse me." She walked away from the agents.

"Sam, we have something that may spice up your interview. Use it to hype the story," he said without saying hello.

"What's up?"

"We've had some serious seismic activity—two locations, lots of movement, but no quakes."

"Where?"

"Are you sitting?"

"No."

"San Andreas fault, LA, San Fran, the entire Western seaboard."

Sam didn't respond.

"Second one's even bigger. *Beijing*."

Sam stayed quiet.

"You there, Sam?"

"Yeah."

"Hey, don't worry yourself, Sammy. This Adam is just some guy looking for publicity. The world's not ending anytime soon. Besides, I've got a great retirement plan that still needs to be executed, so you can be damn sure I'm not going to let any world end until I've spent my three children's inheritance."

Sam smiled. "Thanks. You always know how to cheer me up, Barry."

"That's my job. Just remain objective and get the truth, the story. That's what you're good at."

"Oh, one last thing, boss—what time did seismic activity start?"

"Around seven last night, the computers reported light activity, and it built through the night. Why?"

"Seven, huh?"

"Forget about it, Sam. Don't worry; just do what I pay you to do and *have fun*."

"Right. Fun. Fourteen hours a day of pure fun." Another call came in. "Bye, Barry." The incoming call was from *Sunshine*. She pressed a button to switch over. "Honey, Mommy's real busy."

"Mom! I got over two thousands hits on my YouTube! Lots of people want to see my message! Thanks for being the best mom ever!"

"That's super, Sunshine. When I get home tonight, we'll kick it up another notch, promise." Sam rubbed her temple.

"No, Mommy, I'm okay. I can do it myself. I'm going to add a new message tonight. I'll show it to you when you get home, 'kay?"

"Kay. Now you help Benita clean up after dinner, and I'll see you in a couple of hours. Bye-bye!"

Sam replaced her smartphone into her phone case as she looked up at a faded painting of Jesus bearing the weight of the cross while kneeling on the ground. He seemed to be staring right at her. She pondered the events of the last twenty-four hours; they seemed so surreal.

She rubbed her clammy palms on her skirt. If the world ended in seven days, would she have any regrets? Of course she would. That she hadn't been a better mother. She knew it, but why didn't she do something about it? That she'd never taken Lucy to Disney World—what had stopped her from fulfilling that promise? That she hadn't started dating again; it was time. She sighed. *Maybe I should go back to seeing my therapist every week.*

Sam shook her head, took a deep breath, and pulled out her smartphone to check her email; she needed a dose of reality.

A cameraman tapped Sam on the shoulder. "We're all ready, just waiting for you."

"Right. Let's get the show going." *A show,* she reassured herself as she put her phone away. *That's all this is. Get it done, and get home on time.* "I just need a couple of Advil. I feel a headache coming on." She grabbed some from her purse, swallowed them with water, and went to the stage.

The producer counted down for a start at precisely six p.m. "Good evening. I'm Samantha Cott, and I am your host this evening for this live broadcast from the beautiful St. John the Divine Cathedral in New York. We've assembled the one hundred sixty-four 'Roxy's Apostles,' as they have come to be known, to testify in front of our expert panel regarding the so-called holy event that happened last night at Roxy's Bar in New Hyde Park, New York. At the event, it was prophesied that the world would end in seven days, on this coming Friday at seven p.m."

In the back of the room, a young man, probably in his early twenties and dressed in a suit and tie, yelled, "*Bullshit*!"

A security guard quickly escorted him out of the church, covering his mouth with a leather-gloved hand.

"The disciples were visited at Roxy's by this man, Mr. Adam Johl, a thirty-six-year-old computer programmer with Conestry Technologies."

The camera zoomed in on Adam's shiny face.

Adam wore a black suit and red tie. Sweat dripped from his brow.

"Adam Johl seemingly performed miracles to prove he delivered a dire message from... *God*."

Hushed background chattering filled the gallery.

"I'll ask you a few questions to open it up, then pass it on to our panel of experts."

The camera panned the panel seated at the front of the room.

"Mr. Johl, you seemed to have convinced a restaurant full of people that you indeed were delivering a message from God. How and when were you aware that God spoke through you, and why did you deliver the message at Roxy's?"

After a well-timed dramatic pause, Adam answered to a patiently waiting crowd, "All I know is I was somehow guided toward Roxy's last night while on my way home from work. I had never been there before, though I'd passed by a few times. I thought I'd maybe grab a burger and a glass of wine. But when I walked through the doors, I was no longer in control. I felt a warmth rush through my body, mind, and soul; the words, thoughts, and miracles just came. It was as if I were having an out-of-body experience—"

"And what about now? Do you still feel special?" Sam interjected quickly.

"I feel... awake. As if I've awoken from a coma that I've been in for years. And I still managed to burn my toast this morning, and my soft-boiled eggs were overdone, so I'm not feeling that special."

A few people chuckled.

"That's funny." Sam smiled. "God is blessed with a sense of humor?"

"I'm not God, but I'm sure He is. Just look at the Yankees, this year."

No one chuckled.

"This is serious threat. Your message is that the world will end next Friday at seven p.m. Why is the world going to perish, and why only a seven-day warning?"

"My feeling is that the seven days is just a token extension, and that the world was supposed to end without notice last night. God choose me to deliver a one-week notice, I guess."

Sam thought of the seismic activity that had started the night before at seven. *Coincidence! Don't mention it.* "Why should the world believe in the message?"

"Great question, Ms. Cott. They should believe if they want to save the world."

"I guess it wasn't a great question. Why should they believe God actually spoke through you?"

The majority of the crowd clapped.

Adam held his head high. "Because He did. He spoke through me. He allowed me to try to convince everyone by performing miracles—real miracles. Not magic. It is all up to your faith and belief. God cannot be proven. He just is. We will all find out by Friday, when it may be too late if what happened at Roxy's is dismissed as magic and trickery." Adam paused and looked into the cameras. "A final tenet."

"Do you know how hard it is for an average person to believe God picked a—one—computer programmer—and two—a bar to deliver his message?" Sam asked.

"Yes. He hasn't made it easy, picking me and a bar to work through. Sounds like the start to a bad joke: 'A guy walks into a bar...' I guess if I wasn't there and tuned in to this broadcast, I would have doubt, too."

"Great. We agree. It sounds unbelievable."

"Yes, Sam, it does," Adam said, smiling. "But you were there. What do you believe? I bet you could convince a very wide audience with your journalistic integrity."

"I want the viewers to decide. I don't want to sway them one way or another."

"I'm sorry to hear that," Adam replied.

"Give us another sign, a miracle. The whole world is watching!" a reporter yelled out of turn. "And don't just start my car!"

"Please, wait your turn," Sam said. "You—"

"That's fine, Ms. Cott. If I had a dime every time someone's asked me that," Adam said calmly. "The miracle, Mr. Klein, is that you are all here tonight. You are all here because you think there is a story—a story that will affect every man, woman, and child on the planet." He paused. "How many miracles before everyone believes? Do I have to go on a world tour? Do back-to-back shows? Float entire stadiums? I've already performed miracles for a small number of random people, random believers that must convince the world of what's happened. If I or God created some stupendous miracle, of course you would all believe, but out of fear, fear of the wrath of God. That's why it's called faith. You just need faith."

The panel of experts were sitting at the edges of their seats, all leaning forward.

Sam sensed the tension and thought it was a good time for a segue. "With us tonight, we have invited several experts in religion: Father Radcliff, Catholic priest; Pastor Weibe, non-denominational leader; Rabbi Samuel, of the Jewish faith; and well-known author, speaker, and doctor of theology, Mr. Babbitt."

Adam took out a tissue and dabbed his forehead and temples.

"We'll start with Dr. Babbitt," Sam said.

Babbitt shifted to sitting at the edge of his chair, almost tipping it.

"You speak of God not wanting to perform a grand-scale miracle to weed out those who would fake their faith out of fear, but God can see into the hearts and souls of everyone. He doesn't need to test man. He knows all."

"True, Doctor. He can see everyone's true heart and intentions. But the whole point is to give everyone a chance, a chance to believe out of faith. After all, that's what the divine tenet is, isn't it? It's a religious doctrine that's proclaimed as true without proof. Those that will be able to reach down deep into their souls, to believe in the savior and change, will be saved."

"Father Radcliff," Sam said.

"Yes. Well, I can only say it's about time we had an event to put religion and the goodness of mankind back on the map. Here we are, being televised all over the world, speaking about the word of God, over two thousand years after he sacrificed himself for all of humanity. I say that is a miracle, and no matter whether Mr. Johl is a fake or not. Either the world doesn't end in a week and we are all acting as better people because of it, or the final Judgment Day is finally upon us. Amen."

The gallery broke out into mixed responses. Half clapped and cheered wildly; the other half murmured.

"Father, do you have a question for Mr. Johl?"

"Yes, I do—and for the record, I believe God has chosen you to deliver his message. Do you think you will be saved in the end?"

"No one knows who will be saved."

"Rabbi Samuel, your turn," Sam continued quickly, trying to keep the tempo up.

"I've read the press releases about the future TV broadcasts of earthquakes, fire, and tsunamis. Were you aware of the major seismic activities last night in California and China?"

"No, I was not," Adam said, shaking his head.

"Just wondering if it was a prophetic sign, a warning," Rabbi Samuel continued.

Sam smiled as the rabbi asked what her boss had wanted her to ask.

"Yes. I believe it is definitely a sign. I would expect more in the coming days, especially if we don't change our ways."

"Mmm. One more question," the rabbi continued. "What can you tell us that would help us truly believe God spoke through you and that the world is really going to end on Friday?"

"I think I've answered that question a dozen ways. Why not hear from those that were there? Dove can take it from here," Adam said.

"Okay, Nat Fossano, aka Dove, can answer that question," Sam said. "Dove was present in the bar during the events and was voted as spokesperson for the group."

Dove stood up in the front row closest to the stage and turned to the crowd. "Ask away," he said clearly.

Father Radcliff raised his hand.

"Go ahead, Father," Sam said.

"Son, after witnessing the events at Roxy's Friday night, what would you say truly sold you on the authenticity of what is professed to have happened?"

Dove, who was dressed in a navy blue suit, white shirt—with the top two buttons undone, bowed his head slightly as if he were about to make the sign of the cross but scratched his forehead instead. "I believe in God, I guess, like a lot of people. But it was always at arm's length. Not real. Because if you really believed, then you would believe there is really a devil and there is really going to be a day when it all ends—or restarts, I guess."

People smiled. They nodded and stared at Dove intently.

"When the bees filled my mouth—well, it would be pretty hard not to believe, if it was happening to you." Dove pulled his lip down to show the remnants of the stings. A KCOD camera got a tight shot. "I felt like a big hand swooped down and picked me up, like King Kong did to the woman. I felt safe. I was a believer."

Sam sensed that Dove would be an instant celebrity. He had the look, allure, and magnetism of a hero. "Please come to the front of the room. I'm sure there will be more questions."

Adam got up from his chair at the front of the room to give it up to Dove, then walked toward a reserved seat waiting for him in the front row.

A slender middle-aged man, halfway into the crowd, stood up and sidestepped out of his row to the main aisle down the middle of the room. He took a few quick, large strides toward the front of the room and raised his arm.

When Adam was within a few steps of the seat, a crisp muffled shot echoed through the hot and stuffy room. Adam crumpled to the floor; screaming and hysteria broke out. People dropped to the floor, hiding behind their chairs. Those close to the exits ran out.

Lobato ran toward the shooter, who tried to aim a second shot at Adam. He tackled the shooter before another shot was fired, face first to the yellow tile floor.

Arena was one step behind Lobato.

"This has been a very interesting couple of days," Lobato said as he took his PlastiCuffs out of his pocket.

Arena helped him cuff the man with the plastic ties. The shooter did not resist. "It's just getting started."

9

"You called this happening, back in the car," Lobato said to Arena as he forced his knee into the perpetrator's back, keeping his face to the floor.

Arena quickly surveyed the room. "Secure the building! No one in or out until we get statements," Arena said, quickly surveying the room for other threats.

"Someone call an ambulance!" Lobato yelled as he headed over to Adam.

Arena mobilized the rent-a-cop security guards to assist in locking down the building as her partner tended to Adam.

"Looks like it caught you in the arm—tricep, I'm guessing. You'll live, but it's bleeding pretty good," Lobato pulled off his favorite blue tie and tied a tourniquet around Adam's upper arm, just in case his diagnosis of the wound was wrong.

Arena rejoined Lobato and inspected Adam's arm. "Flesh wound. You're lucky he's a lousy shot, Mr. Johl."

Adam nodded.

"Looks like our interview with Adam will have to wait a day," Lobato said.

"Yep, this could mean Sunday off," Arena added.

"Perfect. You can come over with some beer and watch football—the soccer version, Cass. Portugal's playing Croatia. It'll be a screamer, they had three goals last—"

"Still on the job, here. Focus." Arena gave Lobato a cold stare. "Just sit here, Mr. Johl. Don't move, please. We'll be right back," she said, then pulled Lobato's arm.

He moved with her, a few yards away from Adam. "So...?"

"My phone is vibrating like mad." Arena answered her phone. "Hello." She listened intently. "Thanks," she said, then hung up. "Looks like our janitor corpse had one other thing in common with the other corpse. They both deposited close to seven thousand dollars in cash within the last week, using the same bill of sale for a car."

"These guys are not very bright—careless, even," Lobato replied. "Seemingly depositing all of the cash and using the same bill of sale."

"It was only careless if they were caught."

"Right."

"And they're running a scan of victim number one's hard drive. Should have results tomorrow."

Adam seemed to be trying to listen in on their conversation.

The sound of distant sirens echoed in the hall. "That's probably for you, Mr. Johl," Arena said. "They'll get you patched up here before taking you to the hospital. We'll wait upstairs. Make sure the premises is secured."

Lobato and Arena sat in a church pew, staring up at the altar as they waited for everyone to leave.

Lobato looked up at the cross bearing Jesus, nails pounded through his palms and feet. The blood looked so real. "I could never understand why they use that image—and the cross—to remind us of Jesus. Why not an image of him smiling? Catching fish or something."

"First it's not *the* reminder. It's *a* reminder. Of the sacrifice he made," Arena responded.

"I know why. I just don't see it. If someone killed my father with a gun, the last thing I'd wear around my neck is a gold chain with a little gun on it to remind me of him. Or the bullet that killed him." Lobato whispered a short prayer under his breath, made the sign of the cross, and sat up. "Cass, I know you are an expert in theology—"

"I'm not an expert, just well-studied. Finding the truth has always interested me."

"What are you?"

"What do you mean?" She sighed.

"Are you of any particular faith?"

"Futurist and Preterist. And daughter of a Baptist minister."

"How come I didn't know that you were the daughter of a— We need to talk about that more. But do you have faith? *A* faith?"

"Get to your point, Bren."

"So it's finally *Bren*. I like it. Point is, the one intangible you can't measure is how a religion makes people feel, think, act."

"I can measure that by how many times a religious person walks into a crowded market or theater and blows themself up. I fully understand how it makes them feel."

Footsteps echoed through the cathedral. Lobato and Arena turned to see the elderly priest shuffling down the aisle.

"Closing time, officers," the father said. "Adam is on his way to the hospital."

"Saved by the bell," Arena said. "I still have plenty to teach you, Grasshopper."

Arena and Lobato left the pews. Lobato faced the altar, genuflected, and signed the cross.

"Say, Father, what do you think about this whole message about the world ending Friday?" Arena asked as they made their way to the door.

"No one knows when it will end, dear. And I think the expert panel should have mentioned that. They may have, if they had had more time." He stopped walking, grabbed her arm, and looked straight into her eyes. "Mathew 24:35–36. 'Heaven and earth will pass away, but My words shall not pass away. But of that day, and hour, no one knows, not even the angels of heaven, nor the Son, but the Father alone.'"

They continued for the door. "That sums it up nicely. Thanks, Father," Arena said.

By the door, Lobato dipped his hand in the well of holy water and again made the sign of the cross.

The agents left the church and silently made their way to the car. Arena stopped on the west side of the building and looked up at the bizarre stone carving in a pillar, one that chillingly depicted the destruction of New York City, including the Twin Towers, but had been carved four years before 9/11. Arena remembered the controversy when the carvings were unveiled. The pillar also had the Chrysler building and Citigroup Center crumbling.

"Confused?" Lobato asked, turning to see why Arena had stopped. He looked up at the pillar. "That's just a conspiracy theory." He pointed up. "The Freemasons funded this building. Since day one."

"I'm not confused at all. Why do you ask?"

"No one knows when it will end, yet Adam Johl could be legit and gives the date. According to your 'Anything's possible' theory."

Arena continued toward the car. "Thanks for trying to comfort me. But I'm totally fine. Just thinking."

Lobato opened the door, one foot on the curb, one on the road.

"Adam Johl may just be giving us a warning shot. Maybe he's not talking in days... *Yôm*? So maybe he told us, and maybe he didn't. It's all perception." Arena got into the car.

Lobato nodded slowly, closed her door, went around, and got behind the wheel. "I never stop learning from you."

"And when you can snatch the Skittle from my hand, you will be worthy," Arena said, shaking a Skittle into her palm from a bag that she kept tucked in the door's cup holder.

Lobato made a move for it, but it was already in her mouth.

She shook some out of the bag into Lobato's hand. "Enjoy. If I have to wait for you to snatch one, you'll starve."

Lobato ate the Skittles then pulled out into the road. "You Baptists are pretty quick."

Arena ignored him.

"Isn't Cassia Arena a Greek or Italian name? Shouldn't you be Orthodox or Catholic?"

"My father's great-grandfather was Italian."

"Nice. Did I mention I was Portuguese? That's close to Italy. Something else we have in common."

"Did I mention I was raised by a strict Baptist minister who hated boys? Especially those of Latin decent?"

"I love those kinds of girls."

Arena shook her head. That was going nowhere fast. "Take me home, Latin lover."

Sam leaned against the cold stone column midway down the steps leading into the church as she watched the FBI agents drive off. She gazed up at the hazy grey-blue early evening sky above her and took a big breath. She looked back down at the street and the continuous stream of Saturday night traffic funneling into Manhattan. People continued on their quest for normality, whatever they perceived that to be.

Sam's reality was her daughter. She pulled her smartphone out and speed-dialed Sunshine. Nothing else mattered more than her daughter, and she needed to show it. Now.

Her daughter answered after two rings.

"Why are you answering the phone? Shouldn't you be in bed?"

"I'm waiting for you, Mommy!"

I'm glad, she thought. "Sorry I'm late. Things took a little turn tonight, but I'm on my way now. You can wait up for me. I still want to help you with your project."

"Okay, but if my eyes close, just open them when you get home."

There was a call waiting beep on Sam's phone. "See you soon. Love you." Sam disconnected and checked the number calling. It was her boss.

Sam hesitated for a moment, let out a massive sigh, pressed *Ignore*, then went to the street to hail a cab.

Pressing *Ignore* was hard to do when she was in the habit of always answering her boss. She was proud of herself; there might be hope yet for her reform. Maybe she would learn to uni-task next?

10
Sunday - Day 2

Claire Nadeau attended the seven thirty a.m. Mass at the Holy Spirit Church.

At the end of the Mass, the priest invited Claire to the pulpit to address the congregation, and for the first time in her life, she spoke before a large audience.

"Thank you, Father Jaworski, for letting me speak today," she said, her voice shaking. "I..."—she cleared her throat—"I witnessed..." She paused and looked into the attentive eyes of the parishioners. "Listen. Many of you know me. I've lived in New Hyde Park my whole life. My parents went to this church; I buried them here. I got married to the wrong man here."

The congregation laughed.

A few people came to the front to video record her speech.

"I see most of you know him." She smiled. "And we baptized our daughter here." Claire took the mic and went out in front of the pulpit. "I haven't been sure of much in my life, and the last five years have been dark and confusing for me. I've felt as though my heart and soul were ripped from me since I found out my husband had been cheating on me for years—and Friday night, at Roxy's, it felt as if God himself reached down and picked me up into his very own arms."

People closed their eyes, clasped their hands, and bowed.

"I can't make you believe or see what I saw and heard. But I can and have prayed that you have faith and believe through me." She took a big breath. "This may sound out there, but I feel like this is the reason I was born. I now have purpose. And I know, without a doubt, that if any of you were in that bar on Friday night, you would say the same thing. I must deliver this message, and I am praying that you will all help me."

The congregation stood and clapped. A few overzealous people cheered. The priest smiled.

"Thank you." Claire smiled and held her head high as she left the altar. *I haven't felt this alive since I was eighteen and unmarried.*

***

The smell of slightly overcooked waffles and coffee wafted in the air. Marty Graham could hear his children talking softly to their mother in the kitchen. He looked in the mirror at his unshaven face and the dark circles around his eyes. He popped three aspirin. His mind had reeled all night, confused about what to do about God and booze. His hand shook as he placed the bottle back in the medicine cabinet, then he dialed his sponsor on his cell.

His sponsor answered after several rings.

"Hey, Jim. It's me, Marty."

"You okay?" Jim asked. "You missed the meeting again. And I've been leaving you messages. Talk to me, man."

"I need to stay sober this week, and I need your help—by the hour, if necessary."

"I know. I saw you on the news. Nothing like the end of the world to sober a guy up."

"For a week, anyway."

"We'll start with one day, friend. I'll be over in half an hour."

"Thanks, Jim."

"Don't thank me. Thank God."

"I'll drink to that."

"*Marty.*"

"I know, bad timing. Later." Marty hung up, held on to the sides of the sink, and stared into his bloodshot eyes. His first drink had been at thirteen years old, a mickey of Southern Comfort, on a dare. He'd thrown up and swore he'd never do that again. The following weekend, he switched to beer, then a few years later, Jack Daniels. It made him fit in with a certain crowd. He had been the life of the party, when he was young. Now he was the drunk of the party. And the drunk of every other place.

He splashed cool water on his face and let it drip as he looked up again. *Party's over.*

***

"You're seventy-nine. You can't be running all over the world for this. Your heart! The doctor said to take it easy," said Mary Beech, sitting on the plastic-covered sofa.

"Seventy-nine is the new fifty-nine, haven't you heard?" Daisy laughed then drank her coffee. She loved her daughter but felt like an invalid around her. Mary was always controlling her. "No one's going to stop me. I'm off to the Caribbean tomorrow, and I will visit every island in the West Indies."

"You know I can't go with you. I just started my job, and I have the kids. How will you get around safely?" Mary took a big breath. "And there's lots of nutbars out there."

"I don't need anyone. You stay here and spread the word, dear. Besides, I'll enlist the help of all four ex-husbands. I have one on each of the big islands, plus boyfriends on the others." Daisy slapped her own knee. "And then there are all your brothers and sisters—too many to remember."

"Right. So many. You were such a player, Mom. No wonder your men all left you."

"Still am! And this should redeem me with Him," Daisy said, pointing up.

"That's a stretch."

"Well, if I'm judged at the pearly gates and they're humming and hawing whether to let me in, I'll do what I do best—"

"Mom!"

"Dance, dearie. Dance. What kind of girl do you think I am?"

"I know what kind, Mom. And yes, dancing was a part of it."

***

Arena and Lobato spent the drizzly grey Sunday morning drudging through news reports and paperwork and analyzing doomsday and fanatical groups. Lobato had brought a ten-cup container of coffee and a box of six donuts.

The news broadcasts and newspapers were filled with events of the past two days, especially the coincidence of tremors around the world. While the shooting of Adam at the church was the most popular new video clip on YouTube, the Roxy's miracles continued to be analyzed, and those reports banked the most total views. Academy Award-winning Hollywood special effects experts, Vegas magicians, and well-known news celebrities all had their opinions on how the miracles were pulled off.

A famous magician explained how he could possibly do almost everything that happened in the bar—including the floating chairs, flying, and mind-reading. He explained that the news broadcast could have been created in a few ways, such as in collusion with the anchor or with audio strung together to match lip movement, the latter of which could then be manually manipulated to polish it off. With the confusion, excitement, and distance of the monitors, those watching may not have noticed if the speech and lips were not entirely synchronized. He also said if what happened at Roxy's were illusions, he would want Adam to teach him. The tricks were flawless, the best he had seen, and would involve tons of planning.

In coffee shops and at Sunday buffets, people discussed the possibility of God, what they would do in case it were their last week on earth, and what size tips they should leave their servers.

Blogs and social network sites chugged and sputtered due to the massive volume of opinions aching to be heard. Since the event at Roxy's, Twitter had a record number of tweets, overloading their capacity. Debate about the existence of God was as common as discussions about the weather.

The media had been camped out at Adam's home around the clock, broadcasting everything possible that they could learn about him. Even Adam's last name and its Hebrew origin and meaning of "as chosen by Jehovah" was analyzed. People who knew Adam—his neighbors, his coworkers, and even people at the coffee shop that he frequented—were interviewed by reporters. The reporters competed to get the newest and most interesting piece of information.

The media had been void of a sensational story for weeks, and Adam Johl performing at Roxy's fed the bulimic beast by the shovelful.

"It's getting a little crazy out there. We're going to have to step up the investigation." Arena tapped her pen on the desk. "How is our prophet doing today?"

"They're going to release him tomorrow."

"We'll get over to the hospital later today, have the chat. We may have enough to hold him on terrorist threats."

"What does the report on the shooter say?"

"Are you sitting down?" Arena asked, picking up a piece of paper from her desk printer.

Lobato gave her a weird look, as he was already sitting. He drank his coffee then bit into his chocolate glazed donut.

"Muslim extremist and part of the terrorist sleeper cell we've been watching. We have a team drilling him right now."

"Ballistics from the church shooting match the dead guy in Queens and the janitor in Brooklyn."

"Why is it everyone we're watching is not being watched when they do something?"

"This shooter was cleaning up loose ends. The Queens victim was also known as an expert forger—passports, birth certificates. One of the best. And he ran a machine shop for fabricating as a cover—not sure how that fits in yet. And it looks like our old janitor wasn't a janitor."

"Let me guess, house cleaner?"

Arena smiled. "Retired cameraman. Did movies, mostly."

Lobato nodded. "That could mean that the cameraman filmed the 'miracle' TV sequence at KCOD, the Queens guy maybe supplied Adam and others with fake papers, and the shooter was cleaning up everyone."

Arena raised her eyebrows. "Good summary. Still sitting?"

Lobato raised his hands in the air and shook his head. "I guess you mean, am I ready for what you're going to say?"

Arena didn't answer him. "One of the communications this shooter made was to the same IP address that our Queens victim had also been in contact with a few months ago. Both made hotel reservations in Florida. Disney World."

"Holiday?" Lobato asked.

"Meeting. Or a point of departure from the country."

"Why not next to an airport or port city if they were going to leave the country?"

"Good question. And if we knew the answer, we would be closer to solving this."

"What was the date for the reservation?"

Arena quickly read the page. "This Thursday night."

"A terrorist summit in Disney World? But for what? Magic acts? Maybe they're all going there to help with some bigger illusions?"

Arena looked pensive. Lobato strummed his desk.

"But why? Why all this magic? The prophecies? Motive is what we need now," she said.

"What would happen if the world were hypothetically to end on Friday? Chaos."

"They're trying to attack us with chaos?"

"Psychological warfare. Terrorism in its purest form."

Arena nodded. "Yes. Possible. But they would need more. The magic isn't enough to throw the world into an apocalyptic craze."

"The tremors that started—lucky timing for Johl? And something is going to happen in Disney World?"

"I'm impressed, Breno. You are truly contributing to this investigation." Arena sipped her coffee and opened the box of donuts to see only two left, and she hadn't eaten any yet.

"Thanks. That means everything, coming from you."

"I know."

"Okay, while I'm contributing, I say we go to ground zero: Roxy's. Give it a real close look and shake that bar owner."

"Already called him. We're meeting him there in an hour." Arena stuck a note on Lobato's laptop screen with the time. "Then off to the hospital."

Lobato smiled and shook his head. "I hope our children are as smart as you."

"Infatuation with your first partner is normal. You're just lucky I'm a woman."

"And I guess you're lucky I'm a man."

Arena gave Lobato a two-fingered gunshot to his face. "Right, Brenda."

"I prefer Bren."

"I think I'm going to leak something to the press through my contact."

"What?" Lobato said as he stood up and stretched.

"I want the press to raise the question that this could all be psychological terrorism, a plot to throw the world into chaos. That may turn the heat up a little on Johl and Darnell. It's just a matter of time before we prove it."

"How do you do that without compromising confidential information?"

"You don't want to know yet. Go get the car. I'll be a few minutes."

Lobato nodded and left.

The two agents pulled up to Roxy's fifteen minutes early to survey the exterior. There were empty crates and cartons piled at the rear, along with a truck-sized garbage container. Someone had sloppily spray painted across Roxy's front windows, "There is no God! Get over it!" in red.

The front doors were locked, and a sign read, "Open for Business Monday at 4:00 p.m. - Sorry for the inconvenience."

There were a shrine of flowers, small statues of Jesus and Mary, and letters of prayer adorning the entry vestibule. There were at least two dozen candles lit in clear jars.

Darnell Williams opened the front door a few minutes late. The smell of fresh paint, vinyl, and sawdust hit them instantly. Rolls of carpet and cases of tiles were piled on the floor. After semi-cordial introductions, Arena asked, "Are you alone?"

"Yes."

"Where are all the workers?"

Darnell hesitated. "Lunch."

"Mmm," Arena said, rubbing the backs of the new chairs. "Looks as if you've been... busy?"

"Renovations. Had them planned for months, *years*."

Before entering, the agents had decided—through a game of rock, paper, scissors—that Lobato would manage the questioning, and he gave her a look to keep quiet.

"Bad timing for renovations?" Lobato questioned.

"Bad timing? Not really. Besides, couldn't cancel the orders. Trucks were rolling; staff, scheduled. It was a lot of work, timing this to have it done in two and a half days."

"Yeah, I can imagine that it's tough closing for two days. Lose a lot of sales."

"That's for sure. Weekend's my busiest time."

"So why the weekend? Why not do the renovations on Monday, Tuesday?"

"That's just when I could get the stuff delivered."

"Why not put it in storage for a few days? That's got to be cheaper than losing weekend sales."

"It was the workers, too. A lot of my friends. They could only do it in their spare time; they were off on the weekends."

"You hired friends? Why not just hire professionals on slow days? After all the sales you would lose on a—"

"What's your point? Are you here to talk renovations or about what happened here Friday night?"

Arena and Lobato looked at each other and smirked openly.

"Just curious. You know when someone claims to be speaking through God and threatens that the world could end in a week spreading chaos, we've got to check everything out," Lobato said.

Darnell gave them a stern look, his left brow raised. He tapped his toes. "What does this have to do with me?"

Arena made her way behind the bar, poking around.

"Did you know Adam Johl before Friday night?" Lobato continued.

"He had never been in my place before."

"I never asked if he had been in your place. I asked if you knew him."

"No."

"Are you positive? You remember every single customer that has ever walked through your doors?"

"What does 'no' mean? I'd never seen him before. Should I get a lawyer to start answering you, maybe a Bible to swear on?" Darnell fumbled a cigarette out of his shirt pocket and lit it.

"What about Nat Fossano, aka Dove. Did you know him?"

"Didn't know him, but he's been in here before, maybe once or twice. The girls love him." Darnell headed behind the bar.

"Ever talk to him before Friday night?" Lobato followed him.

Arena poked her head into the kitchen.

Darnell grabbed an ashtray. "Probably said 'Hello' or 'How you doin'?' That's about it. Why these questions?"

"We told you why. What did you do with all the old chairs and furniture?" Lobato asked.

"They took them away."

"Who?"

"The guys who delivered all the furniture. It was part of the deal I made; they would get all the old equipment. It reduced my cost." Darnell grabbed a broom and swept sawdust around the bar, cigarette dangling from his mouth.

"Can we get up onto the roof?"

"They just re-tarred and graveled it, so you'll have to wait a few days."

"How convenient."

"What the hell are you insinuating?"

"What about the sound system? Can we take a look?"

"No, the stuff that was here Friday night is all gone. Swapped it all out. Got a brand new updated DJ system. State of the art."

"Must have been a huge investment."

"Big enough."

"Where did you get all the money for this major reno? Private investors?"

"I cashed in my rolled pennies."

"Where did Mr. Johl fly up through the ceiling?" Arena yelled from the other side of the room.

"Straight above the stage over there," Darnell said, pointing.

She shone her flashlight up at the twenty-foot-high ceiling. "Is that fresh paint?"

"We're doing renovations! Painting is part of that." Darnell rolled his eyes.

"You'd think you'd want to keep this place like a shrine... I mean *God* speaking here and all... You could make a lot of money from curiosity seekers," Lobato said.

"Those types of people don't drink," Darnell threw back. He dropped the broom, went behind the bar, and poured himself a glass of cola. "Besides, it wasn't God who spoke—"

"What about the news anchor, Paul Mansfield. Do you know him?"

"Everyone knows him. He's on the news every night."

"Let me make it a simpler question. Has Paul Mansfield ever visited your bar, and have you ever met him in person?"

"No," Darnell snapped back with a sneer then gulped his cola.

"What religious denomination are you?"

"Money-istic," he said, dabbing his temples with a cocktail napkin then taking a drag of his cigarette, hand shaking slightly.

"You've been a little short with us. I could call you uncooperative. Maybe you'd be a little nicer answering some questions downtown," Lobato said, stepping closer to Darnell.

"Downtown? What charges?" Darnell asked. "That's an empty threat."

"Obstructing justice," Arena responded.

Darnell laughed. "Whatever. I'm sort of a Catholic. Okay? Obstructing justice, what a joke."

"Sort of Catholic?" Lobato continued.

"Haven't been to church in years, but I'm going Sunday. You would, too, if you'd seen what happened here."

"That wasn't too convincing," Lobato said.

"Wasn't trying to convince you."

"Clearly. We're done here for now. One last thing—what's the name and address of the company that took your old equipment?"

Darnell reached into his pocket and pulled out a crumpled business card. "Here. Call them, go see them—whatever makes you happy. Don't want to obstruct your mission..."

"How cooperative you've become. Let's go, Cass," Lobato shouted to Arena.

As Arena came from the other side of the bar, she bent down, picked something up, and placed it in her pocket.

Darnell tapped the bar with a straw while he sucked the life out of his cigarette.

"We'll be in touch," Lobato said.

Darnell escorted them to the door then quickly locked it after they left.

As the two agents walked to the car, Lobato asked, "What did you pick up from the floor?"

"This. A small, slender steel spring." She showed him. "Looks like high-strength steel. Aviation, maybe."

"Used in the chairs, *maybe*?"

"Maybe." Arena laughed. "We'll have the lab check it out."

Lobato nodded. "We're losing it. I'm thinking it's time for lunch: great Italian food and nice dry red wine."

"Lobato, you're relentless. And you drink too much wine."

"What? A guy's gotta eat. And wine goes with food. Ask Jesus. It's not always about you-you-you."

"So, it's all about Italian food and booze?"

"Yeah. Italian food, it's close to my heritage." Lobato paused. "Wine complements food. Okay, and you. It's also about you. If you didn't know..."

"You're buying." Arena undid her ponytail and let her hair drop to her shoulders, then checked her watch. "But it's a quick lunch. We have to get to the hospital. No *vino*."

"Do you have to do that thing with your hair? You know, like a shampoo commercial."

"It simply dropped. I didn't even shake it."

"Still. It's all loose and wavy now. And so red."

Arena rolled her eyes and gave it an extra toss as they walked.

"I love you."

"*Breno...* Seriously, it's unprofessional. Stop. That's an order."

"I meant to say, sure, I've got the bill. It's my turn."

Arena passed Lobato and double-timed it to the car, hiding her smile as she gathered her hair and retied her ponytail.

11

"I am not eating any more carbs for a week," Arena said as they pulled up to the emergency entrance to the Harlem Hospital center. Lobato parked next to the curb, twenty feet from the doors.

There were roughly thirty to forty people close to the entrance. Divided into two almost equal groups, they were yelling back and forth about Adam and the prophecies. Two security guards were at the door. One spoke on his phone, the other had his arms crossed and watched the crowd.

"Looks as if we may burn them off quickly. That half loves them." He indicated the half who looked as if they just came from either a church or a Green Peace rally. "That half—well, just look at them. Weird mix. Some probably worship Metallica and 7-11 corner stores; others look almost normal."

Lobato and Arena both looked at the rough-looking side of the mob, and Arena chuckled at the sight of a young man wearing a Metallica hoodie next to a guy wearing a white short-sleeved shirt and bright yellow tie. "What a mixed crowd. This is what he wants," Arena said, as they exited their dark blue sedan. "He wants them fighting, everyone fighting."

A middle-aged woman, who sort of looked like Oprah, waved a sign that read "Finally!" at the agents as they passed by the crowd.

A slim, young, pale man wearing a black trench coat grabbed the sign and broke it over his knee and yelled, "*Finally*... someone broke your sign!"

"Okay, settle down!" Lobato said as he stopped, standing toe-to-toe with the young aggressor.

"Johl's gotta pay! They should hang 'em!"

A few more yelled, "Johl's a fake!"

"Kool-Aid maker!" someone shouted.

"Repent, sinners!" and "God is Great!" was shouted in Adam's defense.

All six of the hospital's security guards stood in front of the shouting crowd. Invectives were hurled at the guards and at Adam's supporters.

The quick chirps of a police car's siren announced the arrival of two cruisers with four officers. They parked staggered in front of the group, quickly left their vehicles, and worked with the security guards to move the mob off the property.

Lobato and Arena continued on to the doors and watched.

After shoving, spitting, and a string of vulgar words not in the Bible, the groups were moved off hospital property to the sidewalk. Believers stood on one side of the entrance to the hospital; everyone else grouped on the other. The police cruisers positioned themselves at the entrance and would stay for a while to ensure compliance.

Arena and Lobato made their way to the fourth floor and Adam's private room. The police officer who was stationed outside the room tipped his hat after the two agents flashed their credentials. Arena handed Lobato another mint to cover up garlicky breath from their spicy, alcohol-free lunch, then entered the room.

The room had one bed, two chairs, a TV suspended from the ceiling—tuned to a news station—and one large window with blinds. Adam was sitting up in his bed, reading the paper.

"Hello, I'm FBI Agent Breno Lobato, and this is my partner, Agent Cassia Arena. We met at the church."

"Yes, thanks so much for your help yesterday. I never thought anyone would try to kill me—so soon, that is."

Lobato moved to the window, slightly fidgety. "Well, there's a mob out there waiting for you, as well. Be prepared for more of the same."

Arena crossed her arms. "Tact, Breno?"

"What I meant to say was, you're still not out of danger, Mr. Johl. But we're here to help you, if you help us."

Adam sat up a little straighter. "Will you escort me out of here today, past that mob? I would really appreciate it."

"What I had in mind, actually, is the truth. The truth shall set you free."

"Truth?" Adam asked, shaking his head.

"If you want all this to end, tell the truth. As it sits now, the charges will be minimal. You'll probably just get community service time for public mischief. Maybe even a spot on a TV talent show for your magic acts."

Adam's mouth tightened. "The truth is you have a little over five days left to do everything you've ever wanted to do in your life, because on Friday night, it's all over. I'd call in sick the rest of the week, if I were you."

Arena and Lobato looked at each other.

"That's one cold look. Frightened, maybe?" Adam questioned.

"That's funny. Let's start with who you were eight years ago?" Arena asked.

"A younger version of myself."

"Who forged your identity? Seven years ago?" she continued. "Or are you like Obama? No real birth certificate?"

"That's really funny, Agent Arena. Besides, he does have a real birth certificate."

"Not according to Donald Trump. Where were you eight years ago? Where did you live, work?"

"Here, in New York. Just started with Conestry."

"The truth, please."

Adam examined Arena's face. "That's the truth."

"We can't find any history on you past seven years ago. Would you know why?"

"I've been Adam Johl for thirty-six years."

"You've paid no taxes for your first twenty-nine years on this planet."

"Maybe I was unemployed."

Arena stood a foot from the side of Adam's bed. "Maybe you worked and didn't pay your taxes? That's enough for us to hold you, until we check that out. Tax evasion can put you behind bars."

"My history goes back to day one of my life."

"Yes, but the 'real you' has no footprint past seven years ago. Forged papers can't leave footprints. Credit card bills for restaurants, gas. Ordering things online to be delivered to your house." She slowly walked to the other side of the bed.

Lobato sat on the edge of the window ledge, occasionally looking down at the parking lot and street while Arena continued the questioning.

"Your forgers are very good. You must have connections within government agencies, too, and we will find them all. We have a team on it, so it will just be a matter of time, and it will serve you best to come clean now. Stop this before it really starts."

Adam said nothing. He sat up, arms crossed, staring straight across the room at the wall.

"Are you Muslim?" Arena asked.

"I believe there is a God."

"Of course."

"Do you believe there is a God, Ms. Arena?"

She ignored the question. "Are you part of a sleeper terrorist cell?"

"What's that?"

"The 'cell' part is where you'll be spending some time if you don't cooperate."

"Funny again." Adam adjusted some of the tubes on his bed and looked out the window, not making eye contact with the agents.

"How long have you and Darnell Williams been planning this at Roxy's?"

"It wasn't planned. It happened."

"Why can't you answer a question honestly?"

"Why won't you answer a simple question like do you believe in God?"

"I don't have to answer that."

"But I do?"

"You are the one threatening the lives of every American."

"No, I am not."

"What do you call the threat the world will end next Friday? A date?"

"I'm not threatening anyone, just warning." Adam shifted in the bed and scratched his head.

Arena shrugged. "Same thing in the eyes of the FBI. You are a threat to the safety of American citizens, and until you can prove to me that God really did speak through you or admit that you are just a wannabe magician, then you are a threat. And a threat like this is an act of psychological terrorism. Maybe you'll disclose that there is a bomb that will go off next Friday if the world doesn't repent? Maybe it will be in a crowded stadium? So answer my questions."

"You are asking questions I can't or won't answer. Ask me something clever that I don't think would incriminate me." He shifted again in the bed.

"I've already asked you clever questions. Your response, or lack thereof, and your body language gave me all the answers I need—for now."

Adam's smile disappeared.

She looked out the window. "Yes, you clearly have been well trained and are extremely well connected. I would think if we rushed you off to our special camp for an intensive 'chat,' you may answer a few more questions, honestly. Or maybe the pressure from the fanatical groups out there will do our job for us. Did you know that the atheists actually have large groups—churches, so to speak?

They are all over the country, and they are hating you right now."

Adam shook his head. "Keep trying."

"Those atheist groups probably have some people who are extreme. Radicals. Sort of like the Muslims. One or two bad seeds trying to cause terror. Maybe blow something up. Maybe you."

"I guess the police will get me out of here safely."

"Maybe, but what about at home? What about your car? Are you sure you can turn the key without it going 'boom'? This won't be over until you come clean, Mr. Johl. You'll be running for a long time, in jail, or dead. With this charade you've conjured up, there is no in-between with radicals. People are wound up very tight these days, about religion of all faiths. Or about the battle in the schools over the Lord's prayer. Or about the phrase 'One nation under God'."

"I've done nothing wrong."

"Agent Arena and I are here to help you. Let us," Lobato piped up as he paced.

"There's nothing else I can tell you than what's already been told. If you don't believe, then you'll be two more reasons mankind fails."

"We can hold you indefinitely."

"For what?" Adam asked, sounding shocked.

"We have information that could link you to known terrorist cells."

"What information?" His forehead glistened.

"Information that gives us enough cause to lock you up until we verify and review the information. Could take months."

"How is a message from God an act of terrorism?" Adam asked. "Besides, terrorism suspects who are not declared enemy combatants—which I *have not been*—are subject to the laws of the state in which they are apprehended. In New York, that's twenty-four hours in lockup. Maximum."

"See? You told me something again without telling me anything." Arena smiled.

"You can leave now, please. Unless you want to detain me under your *information*."

The patrolman in the hallway poked his head in the room.

"We're just leaving," Lobato said to the officer, then turned back to Adam. "Here are our cards. If you change your mind or it gets too hot in hell, give us a call."

"No handcuffing me to the bed? Sticking me in a damp, dark cell as a terrorist?"

"You would just magically escape, fly through the ceiling. We'll be in touch very soon, Adam. Don't leave town. Or magically disappear."

The agents laid their cards on the end of the bed and left the room.

"Do you think it was my breath that made him so friendly?" Lobato asked, huffing into his hand and sniffing.

"We need to have one of our people tailing him when he gets out," Arena said, pressing the parking button in the elevator. "What he does next and who he meets are more important to us than detaining him. He wouldn't say shit."

"We're so thin with Code Orange up again. Will they even give us more manpower on this? I mean, it's just a bunch of magic acts so far, with loose connections to some dead people. No hard evidence."

"For this, yes. They can see where it's headed fast. We have to talk to Dove next. He's in on it, too. See if we can shake him up and—" Arena's phone pinged.

"Work faster and harder. We're turning into corporate America," Lobato said as the elevator opened to the main floor.

"It's my phone," Arena interrupted.

"Oh, mine just started too." Lobato reached into his pocket to check his phone.

"Death threats to the Pope," Arena read.

They stared at each other then exited the elevator on the main floor.

Lobato broke the silence. "Wow, this is nuts."

"Like birth pains," Arena said.

"What?" Lobato asked as they exited the hospital.

"Biblical reference. I am a religious specialist, you know—"

"You've told me. Twenty times," he said as they got to the car. He opened the door for Arena.

Arena waited for Lobato to get into the driver's seat, then continued, "If it were twenty times, you'd think you get it by now," Arena jabbed. "Armageddon comes like birth pains. The signs start out slow, and as it gets closer to birth—or Armageddon—the pains happen more frequently and are more intense. And Adam and his group are fueling it."

"You've had a baby?"

"No..."

"Do you want to have one? I mean, in the future."

"Why does it always have to end up there?" she said, as Lobato started the car and pulled away.

"What's it? And where's what?"

"In your tiny brain, the one between your legs."

"Hey, unless you've seen my brain, please don't comment on its size. There's a lot of grey matter there."

"I would say it's probably more like 'Doesn't matter.'"

"We'll take this up at a later time, real late, after dinner... and wine, two or three bottles. Then I'll show you who matters—me and Einstein, that's who."

"It'll take a lot more than three bottles." Arena turned her head and looked out the window, trying not to laugh. "It would take the entire Sonoma Valley of wine. And if I did call you on it, you'd back down like a frightened school boy at his first dance."

"Ouch." Lobato winced. "But you've got me wrong. I could win the mirror ball on *Dancing with the Stars*."

"Don't tell me you've watched that," Arena said, as their smartphones pinged again while they passed the placard-waving mob on the street. They glanced at each other, then Arena read, "Seismic activity—Caracas and the Mid-Atlantic, east of New York."

"Birth pains?" Lobato asked.

"Is there one of those seismic places close to us, here in New York? I'd like to talk to someone about this. It's too coincidental."

"Actually, in 2004 I was invited to the grand opening of the Gottesman Hall of Planet Earth at the New York Public Library. They have a real-time earthquake station there." Lobato inflated his chest as he maneuvered his car around a stalled pickup truck.

"Were you a science nerd?"

"Nerd? Do I look like a nerd? I had them lined up, let me tell you—"

"At the exit door."

Lobato ignored the remark. "My girlfriend was Gottesman's niece, Pat Meadows. Thought I'd be bored out of my mind, but it was very interesting. They have a large, three-drum seismograph that constantly monitors and records ground shaking as it occurs at stations in Fairbanks, Alaska; Tucson; and Japan."

"Boy, that must have been some date."

"For her, it was. She's a seismologist, and she still works there." Lobato slammed his breaks to stop at the congested intersection. "Not that I've checked in on her lately. Damn traffic."

"Maybe we could talk to her."

"We could. I'll try to set it up for tomorrow. And don't worry—I broke things off with her years ago. She never had enough time for me."

"Oh, good. I was worried," Arena said, shaking her head. "I wouldn't want to scratch her eyes out in a cat fight."

"What's that asshole doing?" Lobato rolled down his window to get a better view at the street. "Traffic has stopped dead."

"He's stalled… or he can't—"

Crack! Bang! came two loud shots from out front of the vehicle.

Arena and Lobato ducked and drew their weapons.

She peeked up over the dash after checking her side-view mirror. "Backfire," she said.

"This case has us spooked," Lobato said as they sat back up and holstered their guns.

"Has *you* spooked."

"You can't tell me it doesn't creep you out, even a little? I think you're hiding it."

"Will you look at that?" She pointed at the hazy Manhattan sky as the sun set.

Lobato strained to look up out the window. "What?"

"That cloud! It's unbelievable."

"Which one?"

"The incredible one that looks exactly like Jesus carrying the cross—right there. Must be a sign."

"Where? I don't see it."

"It's right next to one that spells out 'sucker.'"

The car in front of them had pulled away. The car behind him honked.

Lobato pulled his head back in the window and put his foot on the accelerator. "That'll be ten Our Fathers and a couple of Hail Mary's." He paused. "I'm a spiritual person. I was an altar boy, went to church every Sunday. I'm just saying, you can never be too sure."

"Be sure of this, Breno: Adam Johl is no more a prophet of God than Elvis is alive and a grill cook in Memphis."

"Maybe we should go check out the Memphis diner. If Elvis is there, then..." Lobato smiled.

Arena smiled back, wondering if she had let their partnership become too lax, too quick. Allowing Breno to joke around a little too much and to flirt with her could be dangerous in the field, and as the senior partner, she should put a stop to it. The problem was, she enjoyed it as a welcome relief in a stressful and sometimes excruciatingly boring job. She needed to be worrying about the two minutes of heart-thumping chaos that tended to follow the weeks of monotony—that was when they would both need to be one hundred percent on their game.

Maybe she would find an appropriate time to have a heart-to-heart with him. *Soon.*

They drove quietly, both in thought.

"Do you?" Lobato asked.

"Do I? That's random. Do I what?"

"What Johl asked you at the hospital. Do you believe in God? Really believe?"

Arena hesitated. "Yes. I do."

"Oh."

"Oh?"

"Just oh. And good."

Arena shook her head, and they continued on in silence.

12
Monday - Day 3

The mob that had been ushered off the hospital property was tipped off by Arena's contact as to when Adam Johl would leave the hospital and that the police would try to slip him out the back door by the delivery dock.

They rushed the doors as Adam was escorted through them. The security guards attempted to move them back, but the crowd had grown to more than seventy-five and overwhelmed the six guards.

Flanked by four policemen, a nurse pushed Adam in a wheelchair down a ramp to the police car. One officer opened the back door while another watched the crowd. Just before Adam entered the vehicle, someone in the mob tossed an egg and nailed Adam on the side of the face—another egg hit an officer in the chest. The eggs smelled as if they had been left on a hot sidewalk for days. A scuffle broke out in the crowd as profanity was shouted at Adam.

A man with a knife broke through the front line of the crowd, yelled "Die!", and lunged toward Adam as he entered the car. An officer drew his weapon and fired at him. The man dropped to the ground, blood oozing from his chest. One officer whisked Adam away in the unmarked car.

The officer looked in his rearview mirror. "I hope you know what you're doing, Mr. Johl."

"Please, I need police protection. At my house."

"Sorry, but we've been told to drop you off. But you can take it up with my boss or his boss." The officer looked concerned. "It doesn't make sense to me, either, but an order's an order."

"You just saw what happened. That's the second attempt on my life in less than two days."

"Do you own a gun?"

"No! I don't believe in guns."

"Listen." The officer glanced in his mirror. "We'll have someone drive by and check on you, off the record. I don't think it's right either, but you must have really pissed someone off."

"Maybe, but they are upsetting a much higher power."

The officer raised his eyebrows.

He took Adam to his house, escorted him to his front door, and gave him some basic advice on safety. Adam thanked him. The officer seemed sincere and did what he could.

Adam watched him as he parked outside his house for thirty minutes, doing some paperwork. Then a car came by to relieve him, which only stayed for fifteen minutes before they left, seemingly in a hurry.

He checked out his kitchen window, which was at the back of the house. All looked quiet in his backyard.

Adam returned to his front room. He parted the dark red curtains in his living room and looked out to his street that was lined with vehicles, buses, news vans, and people mingling about holding mugs, cameras, and Bibles. He closed the curtain and looked at his scantly decorated living room. He had no family photos or pictures on the wall to pack. On a table next to his Moroccan couch was a lucky bamboo plant in a square, clear glass vase. It had been his lone living companion for almost seven years as he'd worked on his laptop.

Smash!

A rock with a newspaper wrapped around it broke the window, rolling along the carpet and stopping by Adam's feet. He calmly picked it up and unwrapped it. The newspaper clipping contained an article from that day's newspaper, about him possibly having terrorist ties. Written in red felt pen over it was the message, "Burn in hell with your seventy virgins!"

"Fan mail... And I wish they'd get their facts right. It's seventy-two virgins." He laughed to himself. "Time to pack the lucky bamboo and laptop."

***

Lobato and Arena rolled up to century-old New York Public Library thirty minutes before its opening. Lobato's ex-girlfriend, Pat Meadows, met them at the large bronze front doors to take them to Gottesman Hall. Lobato loved the powerful old architecture of the library. It seemed as though it should've been a palace or a building in the Vatican. Many times, he had met Pat there on sunny days, and they'd sat on the expansive stone steps, enjoying coffee.

"Long time." Pat's shimmering black hair was tied up in a bun, and a large silver pin protruded the sides like a speared apple. She wore a white silk blouse, buttoned right up.

"Yes, it's been a while," he said, nodding too long. "This is Agent Cassia Arena. Cass, Pat Meadows."

"Hello, Ms. Meadows. Thanks for seeing us on short notice."

"Bren said it was urgent and that you guys were working on something important. Homeland security stuff."

Arena glared at Lobato. "*Bren* said that, did he?"

Lobato sped up to be closer to Pat as they followed her down the marble-tiled hall.

Pat's boot heels clicking on the polished floor accentuated the wiggle of her butt in her black, knee-length skirt. She seemed to be putting a little extra twist in each step. Pat knew how that drove him crazy.

Lobato shook his head. "You been working out, Pat?"

"Actually, working mostly in."

"Nice," Arena said.

Sensing Pat was still a little bitter on their breakup, Lobato wanted to try to keep to business only for this visit. He'd told Arena the reason they broke up was that Pat never had enough time for him. Actually, Pat had wanted to move the relationship forward, quicker. She wanted to move in with him. She talked about weddings and babies while Lobato was mostly interested in her naughty librarian persona and partying. Both of which he enjoyed a lot of.

The main exhibit room featured LCD screens, on one of which a map of the world alternated with one of the United States, showing real-time seismic activity.

"What are all the different-colored dots?" Arena asked.

"Red ones are what happened today; orange is yesterday; yellow is the last two weeks; purple, the last five years."

"There is a lot of red and orange," Lobato said, clearing his throat.

"And what about those rings around the dots?" Arena added.

"Those indicate the magnitude. The wider the yellow rings, the more severe the activity. So why is the FBI so interested in seismic activity?"

"Sorry, Pat. That's confidential," Lobato replied.

"More confidential than your special haircut?" She winked.

Arena crossed her arms. "This I have to hear."

"We're here to check out the frequency of seismic activity and if there could be any relationship to terrorist activity or possible tampering," Lobato spouted in one quick breath, then muttered, "I hate blackmail."

"I still want to know about this special haircut," Arena said. "It did just cost us some confidentiality."

"Not that confidential."

"Since when is there grey area in confidentiality, partner?"

Pat giggled. "Let's go for coffee sometime, and I'll fill you in on a ton of fun facts, Cass."

"So this is all in real time?" Lobato cut in.

"Yes, you're seeing it as it happens."

"There's a lot of activity. Is this normal?"

"Almost. There are normally fifteen to seventeen hundred earthquakes a year, and twenty times that for measurable seismic activity."

"Have you noticed an increase in the last few days?" Lobato asked.

"We've had measurable increase in seismic activity throughout the network, and a major number of swarms over the past month."

"What network?" Arena asked.

"And what's a swarm?" Lobato asked.

"We have a global network of seismic stations accessible to this and other museums. The data is updated every ten minutes. We're just about due for another update, any minute here."

"These stations, are they run by seismologists or scientists?" Arena asked.

"Most are just computers that feed information back to a main monitoring station."

"And swarms?" Lobato pressed then cleared his throat.

"A cluster of smaller seismic activities. But they're not telltale of an impending big one like a layman would think—well, not normally. There were swarms, followed by a big one, in L'Aquila, Italy, in 2009. Three hundred people died. Six scientists and a government bureaucrat were sentenced to six years in jail on manslaughter charges for their failure to predict the earthquake and forewarn the people."

"So, you can predict earthquakes?" Lobato asked.

"That's the funny thing—well, not for the jailed scientists. No. No one can. I mean, we can guess the probability over maybe ten to one hundred years, but it's just a numbers guessing game."

"But someone could figure it out? With physics or something?" Lobato asked.

"Maybe down the road, a long way down the road. But it's like guessing what shape the next snowflake will be, it's so random."

A beep sounded, warning of an update. Arena and Lobato looked at the plasma screen.

"See any difference?" he asked.

"Yes. There." Pat pointed to a small island in the Caribbean. "That's new, major activity by Barbuda. New swarms. There is an active volcano there, so that's not good."

"So do you think all of this activity is just a blip? An acceptable anomaly?"

Pat looked down at the floor, took her glasses off, and scratched her temple. "Like I said, no one can predict, but this isn't normal. I would think something big will happen... within ten to one hundred years. Probably closer to the ten-year mark, with all this activity."

Arena and Lobato looked at each other.

"Can't you give a better estimate of where and when?" Lobato questioned.

"I'm not an expert in that, but this activity is spread out all over the globe. It's very erratic."

"Erratic?" Lobato asked, scratching his ear.

Pat smiled at Lobato, let it linger as if to say she still loved him or wanted him. She looked at his lips, then answered, "Unbelievable, but not impossible." She put her glasses back on and looked up at the monitor. "Do you think it's related to the seven-day warning? I mean, it's on everyone's mind—I know *I've* been thinking about it."

"That's why we're here, trying to differentiate fact from fiction." Arena walked toward a model of the earth's crust.

"And what it looks like to me is that until we have a real earthquake, it's just computers spittin' out numbers," Lobato said.

"Numbers that anyone can tamper with," Arena pointed out, examining the detailed creation of the inner core of the planet.

Pat let out a deep breath. "It would be hard to tamper with these computers; they have firewalls that are second to none."

Arena rejoined them at the monitor.

"You'd be amazed at what hackers can get into these days," Lobato said. "They've even hacked into our systems."

"Maybe, but we were told we're tighter than Fort Knox. Same security system and encryption as the White House computers."

Lobato and Arena walked around the monitoring room, looking at control panels. "Okay, we believe you," he said.

"I sense a little patronizing," Pat said softly, walking away from the agents toward a computer monitor. "Conestry Technologies *is* the best in North America for security, maybe the world."

"What was that?" Arena asked from the other side of the room. Lobato turned sharply to look at Pat, who was typing something into a computer keyboard.

"Best in the world for security," Pat repeated as she looked at the computer screen.

"Who?" Arena asked, as they closed in on Pat.

"Conestry Technologies. They also created the programs for the seismic stations in the US. Right here." She tapped at the Conestry website on her monitor.

Arena and Lobato immediately looked at each other, eyes wide. They looked at the screen for the Conestry homepage. A banner scrolled saying, "We provide Internet security to the White House."

Pat noticed their expressions. "Is there something I should know?"

"No," Arena responded quickly.

"Gotta run, Pat. Thanks so much for all of your help," Lobato said smiling.

"Don't be a stranger, Brenny. Maybe you could buy me a drink sometime, get caught up." Pat adjusted the spear in her hair.

Arena smiled.

"Yeah, for sure. I'll call you sometime," Lobato squeaked out.

"Right, 'sometime.' That's a Breno-style commitment," Pat said, leaving the computer and walking toward the doors.

They followed her out of the room and toward the front exit.

"That's not what I meant. What's your new number, Pat? I'll call you." Lobato motioned to pull out his smartphone from his jacket pocket.

"Actually, I don't drink anymore. And you drink too much."

"Double ouch. Not your day is it? *Brenny*," Arena said.

"Just more of me for you, sweetie," Lobato responded quickly.

Arena and Pat simultaneously rolled their eyes.

They quickly reached the exit. "Haircut," Pat quickly said as she turned the key to unlock the deadbolt. "I had fun doing it."

"I'll call you for coffee," Arena said. "I have to hear this."

Pat nodded as Arena and Lobato left the building.

Lobato regretted letting Pat give him a full-body shave. She called it a 'haircut.' He called it an itchy, pokey mistake.

Lobato opened the car door for Arena just as his smartphone buzzed.

"Mine too," Arena said. "Intel reports, finally."

The report read, "Paul Mansfield, anchor-man, turned Muslim eight years ago. Very low-key, in a private ceremony—the public doesn't know."

Their phones buzzed again with another message, Arena read this one outloud. "Adam Johl made a trip to Iraq five years ago. Made phone calls from a small city called Rutba to his office in New York." She pocketed her phone. "And now I suspect he had something to do with programming at this and other seismic stations based on what your old girlfriend told us. *Pat*."

"Jealous. Love it."

Arena shook her head. "Our suspicions about Johl being a terrorist are a lot more certain." Arena scrolled through her smartphone. "Mansfield could have staged the future TV report and could be working with Adam. As odd as that sounds."

"Just because Mansfield is a Muslim? A very small percentage of Muslims are terrorists. Right, Cass?"

"Correct, but this just ties them all together a little closer. Maybe Johl plays it up as a good thing for mankind? Persuades Mansfield to do it? Maybe pays him a ton of cash?"

Lobato nodded as he strummed the steering wheel.

"We just need some proof of who Johl is. His real identity."

Lobato started the car. "We could wrap this up as a hoax if we had that. Go to the press."

"Right." Arena checked her email. "Our intel team and the CIA's are having a tough time cracking who he is."

Lobato pulled out of the parking lot.

"Where are we going, driver?" Arena asked.

"I'm going to take you home, Miss Daisy."

"Slacker."

"Tired. Too tired to even flirt."

"That's tired, for you."

"Right."

Arena looked at him as if she thought something was wrong with him.

Lobato just felt a little pouty after how Pat had teased him. And Arena was always shutting him down on his advances. Maybe he should give it up. Keep it all business. That would serve her right. Or maybe he just needed some sleep, and a drink. Tomorrow would be a new day.

At eight p.m. Monday night, Adam packed essentials, laptop, and some clothes into a black gym bag. He went to his basement, and behind the furnace, he moved a crate. Under the crate was a safe built into the floor. He removed the fake floor tile, opened the safe, and pulled out all his cash. Twenty thousand dollars. He packed the money in a wrap-around waist belt. The cash would last him for the full month of his plan, he hoped.

Adam left his bamboo plant on the kitchen windowsill, filling the vase to the brim with water and wondering how long the plant would live. He then wrote, "Thank you for everything, Stella; this house has never been cleaner" on an envelope and put two hundred dollars in it. He left it leaning up against the bamboo vase.

His arm hurting, he crawled awkwardly out a basement window into his side yard. There were only four feet between his house and the fence. He quickly jumped the low picket fence into the neighbor's yard, went out the back yard, and headed down the dimly lit alley. Adam's plan was to zigzag through the neighborhood until he got a safe distance away, then call a cab.

Unfortunately, a sharp-eyed punk caught a glimpse of him running.

The punk whistled for some of his friends, and the chase began. The believers who'd been camped outside Adam's house followed them, realizing their prophet could be in trouble.

Adam looked back, then flung the strap of his bag over his shoulder and sprinted. Many in the mob swung bats and quickly closed in. Several of the provokers hurled rocks at Adam, along with insults and curses.

He stumbled on the gravel back alley. He looked backward to see the narrowing gap. Sweat beaded on his forehead as he got up. He looked around for an escape route, but there were garages and six-foot-high fences on both sides.

A punk lunged at him with a stubby bat. Adam tried to avoid the blow, but the bat grazed his head just enough to knock him back to the ground. The gang of punks surrounded him.

Another man picked up an old metal garbage can, dumped the garbage out over Adam, then smashed him with the can.

Adam wiped some smelly wet kitchen garbage from his face, looking up at the man who just hit him, and wondered if he would get out of there alive. The young men looked as though they would have no problem killing him. He tried to slowly crawl to the side of the alley, scraping his knees on the gravel and trash. The tallest punk stood over Adam and thrust his big black boot on Adam's back, shoving him back to the ground on his belly. Adam felt helpless and smelled old coffee grounds and moldy food.

The supporters quickly caught up to Adam. They outnumbered those who were attacking him at least four to one and approached with locked arms, reciting the Lord's Prayer in a melodic monotone. The man who straddled Adam's body whacked him across the back between the shoulder blades with the bat, then joined the raunchy crowd as they prepared to face off with the oncoming wave of Adam's rescuers. His back, head, and arm all hurt.

As the two groups squared off, Adam got up slowly, shaking his head. He stepped backward, then turned and ran. His legs burned, and his head spun. He stumbled several times, then slowed to a power walk, touching the alley fences as he passed to help keep his balance.

Only three days into his thirty-day plan, he thought, and it might be over if he didn't escape. But he'd known the first seven days could be the roughest for him. He picked up the pace to a sloppy run, not looking back.

The battle commenced. The human chain of supporters was soon broken, and many dropped to their knees and covered their heads with their hands as they were ruthlessly pummeled with fists and bats. Not many raised a hand to the violent gang of vulgar thugs. It was a submissive sacrifice to save their savior.

Three of the thugs took chase after Adam.

At the end of the alley, a red sedan rolled up, the window rolled down. "Come! I'll get you out of here!" Samantha Cott shouted, waving Adam in.

Adam turned to see several screaming, angry men running toward him, waving bats and knives. He jumped into the back seat of the car just as one attacker swung his bat at the vehicle. The bat smashed the side window as Sam sped off.

The man shouted, "Die, bitch!" Another yelled, "We know who you are!"

The third man threw a rock, which hit the trunk and bounced off.

"Thank you, Samantha!" Adam said, watching the men through the rear window.

"Call me Sam. And I'm happy I parked outside your home tonight. I didn't get much of a chance to talk to you at the church." Sam ran her fingers through her hair to shake loose some shards of glass. "You will be safe with me tonight, if you want. From there, we'll figure out what to do next." She made a sour face. "Maybe a shower, for you."

"I just may take you up on that," he said, pulling a clump of spaghetti off of his shoulder and tossing it out of the window. "And sorry about the window."

"Company car, no worries." Sam ran the stop sign at the end of the street, made a screeching turn to her left, almost on two wheels. She laughed. "Company tires, too."

Though he listened to her, Adam was preoccupied with the safety of those people protecting him in the alley. He dialed 911 on his cell phone.

They answered promptly.

"Please send police and ambulances to 177 Lark Court quickly! People are getting hurt!" He disconnected.

***

Police helicopters were deployed to the area around Adam's house within minutes of the call. Two people had been killed and dozens seriously injured before the police finally ended the clash. By then, Sam had Adam exclusively to herself in the sanctity of her three-bedroom Queens apartment. She could smell the award-winning story brewing, and it would be a masterpiece, since she had the main ingredient: the prophet, Adam Johl.

Adam took an extra long shower while Sam washed his clothes. It gave her time to think of how she could keep him close as long as possible and how to get the real story out of him. The press was throwing around possible terrorist ties. She needed to explore that without making him feel threatened. She needed to quickly build his trust, and she was good at that. But she was also good at breaking trust, according to Lucy, she thought.

13
Tuesday - Day 4

Daisy sat quietly at her kitchen table, watching the live broadcasts of the battle on the alley behind Adam's home, flipping channels between two major networks. The blood was still wet on the gravel-packed alley as the camera zoomed in. The sensational story of Adam's believers being beaten and two being murdered triggered extreme emotions on both sides of what had become a global religious battle. From rocks thrown through stained-glass church windows in France to mosques being fire bombed with Molotov cocktails in Greece, the news ignited heated passion and hate.

The images terrified Daisy. She sensed something dark was about to happen.

A terrible dream had woken her last night. She was driving down a pothole-filled road through a drought-looking countryside. The clouds were low and grey, threatening a storm. Tumble weeds drifted across the road. Then a shiny, royal blue car approached her at high speed, and just as it was to pass her, it swerved into her lane in a head-on collision. It seemed so real, and she clearly saw the silver emblem on the hood of the blue car smashing straight through her face. It was a Rolls Royce.

What the hell did that mean? She hated her dreams. They were all bad lately.

And the news was no better. In Alabama, a vindictive man led the charge of a bat-toting, beer-swilling mob of believers in retaliating for the burning of a cross on their church lawn. They singled out a well-known group of skinheads that had a private club of sorts in the thick back woods of St. Clair County. The location looked like a modern-day junkyard. A green fridge and a brown plaid sofa mixed with tires, stained white plastic lawn furniture, and piles of rusted stuff.

There was no proof the unsuspecting bunch of misfits had committed the crime, but to the mob of believers, they looked and smelled the part, and that was good enough for the fired-up keepers of the faith. They burned down the old farmhouse where the skinheads took refuge. Three made it out and were beaten mercilessly on a dirt road. Five more died inside when a propane tank exploded, lighting the area like a football field on Friday night.

Similar incidents, on a smaller scale and without deaths, played out across the country.

The media called it the start of the end of the world. Daisy called it Revelations.

***

Lobato waited for Arena outside her New Jersey apartment. He looked up at the renovated warehouse as the morning sun reflected off the upper lofts. She finally appeared in the lobby and quickly walked out to the car.

"Hey, Breno," she said as she got in. "Thanks for driving again, this week."

"Love driving. No problem—are you making a little money on the side?"

"No. Why?"

"These places are out of our pay grade," he said as they sped off.

Arena smiled. "My ex. Well, you know he was a lawyer. But what you don't know is that he was a piss-poor one. I got the condo."

"Remind me to sign a solid pre-nup with you. And not to use him as my lawyer."

"Are you going to start first thing in the morning, Agent Lobato?"

"I'm refreshed and ready to go again... Never mind. Got your favorite. Caramel macchiato, extra sprinkles," he said, then handed her the hot cup with a sleeve and caught a pleasant whiff of her subtle fragrance. It was a sexier scent than the sporty one she had worn all last week.

"You need to tone down the flirting. I know you're joking, but ease up. A lot."

Lobato looked into her dark eyes then looked forward to the traffic. He'd known he was overdoing it, but he enjoyed it and thought it was harmless. "Okay."

"Okay?"

"I respect you. I really respect that you are comfortable enough to tell me this. And it's a long drive to KCOD. I'd like it to be pleasant." Lobato forced a smile.

"Great. Read your reports?" Arena asked.

"Yes. It's getting hot out there, everywhere. And it looks like Pat Meadows gave a little call to the press. Told them of our visit and explained about the unusual frequency of swarms."

"This news will create a ton of panic. You must have really made her angry with your breakup."

"Do we know where Adam disappeared to yet?" Lobato asked quickly.

"He probably left the state, headed south. Disney World?" Arena said then hesitated. "Their plan to cause global pandemonium is unfolding. We have to squash it today with a press release after our interviews. We just need a few more pieces to convince the masses before everyone goes nuts out there."

"They already are going nuts. Did you make appointments?"

"I called to make sure the KCOD station manager and human resources manager were in. We're going to surprise them."

"Perfect." Arena took a sip of her coffee.

"Then we have appointments at Conestry Technology. We're waiting to find Mansfield. He's MIA—never showed up to the station—and Dove is also MIA."

"You've finally managed to impress me, Breno. Imagine, all that work this morning, and you still had time to get my sprinkles."

"And the sprinkles weren't flirting. I would have done it for any partner, if that's how they took their coffee."

"Right."

As they drove through downtown Manhattan, Lobato thought about all the events over the last few days that had happened as a result of the event at Roxy's. He and Arena looked at each other with raised eyebrows and slight smiles, as if their thoughts concurred. He felt as if they were gelling as partners. Almost in sync. He didn't want to let her down by fooling around too much. He had a tendency to do that when he was nervous or insecure. But his newfound confidence, from Arena praising him for a job well done, helped him to curb the antics.

Arena looked at her phone and read a live news feed app. "Someone is leaking intel, or there are some very talented investigative journalists out there."

"How so?"

"His short seven-year identity is now public knowledge. Which raises the question in the public of 'Who is he, really?' It says here some think he divinely appeared on the planet seven years ago to commence Revelations. Others want him dead."

"Social networking will be the death of spy work. News travels so fast now. Shit happens before we have a chance to prove anything."

"We can only work as fast in proving things as we can drive and sleep."

Lobato nodded. "And eat."

They pulled up to KCOD and parked in the handicap zone in front of the newly built two-story contemporary building. Arena pointed at the blue *H*; Lobato moved into a spot that said "Mansfield."

As they entered through the large glass front doors, the receptionist smiled at them. Lobato held his smile a little too long.

After they showed their credentials, the receptionist led them to Robyn Brown, the HR manager.

The middle-aged manager, Robyn, stood up from behind her desk to shake their hands. She was six feet tall and looked strong, but her handshake was weak. She sat down as quickly as she stood up.

"Phil Rutherford," Arena said as she dropped a photo of him on Robyn's desk. "Did he work here?"

"Phil Rutherford? Never," Robyn answered, her voice gravelly like a smoker's.

"Are you positive?" Arena asked.

"Yes. No cash or check has been paid out to a Phil Rutherford, and no hire paperwork has ever been done with that name—that, I can assure you. I know every person hired. I interview them all, and put them through a lengthy interview process." She coughed. "And I review all payroll, W-2's—everything."

"How many employees does KCOD have on staff?" Arena asked.

Robyn scanned a spreadsheet in a well-used file folder. "Currently... sixty-six."

"Here's number sixty-seven's ID card. Ever seen this?" Arena pulled a small plastic baggie out of her pocket and dropped it on her desk.

Robyn pulled her glasses down on her nose and examined the ID card inside the baggie as if it were contaminated. "This is a forgery. See the photo? It's embossed on top of the ID pad. We print our IDs off as one plastic card. What did this guy do anyway? Sneak in and clean some floors at night?"

"Well, maybe, but he's dead, so we'll never know," Arena responded coldly then picked up the ID tag.

"Hmph," the woman said, closing her file.

"Can we see the station manager now, please?" Lobato asked. "We're done with you, for now."

"This way." The woman stood up and led them out. She walked slightly hunched as they made their way down the hall filled with autographed glossy photos of anchors, movie stars, and athletes.

Arena rubbed her finger along the top of the picture as they walked and found a thick layer of dust. "Looks as if you should've hired Rutherford around here," she remarked.

The manager's office overlooked the main news stage with wall-to-wall triple-pane glass windows.

Fielding pored over a stack of papers on his desk. "Come in," he said.

"I'm Agent Cassia Arena, and this is Agent Breno Lobato." They both flashed their credentials. "We'll get right to it, if you don't mind. We're here investigating a murder. Have you ever seen this man?" Arena dropped the ID tag on his desk.

"Murder? Who?" Fielding replied with a puzzled look.

"This man." Arena tapped the ID tag on his desk. "Ever seen him?"

"No," Fielding said after a quick glance at it.

"Take a closer look," Lobato pressed.

"Is this the murderer or the murdered?"

"Murdered," Arena said in her usual rapid-fire style.

"I've never seen him, and I practically live here. So you're done... *Right?*" Fielding asked.

Arena leaned forward, hands on her hips. "How does someone get access to the building after hours?"

"They need a security card."

"Like this one?" Lobato asked, trying to keep pace with Arena.

"Yes, if it works."

"Let's try it," Arena said.

"I can do that right here and now."

Fielding hastily grabbed the card, turned around in his swivel chair, and opened his credenza. There was a card-making machine the size of a small shoebox on a roll-out shelf.

"Can I touch it?" he asked, as he slowly undid the Ziploc.

"Yes, we've already dusted for prints." Arena nodded.

Fielding nodded then swiped the card through the reader. The machine beeped once, and the LED glowed green.

"It's good; it works..." Fielding said softly. He swiveled back around to his desk.

"And how would someone who neither you nor your HR manager have seen get this card activated?"

Lobato stood with his back against the wall, arms crossed, silently enjoying Arena's questioning skills. She knew how to paint a person into a corner.

"I don't know, but it concerns me. It's obviously a fake."

"Who makes your cards?"

"H.R."

"Why do you have a card machine?"

"It's an old one. We upgraded, and instead of tossing it out, I stuck it in here."

"Who else has access to your office?" Arena asked.

"The janitor, admin, anchors who stop by. But they don't have keys to my credenza."

"That would be easy to open. I could do it with a paper clip," Lobato said, unable to maintain silence any longer.

"So, what are you saying?" Fielding asked.

"We're saying that we have a victim who, for some reason, had a security pass for your station. And that one of four people could have made this card for him." Arena took a deep breath. "You, your admin, your HR manager, or your anchor."

"Even so, how does any of this tie in to his death? Was the card a murder weapon?" Fielding glanced at his watch and sighed.

"Maybe," she responded slowly. "We have a piece to the puzzle here that doesn't fit. A man that no one knows who had a pass to this station, and a news broadcast at Roxy's that no one made."

"Okay, is that it? Anything else we can do for you?" Fielding asked. "I have a news deadline to take care of. And there's lots to report this week. Did you hear about the bombing of the mosque in London? Twenty people killed, many more injured." He checked his watch again. "Happened ten minutes ago."

The agents kept straight faces, though they hadn't heard about it.

"You can stay in town. You and your HR manager," Arena said sternly.

"Are you joking? Are we suspects?"

"The FBI has the right to detain in these situations, but we'll just tell you to stay close to home. Just in case we need you," Arena said.

Lobato looked at Arena, who smirked. She loved this part of the job—telling someone who seemed arrogant to stay put, even if she didn't need them to. He smiled, too.

"*Now* that's it," Arena said.

The two agents got up and let themselves out.

"That was a waste of time," Lobato said, as they approached the car.

"I'm guessing that Mansfield made the card for the janitor."

"Why?"

"Maybe he had a part in fabricating the news piece—hey, another message from intel." Arena stopped to read her smartphone. "Will you look at that."

"What?"

"Adam Johl sent flowers to a family in Rutba, Iraq. For a funeral last year. They dug further. Got a match from a surveillance bank camera in Rutba. Johl was there on a regular basis between eight and ten years ago. That's as far back as they had video records."

Lobato opened the car door for Arena. "He lived there."

"Thanks. Yes. They're searching for birth records."

Lobato drove off. "Does the boss think we have enough to arrest Johl for trying to cause chaos and executing an act of terror?"

"Asking the world to be better is an act of terror? I know—it can cause chaos. But we still need something solid."

"Conestry could be our something solid. We might get the director to sign off on us releasing our findings publicly, then we can give a statement in time for the evening news to stop any more fanatics from hurting anyone. We've got the fake news feed filmed by Rutherford, Mansfield a Muslim and possibly terrorist sympathetic, and Adam the master-mind, faking seismic activity through his programming and spreading global panic."

"Agreed. Drive fast."

Lobato put on his flashing lights and sped up. "I can do that."

14

The late morning sun streamed through the kitchen blinds onto the table and natural-stained old oak floors. Sam's daughter Lucy peeked into the kitchen where Sam re-dressed Adam's head at the butcher-block kitchen table.

"Who is this man?" Lucy asked, holding a Barbie doll by the legs.

"This is Adam Johl," Sam replied.

"I saw you on TV." Wearing her pajamas, seven-year-old Lucy entered the kitchen and stared up at Adam. "Are you God?"

"No, dear."

Sam considered stopping Lucy from asking what could be embarrassing questions, then decided to see where it would go. Maybe Adam would reveal something she could use in her story.

"But you are the one on TV—the one who made all the chairs fly? My teacher said you're like Criss Angel."

"Yes, but not quite like Criss Angel." Adam squinted as the sun hit his eyes.

"Can you make a miracle for me now? Can you make a friend for my Barbie? And maybe a pink motorhome?"

"Lucy, why don't you brush your teeth and pick out some clothes for the day? Then I'll fix you some waffles with syrup. Okay, Sunshine?"

"Kay, Mommy." Lucy batted her long eyelashes, smiled, and skipped down the narrow, tall hallway.

"Lovely daughter," Adam said, smiling, then looked at the fridge.

"Did you ever marry? Any children?"

"Who has time?" Adam asked, staring at the cream-colored fridge plastered with photos of Lucy, her colorful artwork, and a picture of her father.

Her father's picture was framed in a hand-drawn red heart—a picture frame Lucy made for him for Father's Day. He held Lucy, and Sam had her arms around him.

The picture had been taken a month before he died.

"Thank you for your help and hospitality, but I need to get going."

"You shouldn't travel yet. Your arm needs rest, I think you may have a concussion, and the stitches I gave you have—"

"I'm fine. I have to keep moving."

"Your face is on every newspaper, every news broadcast; moving's not going to help you. Next time, you may not be so lucky."

"I'm not afraid."

"Adam." Sam swallowed, unsure if she should offer him help, but it was the right thing to do. "Maybe I can help you."

"You already have. And I'm very thankful."

"I can get you out of the city. It's a real hot zone here for you. I'll take you wherever you want."

"Why would you do that?" He pushed away from the table to stand up.

People would try to kill him. Helping him would risk her safety—but in exchange, she'd have a huge story on her hands. "I want exclusive rights to the rest of the week, whatever it is you want to say, whatever happens up until Friday. I'm with you."

"Not much left to say, Sam. You already know everything. Besides, it will be more difficult to hide with two celebrities; you're known, too, and that would put you in danger if someone else decides to take a shot at me." He stood up.

"I may be a little well-known in New York, but not other states." Sam refilled her coffee mug from the carafe, trying to slow down his attempt to depart. "My friend has a motorhome I can borrow, and you wouldn't have to leave it until I get somewhere real safe. I have friends all over the country I can trust. We could essentially go underground."

"No, thank you. I'll be fine. I have people I know, too. All over the country."

"And when you stop for gas or food, or when someone sees you driving, it's all over."

"Please don't take this the wrong way, but the reason you want to help me is for the story. Right? And if I get shot or something happens, you'll be the first one there, with the story. Wherever I am?"

"I guess it would depend where you are... But that's not fair for you to say. You don't know me. I also care about your safety." She looked directly into his brown eyes.

"I'm sorry. I didn't mean to imply— That was rude of me. Can I please have a little more coffee?"

Sam hastily filled his mug, splashing a little on the table.

"Thank you," he said taking his cup but not sitting down.

She nodded.

Adam took a sip, then carried it to the kitchen window, where he looked out over the narrow backyard, which had one large, airy canopy tree in the middle. "I'm sorry. That wasn't fair. I'm just so damn cynical."

He took another sip of coffee. "You've been like a saint, considering the news is now describing me as a terrorist, but I've got to get going."

"I'm not a saint. I just want to tell the story," Sam said softly. "But I'll loan you my car to get out of New York on your own. Give you a little cash, if you need it." She was trying to gain trust. She hoped he didn't see the gestures as false or patronizing.

"I couldn't do that."

"No worries, company vehicle. I'll expense the cash, too. Entertainment." She laughed.

"There must be a spot in heaven for you and your daughter," Adam said. "You seem so kind."

"Hopefully no time soon—besides, it's only an Impala. With a broken window."

"Okay, maybe a spot on the lawn just outside the pearly gates."

Adam and Sam laughed. It was the first laugh she had heard from him.

"I will ask for one favor, Adam."

He nodded.

"Can you call me? Update me so I can report from your viewpoint?"

He nodded again. "I will."

Sam looked into his eyes and knew he would. She handed him her business card. They both held it for a moment before she let go.

There was something about him, something different. She would have to be careful, as the feeling could cause her to let down her guard and write a biased story. She wouldn't go easy on him.

It was the unbiased story she needed to explain. To report and expose the truth.

The morning news had reported the evacuation of dozens of Caribbean towns and some other small towns centered around swarms of seismic activity. Looting stories had popped up all over the world, not rampant, but enough to cause concern. Lineups for goods were long, and clash deaths were reported hourly.

This is like the paranoia of December 1999, she thought. *Except on steroids, and with a volatile catalyst looming.* Earthquakes would be that catalyst. Then, who knew what people would be capable of when they believed the end was near?

***

Claire stood in the middle of a twenty-person lineup for the instant teller. *Why are all these people taking out cash?* She had never seen it like that before. She rummaged through her purse, looking for a mint, and heard a crash. She looked across the street.

A few young men hurled something though the window of a local jewelry store. They reached in through the bars to grab stuff, but the merchandise appeared to have been placed just out of reach.

At almost the same time, she heard the sound of other windows breaking. Claire closed up her purse and ran to her car. People were looting the shops in the normally quiet suburb. *But why? How did this start so quickly?* Was it just thugs looking for a reason to smash and grab? Or was it people who seriously believed something big was going to happen?

Either way, Claire decided she would make a stop at the grocery store to stock up. She sped off.

She then realized that if she was thinking to stock up, a lot of people would be thinking the same way. She hit the gas pedal and surged through a light that just turned red.

Good thing she only needed supplies for one.

***

Arena and Lobato arrived at the Conestry building in Garden City Park, which was a twenty-minute commute for Adam from his home.

Sitting at a small, exotic wood table in Mr. Billings's corner office, Arena couldn't help but surmise the company made a ton of money, demonstrated by the expensive-looking oil paintings, highly polished exotic wood furnishings, and the comfortable-looking leather chair behind Billings' intricately carved pedestal desk.

"Mr. Billings, can you tell us how long Adam Johl worked for Conestry?" Arena asked.

"Seven years, and a great employee. Never missed a day."

"Until now."

"Actually, he put in for a three-week vacation. I approved it."

Arena and Lobato looked at each other.

"Have you ever noticed anything odd or out of place with Adam?"

"If you mean, 'Did he turn the water cooler into a wine barrel or something?', no, never. He was as average as... Joe."

"What was he working on before his holidays?" Lobato asked.

"He was debugging a seismic program we wrote. Some minor tweaks."

"Did he write the program?" Arena asked.

"He was the lead on the team and absolutely brilliant. If anything was weird with him, it was that he was too smart—seemed to know everything about everything—but he was a normal guy. Does that make sense? He never flaunted his intelligence. He was—is—the perfect gentleman."

Arena and Lobato both nodded. Arena scribbled notes on her pad.

"What other projects has Mr. Johl finished in the past twelve months?" Arena asked.

"His latest project was the seismic, but he's done special effects programs, point-of-sale systems, CGI—the list goes on." Billing paused and looked over his shoulder. "We are also on special contract with the US military, classified stuff, which only Adam worked on. He would just give me the billed hours and updates. All kinds of confidentiality contracts are involved—I actually think I'm in breach now, just telling you." He fidgeted with his water bottle, peeling the label a little.

"Who are your contacts?" Arena asked.

"You can take up any further questioning about those projects with the Office of the Deputy Chief of Staff, Intelligence."

Arena nodded, but getting approvals to pull that information would take days, maybe weeks, despite the new cross-agency information sharing policy. They would start the process, but who knew if they would get information in time to be of any use.

"What does this have to do with the prophecies, Ms. Arena?"

"Maybe nothing, maybe everything."

"You speak in riddles, just like Adam."

"What do you mean?"

"He has endless sayings, quotes. Uses old clichés. Does it all the time; drives everyone nuts."

"Give us an example, please," Arena asked.

"One that he wore out like a cheap rug—he used that one, too—was 'You can't see the forest for the trees.' Used it when he was the only one who could find the error in a program. And 'Faith will move mountains.' 'A little knowledge is a dangerous thing'—used that one on me. Oh yeah, and, 'All the world's a stage, and all the men and women, merely players.' Shakespeare, methinks. And on and on."

Arena and Lobato raised their eyebrows.

"Can we see his desk?" Arena asked.

Billings hesitated and rubbed his chin. "Don't you need a warrant?"

"We can have one here in a few hours, if you'd like to wait here with us?"

He looked at his watch then nodded jerkily. He pushed away from the desk, got up, and walked out of his office. "This way." He sighed.

Arena and Lobato rummaged through Adam's desk, which was set in the middle of the bullpen of cubicles. Everything was meticulously placed. Pencils all lined up perfectly in a square plastic holder, papers stacked in piles that a laser would find square, books lined up according to size, and spines aligned perfectly with the edge of the shelf.

"No pictures of any family? Friends? Girl-friend?" Arena asked.

"Never," Billings replied, adjusting his glasses. "But he liked women, if you know what I mean."

"His desk is pretty much cleaned out; no files in these drawers," Lobato reported.

Billings unlocked Adam's filing cabinet; it was empty. "That's weird. His entire project backup should be locked in here."

"Who else was on the seismic project?" Lobato asked.

"There were three others authoring small parts. Adam was the gatekeeper and mastermind on the project. He was the only one with all the components."

"Who reviewed the program when it was complete?"

"Adam. He was the one to test and demo it and then sign off before it went to the customer."

"And who was the customer?"

"Pretty much all the seismic research sites in the world. We cornered the market on this one, thanks to Adam."

Arena looked at Lobato, wondering if he'd connected the dots, too. "Could Johl control or override the programs after they were installed in the seismic centers?" Arena asked.

"Adam is the most brilliant programmer I've seen ever. He could probably do anything he wanted, but he wouldn't mess with anything. He was too straight."

"Straight as hell, huh?" Lobato asked.

Billings gave a blank stare.

"Isn't that a cliché, too?" Lobato asked.

"Hot as hell, is the one I was thinking," Billings said.

"We'll be seizing this hard drive, as well as the others that worked on the project. I'll call it in now. Our department will be here soon."

Billings gave an exaggerated groan and rolled his eyes.

After a longer-than-expected wait for the proper paperwork and the seizure team to arrive, the computer property was tagged and removed, and Lobato and Arena finally left the Conestry building.

Dark billowy clouds had rolled in since they had last been outside. "That sky looks menacing," Lobato said. "You think Adam ordered it?"

"Absolutely," Arena said, looking at her smartphone. "Mansfield's nowhere to be found; apparently, he took a sudden holiday. He's the last piece to this puzzle. Well, Dove, too."

"Not sure if we should even be worried about him, right now. Time's running out. We need Adam to come clean, now, and stop the madness," Lobato opened the car door for Arena.

"Thank you," she said with a smile. "You're a gentleman, but you really don't have to keep doing that. We're all equal on the job."

"It's how I roll."

Arena shook her head. "I agree about getting Adam to come clean. By Friday, the world could really end at the pace the pandemonium is escalating, created solely by the fear." She got into the car. "We've got to bring in Dove and Adam today. Intel has Dove traced to a motel in Jersey. We're still trying to locate Adam."

"Still time for dinner, though? And good wine, no argument about it. Period."

"Geez, Breno, food again? You eat a lot for such a slight guy."

"I prefer 'toned.' And my rate of metabolism is very high."

"Did you ever watch any movies with the FBI or CIA or James Bond? *Mission Impossible?*"

"Yeah, why?"

"Did you ever see any of the heroes stop to eat?"

"Bond was always drinking martinis... So you think I'm a hero?"

"Maybe the sandwich version."

"I'll take that as a yes to dinner, with merlot—and dessert, for the cheap shot. Cheesecake."

***

Adam backed the Impala out of the single-car garage onto the narrow street. He waved at Sam and her daughter, who were both standing at the front-door window.

He put the car into drive to head down the street. A four-by-four pickup truck came barreling at him, head-on. Adam hit the brake pedal hard, came to a sudden stop, and thrust the shifter into reverse.

He crashed into another truck that came at him from behind.

Adam quickly shifted to drive again and drove back into the garage that was still open. He jumped out of the car as the garage door closed behind him and entered the house through the connecting door.

"Are you okay?" Sam shouted.

"Fine. It's a bunch of those hooligans. How did they find me?"

"Someone must've recognized me when I picked you up."

"Is there another way out of here?"

"I've called the police. They'll be here any second," she said as she led him into the foyer.

Someone hammered on the front door. "We know he's in there! Give him up! No one has to get hurt!"

Adam looked down the hall and through the small front door window. "It looks like the guys in the truck!"

"I've called the police!" Sam yelled.

One of the men shattered the glass on the front door, reached in, and undid the deadbolt.

"We don't have time. Follow me!" Sam grabbed her purse, swooped up her daughter in her arms, and made for the basement. Adam followed her down the steps.

Adam could hear the men running through the house, shouting vulgarities. "You two must go alone; I'll stay. It's me they want! Go, please! They'll keep chasing us."

"Forget it! Follow me! We can all get out of here no problem!" Sam said as she kept moving.

Adam stopped. "No! You go!"

"Adam! Come now! Or I'm not going anywhere!"

She had to be bluffing. She wouldn't put her daughter in danger, but Adam did not want her to have to prove anything that could put Lucy and her at risk; he followed her. She led him through the rear basement door into the fenced backyard.

"Here, let me carry her," Adam said.

Sam handed Lucy over, who wrapped her legs around his waist and arms around his neck. "This way!" Sam lifted a cleverly hinged hidden gate that let them into the rear neighbor's yard. They ran through and on to a street where Sam hailed a cab. "No arguments. We're going to borrow my friend's RV and get you out of here. No one will trace this to me or us."

Adam nodded. "Okay. Thanks."

The cab jerked to a stop in front of them.

They piled into the back seat, and Sam gave the cabbie an address one block from her friend's house.

Maybe the thugs back at Adam's house didn't recognize me and trace him to my home, Sam thought, tapping her leg.

Her little Sunshine sat quietly between her and Adam. Maybe Sunshine had posted something on YouTube that sent a whole different batch of thugs to her home. *Good parents should watch what their children are doing on their computers. Especially ones harboring someone who people thought was the Messiah.*

15
Wednesday - Day 5

Dove carefully placed the stainless steel case into his black bag and quickly zipped it shut. The case contained the ancient three thousand-year-old emerald tablet. The one he and his brother had used to fund most of their plan for world chaos.

He looked up at CNN on the motel TV. The headlines read "Pope Assassinated." "Oh, man. That's going to stir things up big time." He plunked on the bed and turned up the volume just as there was a knock at the door.

The knocking became pounding.

Before Dove could go to the peep hole in the door, there were two quick, sharp sounds of splintering wood, the ping of metal, then the door was kicked open.

"Get on the ground now!" Mark Little yelled, pointing a pistol with a silencer at Dove. "I said *down*!" he repeated, motioning with his gun.

Dove dropped to his knees, his hands slightly over his head. "What are you doing?"

"Collecting the emerald tablet." Little hesitated, as if wondering if he should add something else.

Dove didn't trust him.

"And cleaning up loose ends—now lay down *now!"* Little shouted. "Before I become one!"

"You can't be serious! Adam and I are the ones executing this operation. And we're far from done."

"You're done in my book! *Fired!* Now, where is it?" He glanced at the black duffle bag on the bed.

Little had been ordered to eliminate Rutherford and others that had served their purpose, but Dove wasn't on that list. How did he know about the tablet? Who told him about it, and who was pulling the trigger?

It had to be someone Dove had told. Someone he had to use the tablet to leverage for payment. Maybe someone in the Israeli army he had bought? *Or could Adam have ordered this?*

Dove quickly dismissed that possibility. His brother would never betray him. "It's over there, in my bag," he admitted to get Little to look away.

Little looked at the bag. Dove quickly rolled to his side and swept Little's legs with his. Little fell sideways, firing a shot into the floor as Dove rolled on top of him. The gun was jarred from Little's hand and slid across the floor.

Dove tried to beat him to the pistol, but they grabbed it simultaneously. They rolled together in a desperate struggle for control of the weapon. Another bullet left the chamber with a quiet thud into Little's head, just under his chin, and the wrestling match ended.

"Get *off* me, you fat piece of shit!" Dove shouted as he rolled his limp body off his chest.

Dove touched the blood on his own cheek then licked his finger. "Not mine." He laughed as he stood up then checked Little's pulse. There was no doubt he was dead with the bullet coming right through the top of his head. "I guess it's you that's fired, fucking fucker."

He dragged the body into the bathroom by the ankles and deposited it in the tub. He squeezed a small amount of shampoo out over Little's body. "That's how you clean up loose ends, Mr. Mark. With cheap drugstore shampoo. Wouldn't want to waste any of my good Paul Mitchell stuff on you." He laughed hysterically.

Dove stopped to look in the mirror. He wiped his face, brushed his hair back, winked at himself, and left the bathroom.

He grabbed his bag, unzipped it, opened the steel case, and quickly checked the ancient, timeworn leather box that the emerald was stored in. It was fine and safe.

He packed it all back up, zipped the bag, and left. "My precious." He chuckled.

***

Arena and Lobato pulled up to the motel and made their way to Dove's room. Intel had done a great job locating him so quickly.

Noticing the ajar door and shattered handle, they drew their weapons and flattened themselves against the wall outside the room.

"FBI! Come out with your hands on your head!" Arena shouted.

After they waited several seconds and got no response, she motioned with her gun to go in.

They entered the room cautiously, ready for anything. A quick glance at the budget motel room revealed a pool of blood and trail of blood to the bathroom, an unmade bed, and takeout food containers on the dresser. They found Little's twisted body in the tub with what appeared to be a bullet wound through the top of his head.

"If we didn't stop for food, Mark may still be alive." She checked for a pulse on his neck. "Not that I'd ever shed a tear."

"Or one of us could have been shot. Just saying," Lobato said quickly.

"It's fresh, within the hour. I'll call this in." Arena left the bathroom and made a quick call on her cell.

Lobato surveyed the room. He carefully entered the bathroom and inspected the body at a distance. He noticed what appeared to be shampoo drizzled over Little's face and body, with the small empty bottle resting on his stomach.

"So, what do you think?" Arena asked from the doorway.

"The shampoo is odd. Maybe a sign of cleaning up Mark? Maybe Mark Little comes after Fossano, they struggle, Fossano gets the upper hand and turns the gun on Little, or shoots him with his own gun. We'll have to wait for ballistics."

"That's the easy part. The why is the tough part."

"Little was at Roxy's Friday night. He showed up at the murder scene of the KCOD janitor at the Occidental Hotel and in Queens. And now he's here." Lobato stroked his chin. "Was he chasing Fossano or a partner with him? He may have been in on this whole scam in some weird way. One thing is for sure, Little and Fossano are linked somehow."

"Great observations. I mean, really good."

"Really?"

"Yes. There are other possibilities though. There could have been another person or persons here. Maybe Little got here and

Fossano wasn't here. Maybe a third person killed him. Forensics will help."

Lobato nodded, impressed by her knowledge and experience.

"Backup will be here any minute. Let's do our thing, rope this off, and get going while Fossano's trail is still warm." Arena turned for the door. "Let's get an APB out."

"I'm really sorry, but right there, that moment, you're so hot when you..."

Arena turned and looked him in the eye. She gave a mean squint as she took a few steps toward him.

Lobato held his breath, tightened up his cheek muscles, and closed his eyes, preparing to be slapped. Arena leaned in and kissed him on his tight lips. Lobato opened his eyes and turned grapefruit pink.

"I thought that's what you'd do. All talk. So let that be the end of that." Arena confidently strode from the room.

Lobato stood alone in the room and gazed at Mark Little's corpse. "Mark. It's ironic that you are the reason Cass first kissed me. For that, I am forever in your debt."

"Are you coming, or still in shock?" Arena yelled from down the hall.

"I could answer that one of two ways, Mark. But I'll take your advice: dead quiet." Then he called to Arena, "Coming, Cass."

***

Sam parked the borrowed RV in a fast-food restaurant parking lot. Adam and Lucy ate at the salon table while she called relatives and friends, asking for a favor—could they take Lucy for a few days? While calling, she kept an eye on the TV as they revealed more about the Pope's assassination.

A Russian by the name of 'Ivan the Terrorist' claimed responsibility for the murder. They reported that Ivan had ties to al-Qaeda and that a stinger missile was launched at the Pope as he flew from the Vatican in his helicopter. She wondered how the assassin knew when the helicopter was taking off and that it contained the Pope. Sam doubted that Ivan could have executed such a plan, given his less-than-credible terrorist status that the news was reporting.

One thing was sure, Sam thought: hate had found another race and country to despise, and the world had quickly become a more dangerous place. Sam took a drink of her strong black coffee and continued to watch the news while trying another friend. Adam and Lucy shared ketchup on a plate for their fries.

The news broadcast then showed people in smaller communities who had never locked their doors now locking their doors. They showed politicians flanked by security guards around the clock, even to go to the bathroom.

The broadcast showed Wal-Mart posting extra armed security guards in all of their locations around the world. Sam was stunned to see that even Toys R Us and other family retailers were following the Wal-Mart move. Lucy seemed to be keeping an eye on the small TV screen as well. She was quiet.

The news segment switched to religious gatherings where congregations were trying to disseminate fact from fiction—or in this case, from biblical prophesy. Religious leaders expressed that they felt like targets. One preacher commented that he was unsure how to lead his flock. What message should he deliver? Should he tell them to lay low and stay fairly neutral? Or should he encourage them to lie down in front of tanks, metaphorically speaking. She put the phone down and just watched the news.

They switched to an international broadcast from a London correspondent. The reporter with a British accent explained that halfway across the Atlantic to Europe, beneath the Atlantic floor, a slippage of the tectonic plates had accelerated from the average half-inch of movement per year to one inch in the past twenty-four hours. Experts reported that they were unsure exactly when and if a major earthquake was about to happen, but the mass population along Europe and North American coastlines were preparing, most planning for departure inland.

Sam, not having any luck with her relatives, friends, or housekeeper—none could help on short notice to watch Lucy—decided Lucy would ride shotgun with Sam at the helm of the twenty-five-foot Winnebago. Lucy expressed her joy by doing a five-minute jumping and dancing stint in the RV. After cleaning up and buckling Lucy in, Sam navigated the RV out of the parking lot.

"We'll make our way to Florida," Sam said as she focused on the GPS that was guiding her onto the New Jersey Turnpike. "I know exactly where we can go that no one will find us. It's in Boca Raton."

"Mickey Mouse!" Lucy shouted.

"Sorry, sweetie. Mickey and Minnie will have to wait."

"Why?" Adam asked.

"Why what?"

"Why wait for Disney World? You and your daughter can spend some quality time together. I'll hang out in the RV. I insist," Adam said. "It's the perfect place."

"The perfect place for what?" Sam looked back at Adam, who sat at the salon table with his hands clasped.

"For me to hide. For you and Lucy to have fun."

Sam sensed he had an ulterior motive for wanting to go to Disney World.

"Please, Mommy! Please, please, please! You promised you'd take me to see Mickey Mouse, I don't know how many times!" Lucy pulled on Sam's sleeve. "I can add it to my YouTubes."

"No more YouTube! And I did promise, but the timing is..." Sam's cell phone rang. She checked the caller ID. "It's my boss." She answered it. "Hello, Barry."

Fielding had a bad habit of yelling for everything. Most in the office had become immune to it; Sam hated it.

With him yelling at her again about missing work, she pulled the phone away from her ear. "You don't have to speak so loudly." She never knew when he was mad or just rude.

"You're on today!"

"I know. I left you a message. I'm on my way to... a little vacation with my daughter. Unexpected, sorry." She pulled the phone away from her ear again as he complained about her taking too much vacation time. "I asked you not to yell, Barry. It's getting so old."

He got rude *and* mad. He swore. She pulled the phone away from her ear again.

She then put the phone to her mouth like a microphone. "After everything I've done for you and that station, you threaten to fire me? Are you kidding? You can shove your threats and this job where the sun doesn't shine, jerk!" Then Sam hit *End* and tossed the phone on the dashboard. It flipped end over end in its rubberized waterproof case and hit the window.

"Where doesn't the sun shine, Mommy?"

"My ex-boss's world, sweetie. It's a dark, lonely place he lives in."

"Oh. I need to go the bathroom."

"You know how. I showed you."

Adam helped Lucy undo her seatbelt and held her hand to the rolling restroom, then returned to the captain's seat. "I'm so sorry you lost your job. I've put you in the middle of this."

"Why are you sorry? His constant yelling and ranting was wearing real thin, anyway. Besides, the story you are giving me will land me a job at a bigger and better network. Unless, of course, there are no jobs to go to next week." Sam smiled, trying to make light of the situation.

"Do you believe in the prophecy?"

"I'm not sure what I believe. With all the earthquakes and pandemonium, it sure seems like something's happening. And you seemed to have announced it."

"I did. I know." Adam paused, removed his glasses, and rubbed his eyes. "There will be some bad things happening soon."

"You don't think the Pope being assassinated was a bad thing?"

"Worse than that."

"What are you saying, Adam?"

"Today, maybe tomorrow. The next sign will happen soon. It should happen this week."

"What sign? Did God tell you?"

"No, he didn't." Adam paused. "Sam, I trust you. You've saved my life—probably twice, now. For that I cannot repay you, so I will tell you this: You have family and friends in New York, right?"

Sam trembled. Her knuckles went white gripping the steering wheel. She remembered all the press about Adam possibly being a terrorist. She envisioned the Twin Towers attack in 2001. "Yes."

"Tell them to get out today, soon. Get out of New York City and go far inland."

"*Why?* What's going to happen? A bomb? Is it a bomb?"

"No," he answered.

"I washed my hands, Mommy!" Lucy skipped to the front of the RV and shoved her clean hands in front of her mother's nose for approval.

"That's great, Lucy. Now, buckle up."

Sam turned to look at Adam, but he had gone to the bedroom at the back of the RV and closed the door.

"Damn!" Sam shouted, pounding her fist on the steering wheel.

"That's a swear, Mommy."

"God will forgive me for that, sweetie. Trust me."

Sam looked at her phone. She picked it up then tossed it back on the dash. "*Da...rn*!"

"What's wrong?"

"Everything." Sam picked up the phone again and dialed the first New York number in her personal directory. She would make her way down the list and leave out no one. Hopefully they would all believe what she was about to tell them.

16

Dove drove I-95 South in his 2013 Mustang Cobra. He was enjoying the drive to Florida. The traffic was light, and the weather perfect: seventy-three degrees and slightly overcast. He tapped his fingers on the steering wheel to an AC/DC greatest hits mix from his iPod. The bass was pumping so hard, the rearview mirror images were blurred with every thump.

Dove signaled to pass another semi. He sped up as he passed the fifty-foot truck and trailer, then slowed a little as he settled in front of the big rig.

He heard a quick blast of a siren and checked his rearview mirror. An unmarked police car with lights blazing was right on his tail. Dove hadn't known the car had been behind him. After he slowed down and received two more blasts from the siren, he calmly pulled over and waited for the officer.

"License and registration, sir."

"I was passing a semi. You have to speed up to pass a semi. Right?"

"I clocked the semi at fifty-eight miles per hour. You didn't need to pass him; he was going a safe speed."

"We were going downhill, and I've been trapped behind him for miles." Dove handed him forged documents with the name Bob Smitt.

"Tell it to the judge," the officer said, his nose and cheeks red, and he went back to his cruiser.

Dove looked at the officer through the side-view mirror. He seemed to be talking a fair bit on his two-way radio. Ten minutes passed.

The officer carefully approached Dove's car with one hand on his holster. "Out of the vehicle now, slowly! Hands on your head!"

Dove hesitated. The officer must have some kind of bulletin with his photo.

The officer placed his finger on the trigger. His forehead glistened with sweat.

"Easy, cowboy," Dove said, raising his hands. "I'm coming willingly." His getting caught was planned to happen in England, but now could work, as well. He would have to improvise a little and hope Adam would follow along on the charade.

He looked back at his car. His precious tablet was safely hidden in a compartment beneath the floorboards.

***

The interrogation room was thirteen feet square, grey walls, dimly lit, and hot.

"Let's get this show on the road!" Dove shouted at the mirror on the wall. "Charge me or release me! Damn, I'm roasting in here."

"Mr. Fossano is a feisty one," Arena said from behind the two-way mirror, fanning herself with a file folder. "But he'll be easy to crack. Look at the sweat beading on his forehead."

"You're up first," Lobato said. "Have fun."

"Love this part of the job."

"I know. It's like a dominatrix kind of thing, isn't it?"

"Sick." She left the viewing room and entered the interrogation chamber. She took her time walking to the table, opening the folder as she stood there. She flipped through the pages slowly, pretending to read something.

"We can do this one of two ways," Dove mocked, as he teetered on his chair.

"Dead or alive," Arena finished as she sat down and folded her legs. "I'm Agent Arena with the FBI, and you are not Bob Smitt. You didn't think we would have sent your photo to every agency in the US? That was sloppy, on your behalf."

"Was it?" Dove smiled, crossing his arms. "Or was it intentional? And sloppy implies I'm running from something."

"What do you mean by that?"

"Nothing. That cop was an idiot. There is no way in hell I should have been stopped. Man."

Arena switched gears. "That's a lovely tattoo. Matches the large one on your back of the four intertwined doves holding hand grenades?"

"I was younger. We make mistakes. I'm sure you've got all that bullshit in that file," he said, pointing at Arena's thick file on the table.

"You're still young."

"I'm a good taxpayer now, just like you. I'm in construction."

"Maybe, but what were you and where were you eight years ago? It seems your real file stops about seven years ago. Seems to be a trend with some people that were at Roxy's that infamous night."

"Guess your people aren't that good at pulling history on American citizens."

"Or we're real good at it and there's nothing to find on you because you first came to our country seven years ago..."

Dove shook his head. "Whatever."

"We'll get to your identity soon. Whose initials are on each of the doves? Your real family?"

"Gang members who couldn't get on the right path, unlike me."

"It would be a shame to throw away your road to redemption now, wouldn't it?"

"I didn't do anything."

"If by anything you mean murder, then yes, you're right."

"I need a lawyer if you're going to talk stupid."

"You may, but right now, I just want to talk to you off the record. Taxpayer to taxpayer."

Dove looked at her breasts too long. Arena shook her head then stood up.

"Shoot," he said.

"Exactly. How did it happen? You killed a cop." She paced the room.

"He bust in and tried to kill *me* and accidentally shot himself. There aren't any fingerprints of mine on that gun. But you probably already know that, or you would have charged me."

"By the signs of the forced entry, yes, maybe he broke in, maybe he struggled with you, and maybe the gun went off killing the officer. But, unfortunately, it's still just *maybe*, and you did flee the scene. By the time it gets to court and all the paperwork is shuffled, you'll already have been behind bars for a several months, if you're lucky." Arena stopped pacing and leaned forward on the table. "The prosecution will play up your gang ties that these files say you have. And can really spin a good one with maybe... terrorist ties. Evidence is pouring in by the minute."

His eyes narrowed. "What do you want?"

"We need you to come clean on the prophecies. We know it's a hoax, but we need a disciple to come forward and tell the world, especially the spokesman for the group. Explain how you made bees come from your mouth and the other tricks. We'll drop the murder charges. Call it self-defense. But it has to be stopped now. People are getting hurt, and it's getting worse by the hour." Arena stood straight, crossed her arms, and glared at him. "You'll get a few years' probation for disrupting the peace, inciting riots—even though what you've done probably killed the Pope." She paced the room. "It wasn't just a little magic act in a bar. It had malicious intent."

Dove leaned forward on the table, interlocked his fingers, and looked intently into Arena's eyes. "That's all?"

"We have CNN in the parking lot. They know you're here. I'm sure they'd love to interview your live confession."

"Love to be on TV again, but there's no hoax." Dove sat back in his chair again and crossed his arms on his chest. "Shit's going down, with or without me confessing, and nobody can stop it now. The world's going to end, and I'll see to it. To be honest, you'd be better off locking me up."

Arena sat down across from him again. "I'm sorry you feel that way." She leaned back. "How do you think you'll really fare in prison?

Young, pretty boy. Soft skin, irresistible blue eyes."

"You think I'll make a nice bitch?" Dove puckered his lips and flexed his bicep.

Arena looked up at the two-way mirror. "You're not as tough as you think you are, Mr. Fossano."

"Yes, I am. And you have no idea who I really am and what I am capable of."

She shook her head. "Guess we'll order you a nice orange jumpsuit with a rear flap. Hold you on murder and trump up—or even prove—some kind of connection to terrorism. We can hold you indefinitely for terrorism."

"Indefinitely won't be too long. Friday, probably."

Arena sighed, got up, and knocked on the door. A guard opened it for her. "We're done. Wrap him up for transport."

"Yes, ma'am," the guard responded.

She stepped through the door and turned back. "See you in a few months. Or longer. I can wait."

The door closed. She went back to the other side of the two-way mirror. After a few seconds, Dove looked up at the mirror and said, "Okay."

Arena let him sit for a full minute, then reentered the room.

"Did I tell you you're kind of hot? Tough, sexy. You have a gun."

"See you later." She went for the door.

"And you're good," Dove said, smiling.

"Yes, I am." She hesitated at the door and turned around.

"Chill. I'll do it."

This is way too easy. Why did he give in when he appeared to be so tough? It didn't make sense, and it made her nervous. *He has an ulterior motive.* And the other thing that concerned Arena was that Dove showed no remorse for killing Little. In her book, that meant he had killed before or was a certified psychopath.

"Okay, I'll talk, but on my terms. *And* a lawyer, you pay."

Arena got up and knocked on the door to let in a man in a navy blue pinstriped suit. "Mr. Fossano, meet your lawyer, Mr. Samuel King. He's one of your Roxy's disciples."

"It seems you have something to tell me?" King asked, sitting down at the table and opening his leather attaché. "I knew this was all a big farce."

"I'll tell you what you want to hear, but believe me, it's no farce." Dove winked and smiled. "It's going down."

King pulled out a yellow-lined pad and a red pen and scribbled notes. "Let's start with who put you up to this."

Dove looked up at grey ceiling then pointed like he was shooting a gun. "Allah."

King put the pen down and rubbed his forehead. "I'm paid by the hour, so take all the time you want to tell me what we want to hear."

Dove smiled. "Okay, but God hates a liar."

After two hours of counseling, King and Dove were done. Arena's boss signed the papers, and Dove was almost free. Arena and Lobato escorted Dove to the front steps of the police building, where all news channels were perched, waiting for the live interview. There was a steady stream of camera flashes, and reporters pushed each other to get to the front row in front of the police station. Arena had leaked out that a confession was coming. The sooner she got the message out, the better.

The producer counted down, and the reporter commenced by explaining who Dove was and then asking him for a statement. "My name is Nat Fossano, aka Dove." He flashed the tattoo on his forearm. "I'm here today to tell you that the events at Roxy's Bar were all staged by Adam Johl and that I was paid to participate—"

While Dove spoke, the producer for the main network signaled to cut. Another major story had just broke, and they needed to go to their correspondent in Hong Kong, where a major earthquake had rocked the coast and killed tens of thousands of people.

"Sorry, Mr. Fossano, we have to break, and we will be right back," the reporter said as they signed off. "We'll start from the top again."

Dove, Arena, Lobato, and several others sat around the video monitors in the CNN trailer to watch the incredulous report of the endless amount of damage and death strewn across one of the most populated coastlines in the world: the Ring of Fire in the Pacific.

Before the broadcast got into details, another story broke. A tsunami warning was issued for the East coast from Nova Scotia to North Carolina with the center of impact by New York City.

It wouldn't matter what Dove had to tell the world; they wouldn't believe him.

He laughed out loud. "Oops, there goes my credibility." He tilted so far back in his chair, he fell over.

Twenty minutes later, the makeup girl re-powdered Dove's face. His goal now was to get the public to fall in love with the new, honest, repentful Dove. He would build a large following of supporters that would give him a new celebrity status, one that he would use to further his plot to cause global chaos. The aggressive plan, well thought out, would hopefully lead countries to war.

Dove needed to put on his best show. This was a pivotal moment in the plan.

The reporters resumed pushing and shoving to get in position again in front of the station. The interviewer did introductions again and gave a run-down on what had transpired to that point, then Dove spoke. "I owe the world a sincere apology. I was paid five thousand dollars to go along with what I thought was a harmless prank. All I had to do was put a plastic bag with bees inside my mouth and release them when signaled. I really needed the money, and I feel so ashamed now." Dove frowned. "I thought it was to be some kind of magic act or something. Seemed like fun at the time. I'm so ashamed."

The cameras tightened in on his face. He let a tear leak from his eye.

"His real agenda was chaos. Adam's some kind of psychological terrorist, I guess. Really twisted. Spreads fear and panic."

"When did you realize this was all wrong and that you had to speak up?"

"I saw what these so-called harmless pranks were doing to people around the world. The guilt was killing me. Here I thought asking the world to repent and act nice and do good things was sort of a good idea. I mean, what harm could be done? Right? Preaching never really hurt anyone, but then the Pope, the riots, murders..." His voice trailed off, trickles of tears running down his face from both eyes. "I have been very depressed. Bad thoughts going through my mind."

The interviewer handed him a tissue.

Dove cleared his throat and thrust his head up high with glossy eyes. "It's never too late to repent or ask for forgiveness. That is what I am doing. I've even donated the five thousand dollars to the local youth center that helps keep kids out of gangs. The same center that pulled me from the gang world, too. And I'm going to try and raise more money for them."

"Wow, that's quite the confession, Dove," a reporter said. "So the whole thing is a one hundred percent hoax?"

"Yes, sir."

"And what about Adam Johl? Do you think now that you have come out with the truth, he will as well?"

"I hope so. What he has done is causing a world of problems. I'm sure he's paid more people as well to go along with it, who should all come clean too."

"Do you know who?"

"No. But if they're watching"—Dove looked directly into the camera—"I beg you, confess. It feels good. Donate the money and help stop this chaos we created—if it's not too late. Besides, we didn't really know what this whack job was up to—if we did, we would have never gone along with it!"

The camera went to a full body shot of Dove. One camera cut to the name patch on the pocket of his designer blue mechanic's shirt. It said "Nat."

"Where do you go from here?"

"I want to head up some kind of peace movement. I would love to be a spokesman for everything that's good. I'm tired of people using people, bad things happening. We need to take a step back. There's too much hate and stuff. This has really opened my eyes." He looked up to the sky, held his gaze, then back into the camera. "I guess the message Adam was delivering for malice is one that I'd like to use to really spread the good word."

"That's a lofty goal, and quite a turnaround."

"It's not the first time I've turned my life around. I used to be in a gang, when I was twelve. My parents died—were murdered, actually; I was a mess. Not that I'm using that as an excuse; tons had it worse than me."

The interviewer handed Dove another tissue to wipe his tears.

"I guess Jesus had a lofty goal when he started out, too. Not that I could ever be in the same sentence as him. But it has to start somewhere. Why not with me... and you!" Dove pointed at the camera. "Maybe that's why I was part of this, to really start a movement of peace? Maybe I could inspire younger people too?"

The producer was signaling to wrap up.

"Thank you again, Dove," the reporter said, then looked into the camera. "Well, you heard it here. The acts performed at Roxy's seem to have been an elaborate hoax, one to toss the world into a chaotic tailspin. Next up, Tom Baxter from KCOD, who will present a recap of the events over the past few days leading up to this moment of truth." The network went to a commercial, then Tom came into view from outside the front doors of Roxy's. Dove watched the broadcast on the CNN monitors.

Baxter spoke quicker than normal. "Adam Johl—which according to my sources is an alias—is part of a terrorist cell that launched what they thought was to be psychological warfare. Through a display of incredible magic acts, he was able to convince one hundred sixty-four people in a bar that God was delivering a message of the end of the world in seven days unless the world repented." Pictures of Roxy's and the disciples were shown. "Since then, the controversy over the 'Roxy's prophesies,' as they have been called, has created global tension between religious and non-religious groups, causing deaths and the assassination of the Pope." Pictures of the Pope, his assassin, and clashes in the streets of Rome rolled.

The camera went back to him. "The thing that makes this story all that more sensational is the recent seismic activity and massive earthquakes claiming thousands of lives. One can't help but imagine that these were a sign confirming the prophecies, but now clearly are only a matter of incredible coincidence."

Baxter paused then continued at a slower pace. "Now, to the continuing rescue efforts around the Ring of Fire. Following that, tsunami warnings in New York are now causing evacuation of tens of thousands of people along the coast."

Dove left the tent, stretched, and looked at all the reporters scrambling about. "This is just the beginning!" he yelled. Several paused to look at him. They seemed confused by his statement then continued on their way.

"What? No second interviews? Up close and personal?" He laughed. "Ahh, plenty of time for that."

17

"I know, I saw Dove's confession as well, Sue," Claire Nadeau said to her best friend on the phone. "But somehow I don't believe it—I'm going to find Adam. I need to talk to him and ask him if this is really a hoax. I was there. I felt his words." She sighed. "I'm more confused than ever."

"How will you find him?" Sue asked. "He could be anywhere."

"Social media, maybe. I'm going to keep searching until I find him."

"Good luck, Claire."

"Thanks, but you can help me. Start chatting it up, looking in social media. Let me know if you find anything that will point me in his direction."

"You can count on me. Unlike your ex."

Claire laughed. "Let's go for drinks soon, invite the girls. At Roxy's. Maybe God will show up again."

They said good-bye, then disconnected.

Claire drank her strong black coffee and lit a slender cigarette as she sat at the glass kitchen table. She took that replenishing first drag and exhaled slowly. She thought about the increasing earthquakes and world tension up until that point. It was moving quickly and escalating. But why would Dove say it was all a hoax? *Why?*

She took another drag, then looked up to the ceiling. "God. If you're there, give me a sign. Anything, please. I don't want to believe in another man if he's lying to me, and I just can't tell if he is... again." She bowed her head, "Please."

The buzzer went off on her washing machine.

She shook her head. "I'm a good person. At least, I think I am."

She rested her head in her hands and stared at her designer gas stove and restaurant-sized refrigerator. She felt guilty.

Look at me. Sitting in my big empty house full of useless, expensive shit... I get it now... I really get it! "Forgive me!"

She folded her arms on the table, put her head down, and cried.

After several minutes, Claire wiped her eyes and dialed her only child, Brenda, in Australia, who she hadn't talked to much since her divorce. Her ex-husband seemed to have brainwashed her into thinking it was all her fault. Maybe it was. Maybe it *was* her fault her husband had slept with his secretary...

Someone answered. "Brenda?" Claire asked.

"Mom?"

"Yes, dear, it's me. You sound different."

"Do you know what time it is?"

"Middle of the night for you, sorry. But it's also time to make amends with my only child."

"Have you been drinking?"

"I love you, Brenda."

"*Mom?* Are you okay—what's going on?"

"No. No, I'm not. I'm confused. I feel broken. Everything I thought was real, may not be. Just like with your father."

Brenda hesitated, then said, "I love you too, Mom. I can come visit you soon."

"Soon?" Claire thought of what Adam said at Roxy's... "You wonder if you will see your daughter again. Soon she will come to you." Adam had to be legit! *How else would he know these things?*

"Actually, dear, I think I'm a little better now, talking to you." She smiled. "Thanks! I'll phone you back, at a better time. Love you!"

"Okay, then. Love you, too. Talk to you soon?"

"Yes, soon." Claire hung up. *I need to find Adam, look him in the eyes, and ask him. I need to do this for me, to prove I'm not going crazy.*

***

Marty Graham looked at his wife and shook his head. "I knew it, damn it! Bunch of fake bullshit!"

"Honey, it's not a bad thing."

"Being played a fool again is a bad thing. It's happened my entire life. Always someone taking advantage of me. And I'm fucking tired of it."

"You're a salesman. Who takes advantage of who?"

"Low blow, Tina."

"It got you to stop drinking. The kids are so much happier, as am I." She hugged him while they stood in the mall in front of the TVs of a stereo shop. "And I think the world is a better place, don't you think?"

"Tell that to all the people who have been killed over this. Tell the Pope—oh, you can't. He's dead."

"And all the people who have changed their ways?"

"Yeah," he said with his head on her shoulder, as he watched a beer commercial running on all of the TVs. "For the moment."

Tina sighed. "I'm going to run into tea shop. Be right back."

Marty nodded as she left.

The beer commercial ended with a frosty glass filling with Budweiser on tap.

"Choices. We all have them," he said to himself out loud. "Adam had his choice. Dove had his, and I have mine." His mouth was watering. *Hold on,* he thought. *One more day won't kill me. Give it one more day. You can do that.*

***

The sun warmed Daisy Beech's face as she sat at the outdoor tiki bar in St. John's, Antigua. She took a sip of her beer as she watched Dove finish his confession on TV above the bar. Dark feelings rushed over her. Goose bumps filled her arms; her eyes watered.

"It's too bad, Daisy, you flying all the way out here for nothing," Elias the bartender said as he wiped the counter.

She didn't respond.

"Hello? Earth to Daisy?"

She shook her head. "This trip wasn't for nothing. I saw some of my children, razzed the old men I used to be married to and date—well the ones that are still alive—and I get to have the most handsome bartender on the island serve me beer." She smiled with her sun-beaten wrinkled face. "Wanna dance, cutie?"

Elias laughed.

Daisy took another sip of beer as she twirled slightly on the bar stool, then blurted out, "I ain't quitting this task. I'm sure as shit that this world's coming to a close, and I'm going to keep spreading the word, handsome."

"Somehow, I knew you'd keep going."

"Yeah, well, that Dove's a liar. I saw it plain as day when I stared into his eyes and touched his arm. This is all as real as he is... And he ain't who everyone thinks he is, that's for sure."

"Who is he?"

"If I told you, you'd have me locked up."

Elias laughed. "Come on, mon. Who do you think he is? I won't call da police."

Daisy motioned for him to come closer, and she lowered her voice. "Because I can't say no to a beautiful man, I'll tell you. Just look at your soft skin. You are so beautiful," she said, pinching his cheek. She paused and looked over her shoulder to make sure no one else was listening. The bartender leaned forward over the bar.

"He is evil, pure evil... He is the devil himself. And he is going to take this world to hell with him." She sat back.

The bartender stood straight and stopped cleaning his blender. "That's what you said about your last husband."

"I'm dead serious."

"And how do you know this?"

"I seen it, like I was there. Buildings falling, bombs exploding, and lots of people dying. And in the middle of it all, a smiling Dove."

"Maybe you were just dreaming about what you saw on the TV in that bar. That sounds like what they said was on the fake news broadcast."

Daisy shook her finger in his face. She grabbed his wrist with her hands and closed her eyes. Elias smiled.

"Mmm," she said in a low tone as she squeezed his wrist in a pulsing motion, almost like she was typing Morse code.

"'Mmm' what?"

"You have a pain on your right upper peck." She opened her eyes, released his wrist, and jabbed him with her finger right on the spot close to his armpit.

"Ouch! Yes, that hurts. Cricket ball hit me yesterday. I think something's ripped in there. I didn't tell you that..." He squinted. "Were you there? At my game?"

"No. I see things. Not all the time, but I see things. I'm a body talker, too. I could check you whole body out, if you like?"

Elias wasn't smiling anymore. "You really believe this guy is... bad, don't you?"

"Yes."

"What are you going to do?"

"Stop him."

"How?"

"Maybe I'll marry him."

Elias laughed. "That could work."

***

Lucy was busy tapping at the keys on her mother's laptop as if she had been typing since the womb.

"Whatchya doing, Sunshine?" Sam asked, keeping her eyes on the busy highway.

Adam slid over next to Lucy.

"You won't believe it, Mom. I have over..." Lucy held up nine fingers. "I have that many numbers of people times a zillion who have seen my new YouTube video, Mommy!"

"You're kidding?"

"No, I'm not kidding, Mom." Lucy undid her seatbelt and carried the laptop to her mother. "I have so many Twitter followers too."

"You tweet?" Sam stole a couple of quick glances at the laptop screen. "Wow, that's... over... one hundred and fifty-nine million hits! What the heck did you put on there?"

"I told everyone how nice our new friend, Mr. Johl, is. People are following me now. But not everyone is saying nice things back."

"*What*?" Sam applied the brake and slowly pulled over onto the wide shoulder. She hit the emergency flasher button. "Let me see that."

Sam grabbed the laptop and clicked Lucy's video clip. It wasn't in focus, and part of the top of Lucy's head was cut off, but considering her age, it was amazing. Adam watched with her.

Lucy's clip opened up with, "Hello, I'm Lucy Cott. I'm almost eight, and this is my report on a very nice person, Adam Johl. You guys may know him as the man who made miracles and talked to God." She brushed her hair from her face and took an enthusiastic gulp of air. "I know there's some people out there who want to hurt him, but you shouldn't."

Lucy got off her stool and grabbed the lens of the camera, evidently trying to straighten it out, but only making it a little more crooked. "He's really, really nice and we're all traveling in a nice motor home my mommy borrowed from her friend... It has a bed and a toilet and TV... and we're going to see Mickey Mouse. In Florida."

Sam looked at Adam and swallowed.

Lucy continued, "Adam really talked to God. I know he wouldn't lie. He hasn't made any miracles for me yet, but when we get to Disney World, I'm going to ask him to make five last until nine so I can see more stuff. Anyways, please be nice to each other and do what he said, because I want to be able to spend all weekend at Disney World, and if people aren't nice, the world is going to end. I want to grow up to be just like my mom, and how can I if there is no world left?" Lucy's voice squeaked up at the end.

Sam cleared her throat.

"Signing off—that's what my mom says on TV—I'm Lucy Cott."

Sam hit the power button and closed the laptop.

"What do you think, Mommy?" Lucy asked, plunking herself down on her mom's lap.

Sam wanted to yell at her for not listening, but it would serve no purpose. "How did you find out everything about Adam? And the prophecies?"

"I watch your news. And YouTube."

"You watch my news. And who lets you stay up that late? Benita? I'm going to have a chat with her." Sam dabbed the corners of her eyes with a tissue. "What now?"

"Disney World, just like we promised Lucy."

"People will be looking for us there… Bad people. The police too, probably," Sam said. "We can't go now."

Lucy sat there looking at Adam, eyes wide open, absorbing every word.

"I'll wear a wig," Adam said. "Those large sunglasses and mouse ears. I've always wanted to wear mouse ears."

"Me too!" Lucy laughed.

Unsure if it was stupidity, a lack of reason, or Adam's mental will, she agreed. They would continue with their plan. If it was all going to end, might as well be in the world's friendliest place.

Maybe she would be getting an even better story too. A real exclusive on what may happen next.

18
Thursday - Day 6

After driving all night, Sam pulled the behemoth of a vehicle into a gas station. She filled the cavernous void of a gas tank and went into the gas station with Lucy to purchase food and beverages. When they returned to the RV, Adam was on his phone.

"You should turn that off," Sam said.

"Why?"

"There's a million people looking for you. They can pinpoint your location with that. You of all people should know that."

Adam pressed *End* as though the call didn't matter.

"We need to talk," Sam said, grabbing him by the arm and taking him into the bedroom. He followed, and she closed the door. "Tell me everything."

"What are you talking about?"

"Read this." Sam went through the news channel on her laptop and found the story she had just read on the front page of the newspaper in the gas station. She turned the screen toward Adam. "Hoax! Dove, disciple ringleader and spokesperson, confesses to FBI and makes plea for peace on live broadcast."

Adam scrolled through and read the article. "I see."

Sam waited patiently. "Now. Are you going to tell me?"

"He's trying to make the news. Be popular. He is very vain."

"Apparently, one other of your disciples made the news, Detective Mark Little. He was murdered. It's all on the front page of the newspapers in the gas station too."

Adam sat down on the bed, head hanging down.

"You are messing me up so bad. Come on, Adam! Stop it already! You really think that you did all of those miracles? That God spoke through you? Lies! And to think I told all of my friends to leave New York!"

"You need to believe me. Things are going to happen despite what you believe."

"*Stop* already!" She grabbed his shoulders as a semi roared by the truck stop, tooting its air horn. "You're lying!"

He locked eyes with her; neither one of them blinked.

"Adam, if you aren't completely honest with me, I'm turning you over to the authorities.

You are causing global chaos, and you will be in jail for a very long time."

"I've been betrayed by Mr. Fossano, and it is apparently over," Adam said. "There is no need to turn me in, Ms. Cott. I will be doing it myself. I'll follow his lead and confess, as well."

Adam got up, left the room and the RV, and headed toward the store.

"Mommy, what's going on?"

"Mr. Johl has decided to leave us."

"Are we still going to see Mickey?" Lucy asked, tugging at her mom's shirt.

Sam watched Adam entering the gas station. "Yes. We're going to see Mickey."

"Is he going to be okay?"

Sam buckled her daughter up. "Yes."

"Good! I'm so happy! Let's sing!" Lucy said, as she turned the radio on.

"Sounds good." Sam pulled out of the parking lot and into traffic.

Did she do the right thing by letting Adam just leave? Should she have reported him to the police or helped him? She strummed on the steering wheel. *Just sing,* she thought. *Just sing.*

"Let's find a song we both like." Sam flipped the dial, looking for a good song but not really paying attention.

She stopped on a news broadcast. "The tsunami warning off the east coast of New York is now an evacuation alert. Residents have been told to evacuate immediately as a massive earthquake has been detected seven hundred miles offshore. This earthquake is larger than the one in the Indian Ocean in 2004 that killed an estimated two hundred eighty thousand people. This tsunami will also impact the west coast of Europe. The tsunami is expected to travel at over six hundred miles per hour and hit the coast within one hour. God help us all."

"Damn!" Sam hit the brakes and pulled a two-wheeled U-turn in the middle of the highway.

"What are you doing, Mommy?"

Cars honked and a semi blasted its horn for a solid five seconds.

Sam maneuvered the unbridled beast through traffic back toward the gas station. "Someone's got some serious esplaining to do, Lucy."

Adam went into the station, bought a package of gum, and called the police. Dove getting caught this early was not on schedule, but they had contingencies for these changes. When you have planned to destroy the world, flexibility was essential to success. Like a river being blocked, it will still find its way to the sea, he thought.

Adam sat on the bench at the side of the building. He contemplated how to pull off the Disney departure without Dove. Maybe Dove would contact him? Maybe Adam should *really* pack it in. He felt he had done enough damage. When does revenge end? When is it satisfied?

He hung his head and rubbed his hair. His palms were sweaty. He lifted his head, looked to the sky, and experienced vertigo. He thought of Sam and how she had not judged him. How she tried to understand rather than hate. Could he ever understand how and why the Americans killed his family? Did that matter anymore?

Sam wheeled the bouncing RV back into the parking lot she'd just left and jerked to a stop. "Stay here, Sunshine. Do not move! Do not use YouTube. Do nothing!"

"Mommy! You said we're going to Disney World!" Lucy shouted as Sam left the RV.

She scanned the interior of the store. "Did you see a man that was just in here? He was in his forties—"

"You mean the prophet, Adam Johl?" the clerk asked. He wore a large silver crucifix on a chain around his neck that swung when he talked.

Sam then noticed all the newspaper articles cut out and plastered all over the back wall behind the counter. A large gold plastic cross was pinned to the wall in the middle of the shrine. "Yes. Where is he?"

"He actually bought some gum, grape flavored, then told me he was turning himself in, phoned the police right here in my shop. I can't believe it happened here!"

"Well, where is he now?"

"Right out there, around the corner, sitting on a bench. He signed this front page for me, look!" The man held the newspaper carefully by the corners. The front page picture was of Adam being shot at the town hall meeting.

"Very nice. Thanks." Sam dashed out the door and around the corner. There on the bench was Adam, sitting as if he were waiting for the Sunday bus to go to church.

"Thank God! You have to come with me!"

"No thanks. I'm done running, hiding. It's over. I've called the police as you requested."

"But you don't understand. There's been a massive earthquake, a—"

"Tsunami, I know," Adam interrupted.

"How the hell did you..." Sam stopped as a black van pulled up and four young men, covered in tattoos and wearing red bandanas and baggy clothes, jumped out. They gave cocky glares to Sam and Adam as they passed them on their way into the store.

"If you go to the police, you could be hurt or killed. They can't protect you against what will happen next. You'll be lynched."

She heard sirens off in the distance.

"I really need to go in and confess everything."

Sam glanced through the window of the store and noticed the four men at the cashier, pointing at the newspaper clippings and looking her way. "*Shit!* Adam, you'd better come now, those men—"

Before she could finish, the men had left the counter and were already out the door.

"Come!" Sam grabbed Adam's hand and yanked him off the bench. They made a sprint to the RV that was fifteen yards away. Sam opened the RV door and jumped in. The four thugs caught Adam as he stepped into the RV. They hauled him down to the hot asphalt as Sam stood frozen in the doorway.

One of the men pulled out a switchblade and glared at Sam.

"Leave him alone!" she shouted.

"How would you like to come for the ride too, sweet-ass? Maybe have a five-way, hey, chiquita?"

Sam backed up the steps and looked for a weapon, anything she could use to defend herself. The men laughed and dragged Adam to their van, threw him in the back, and sped off.

Sam tried to get a license plate just as a police cruiser pulled into the opposite end of the lot. She jumped up and down, waving her arms.

The cruiser veered over to her RV and rolled the window down. "Yes, miss. Can we help you?"

"Adam Johl! He's been kidnapped by four men in a black van, New York plates. I think it was RWT6-something... *Damn*!"

The officer grabbed his two-way radio and called it in, then went into the store.

"They went that way!" Sam shouted and pointed down the busy street. The officer ignored her.

Lucy unbuckled herself and came to the door. "Are we still going to see Mickey, Mommy?"

Sam didn't answer. She placed Lucy back in her seat and buckled her up.

"Mommy! You didn't answer me. That's rude."

"Did you also know it's rude for people to keep asking the same question over and over? You're driving me crazy!"

"Well!" Lucy gave a *hmmph.* "If people did what they said, I wouldn't have to ask over and over. Promises." She crossed her arms and frowned.

"How old are you?" Sam asked as she slowly buckled herself in.

"You know that, Mommy. Do I have to tell you everything?"

Sam ignored Lucy's retort. *Stop. Think,* she told herself. *Should I be doing this? Chasing these guys?* It could put Lucy and her in danger. But she couldn't leave Adam alone. They could kill him.

She would go but stay safe. Keep her distance and report it to the police when and if she found them. She sped in the direction the black van had taken.

Sam concentrated on the road and pressed the gas pedal to the floor as she ran a yellow light. The vehicle hit a small crest in the middle of the intersection, bounced, and scraped its tailpipe.

"I'm not going to ask you again. Really. Promise. But... are we speeding to Disney World?"

Sam grit her teeth and counted to ten as she passed another police cruiser that was on its way to the gas station.

"Where'd they go? Where'd they go?" she asked, tapping the steering wheel.

"Where'd who go, Mommy?"

"Some bad men in a black van. They stole Mr. Johl."

"You mean like that one?" Lucy asked, pointing down a side street.

Sam spotted the van Lucy meant and pressed her foot hard on the brake. Their seatbelts locked as they jerked forward. "Yes! Just like that! You're redeemed, for now."

She made an extra wide turn down the side street. The van had parked in front of a bowling and billiards bar called the Pin Cushion. "As soon as we find Mr. Johl, we're headed straight there. Double Dutch promise."

Sam parked on the opposite side of the one-way street. The van looked empty.

"Lucy. I need you to go into the bedroom, and stay there until I get back. I'm very serious. Do not come out of this RV for any reason. And if some people come in the RV, and it's not me, hide in the closet. *Understand*?"

"Oh, Mommy. I understand English very well. You don't have to ask me that."

Lucy quickly bounced to the back and closed the door as Sam grabbed her phone, dialed 911, and gave a quick summary to the person who answered. They said help was on the way and to stay put. She grabbed a steak knife from the drawer and a crowbar from the toolbox.

This isn't part of my staying safe plan, she thought as she left the safety of the RV.

"Dear God, if you're really out there, please watch over my little girl," Sam said as she walked across the street to the van with confidence. "Oh... and me, watch over me, please."

19

The tsunami hit the shores of New York Harbor with a larger force than even the scientists had predicted. The first wave was thirty feet higher than the highest tide; three other waves followed: seventy, forty, and fifteen feet. The crushing wall of water reached all the way to 5th Avenue and reached a height of one hundred twenty-five feet inland.

Although many had been evacuated, many had stayed. Thousands of people were killed instantly. Some drowned. Buildings crumbled on others.

The roads were jammed, shut down, or flooded, so there was no way for emergency vehicles to help. Helicopters hovered, trying to pull survivors from the water. The water was slow to retreat, and half of New York City looked like Venice, with debris floating everywhere.

The news reported it as the second apocalyptic event that week. It then gave a statistic for tornados. The average year in the US saw one thousand three hundred tornados, while they'd had over three hundred touch down that week alone, and the number was increasing by the day.

Agents Arena and Lobato sat in their car at a stop sign behind a dozen cars that weren't moving. They had left the city and were nearly to the gas station where Adam Johl had been seen.

A phone buzzed.

"My phone again," Arena said.

"Ditto."

Both agents read the update about the tsunami with a tear in their eyes. Lobato squeezed out of the lineup to park on the side of the road.

"Hoax?" Lobato asked, raising an eyebrow.

"Coincidence. Global warming has been screwing things up for decades. This was bound to happen." Arena eyed the gas station parking lot from their car.

"What does global warming have to do with an earthquake miles beneath the ocean?"

"You're not going soft on me, are you, Breno?" She raised her eyebrows and rolled down the window. "We have most of the facts from intel now."

"Cass, I'm just saying that maybe Adam did screw with all the seismic readings, maybe he did perform some hocus pocus, but Hong

Kong? The Pacific coastline? New York? How'd he do that? And the timing?"

"Coincidence. *H-o-a-x*. Do I have to spell it out?"

"*Birth pains*?" Lobato rubbed his belly in a circular motion.

"Just when I almost convinced myself one hundred percent that I'm not crazy."

"You need a good man to challenge you, raise your game."

"Why did he want to turn himself in at that gas station if he really is a messenger from God?" Arena pointed with her chin.

"Better than a 7-Eleven, I guess."

They looked at the traffic they had pulled out of. The cars still hadn't moved.

"Dove confessed, so this is a hoax. Intel has confirmed ties and cash movement from known terrorist groups to the cells in New York, to Johl and Fossano. The murders, the profile. It's clearly global psychological warfare... Make everyone go crazy, start killing, burning, stealing. Like the L.A. riots but on the largest scale possible." She shook her head. "It sure wasn't to spread love."

"It's actually brilliant," Lobato responded.

"So, you believe it's a well-planned act of terrorism?"

"To your point, they never launched a bomb or biological warfare. They only put on a forty-minute magic show in a little bar. It is brilliant. Throw in a dash of calculated coincidence, and—*violà*!—world chaos and fear, one of the ultimate goals of terrorism."

"Adam did work on that seismic program. Maybe he figured out a way to detect when major activity was coming, not to alter the readings... Maybe he..."

"Calculated the highest probability of a natural disaster happening and planned his show for that week."

"He could be just that smart. He forced coincidence." Arena smiled.

"There it is."

"What?"

"That smile. It hurts me every time."

Arena looked into Lobato's eyes. They seemed to be calling her. She knew giving in to her feelings for him was dangerously wrong, but she couldn't stop it from developing. Spending countless hours together over the past few months. Getting to know everything about someone and enjoying it. Loving it. *What the hell.* She leaned forward and kissed him, then pulled back slightly.

"Wow... I mean, mmm, you taste great. What flavor is that?"

"Cinnamon."

"*Sin* it is."

"It's just a kiss, Breno. Celebrating the fact the world is not ending on Friday. Not that I ever truly believed it was."

"It just began, in my book."

"You can be very sweet. Too sweet," Arena said, reapplying her lip gloss.

"You're not going soft on me now, are you?"

"It's not me that's soft." She laughed. "Time to roll, lover boy. Our friendly local police actually cooperated with us and gave us the call on Johl, RV woman, and the gangbangers. Let's try to find them. They couldn't have gone that far in the last hour."

***

Sam nonchalantly peeked into the van as she strolled by. She could see a shadowy image rolling around in the cargo area through the tinted windows. "Adam! Is that you?"

Sam heard three muffled thumps. "I'll take that as a yes. Just be still. I'll get you out of there." Sam tried the doors, but they were locked.

She closed her eyes and smashed the side window with her crowbar. Unfortunately, the van's alarm was triggered.

"Of *course*!" She scrambled into the cargo area and sawed through the rope binds on Adam's feet and hands with her steak knife.

He removed the duct tape from his mouth. "Saved by the bell! Again!" He shook his head. "Thank you, you are—"

"Let's go!" Sam said as she led him to the RV, jumped in, strapped up, and sped off, almost hitting a parked car. Would they be chased? What if the men caught them? What would they do to her? What about Lucy? She wished the police would hurry up!

She looked in her side-view mirror. Two of the thugs came out of the bar and checked on the alarm. One yelled into the door of the building and the two men jumped into the black van, leaving the door open as they waited for two others to join.

Sam kept an eye on them in her mirror as long as possible. When she was two blocks away, the van pulled out to take chase down the narrow side street.

"They're gaining on us!" Adam shouted as Sam took a sharp right onto the busy main street.

"Isn't that an RV traveling at high speed with a black van chasing it... straight ahead of us?" Arena asked.

"Yeehaw, Cass."

Arena pulled up the emergency light and slapped it on the roof. "Let's get 'em, cowboy."

"I could just spank you when you call me cowboy."

"I may just let you do that if you can catch Adam *and* the thugs."

"Incentives—that's what motivates me!" Lobato responded, with an ear-to-ear grin.

Sam immediately noticed the flashing light on the grey unmarked police car behind the van. It had been weaving at high speed through traffic. She watched in her rearview mirror as it gained on them. "Help is on the way!" she shouted.

The thugs rolled down their windows. Two of them raised sawed-off shotguns and blasted behind them at the agents.

"Here we go!" Lobato veered right, then left.

Arena drew her weapon and returned fire as Lobato focused on weaving through traffic that was randomly pulling over.

They heard a helicopter overhead.

Arena hit the van's rear window. The driver seemed disoriented from the shot, and the van screeched off to the side, scraping parked cars until it crashed into the back of a large delivery van.

"Nice shot, Tex," Lobato said.

"Note the license of the RV. We're gonna wrap up these guys first!" Arena instructed as Lobato pulled up behind the van that had smoke steaming from the hood. Arena opened her door. "Freeze!" she shouted from behind her door.

Four thugs jumped out of the van, and they unloaded their weapons at the agents while backing down the street.

"On three!" Lobato shouted. "One... two...." Then the two agents unloaded their guns at the perpetrators.

One of the young bandits dropped to the pavement, holding his leg.

"I think that was yours, Cass. Nice."

Arena and Lobato each loaded another magazine.

"Throw your weapons aside!" Lobato shouted.

The wounded man, writhing in pain, released his pistol into a puddle of blood, and kicked it along the sidewalk. The men that were with him ran.

"Does one count toward my bonus?" Lobato asked as they shuffled toward the downed man. "We don't *really* need them all."

"You mean 'boner,' don't you? Well, I shot him, and the three others are gone, so unless you have a real lucky afternoon and can run like hell after them, there'll be no spanking today."

"You'd never pay that debt, anyway." He handcuffed the wounded man.

Arena grabbed his ass cheek. "I had every intention of paying, partner."

"You two want to get a room? I'm bleeding here!" the man said.

"That's a good idea. Maybe we could just cuff him to the parking meter. Someone will stop by and pick him up eventually," Lobato said.

"You're three thugs and an RV short of paying for that room."

Lobato holstered his weapon, grabbed his radio, and quickly barked orders for tracking the RV. Then he picked up the thug by the scruff of the neck with one hand and punched him hard in the kidney with the other.

"Son of a bitch!" the thug said then coughed. "What the hell?"

"You're going to tell me where your punk-ass friends are headed to, or you won't be needing an ambulance!"

"How the hell do I know? That way!" he smirked.

"Incentives... The only way to get a job done." Arena smiled as she walked back to their shot-up car.

"They're gone!" Adam shouted from the back of the RV.

"Great, but we're going to have to hide this vehicle. Rent another."

"Why are we running from those people, Mommy?"

"They're trying to beat us to Disney World."

"Oh. I thought they were after Mr. Johl."

"Actually, they were, honey. You see, those bad—"

"How long before we get there?" Lucy interrupted.

Sam smiled. "We should be there by morning, sweetie."

"Finally! I've been waiting forever and ever for this!"

"You're like a savior, Sam. You're a saint with the soul of Mary."

"Listen, Adam, I'm not that much of a saint. While I am trying to save you, I do have an ulterior motive."

"What are you saying?"

"The story. I'm a reporter. I'm writing a story, remember? The story of the century."

"I know you're a reporter, and that ultimately, it's the story you are after. That's not an ulterior motive. And I'll give you the story, the whole story. You deserve it. Beginning to end."

"Great," Sam said, surprised. "I'm going to swap out this RV. That will buy us a little more time until they track the next one. Then we can get right into it."

Sam drove one-handed as she Googled rental RVs on her smartphone. Her hand shook as she typed with her thumb. Her heart raced. Lucy scolded her for texting while driving: just one more bad example she was setting.

Sam discreetly parked the RV in a Wal-Mart parking lot next to rows of other RVs, and she rented another one from Avis. They drove a few blocks, found another busy mall, and parked for the night.

Lucy slept peacefully in the back as Adam finally commenced his story. He picked up the mini recorder Sam had given him and turned it on. "What if I told you I am a Muslim, and was blinded by my cause, and that this was all one big act to bring about the true prophecy?"

Sam's eyes widened as she held back an emotional outburst. *Be the professional you are.* "Wait. How is that possible? You knew of the tsunami that hit New York? And all of the other disasters?"

"I did."

"No one could have possibly known that. If this isn't divine intervention, how?"

"There could well be some divine influence here, as well. You never know the will of God."

Sam examined Adam's eyes, his lips, his jaw, looking for any telltale signs of lying. He was as calm and cool as an autumn evening in Alaska. "I will need you to explain to me, in specific detail, how you knew about the earthquakes."

"I am an expert in the seismic field. I also worked on a top-secret project for the US military—one I told them failed, and they shelved it. I secretly kept working on it, perfected it. Combined with my computer programming excellence, I can, with certain accuracy, predict major earth crust movement almost to the day. Most definitely the week."

Quickly, all the pieces of the puzzle fitted together in her mind. Adam was brilliant, using his expertise in programming and seismology to predict the probability of an earthquake. His "prophecy" was a hoax, possibly one of the greatest global hoaxes of all time.

Sam looked over at the bedroom door. Lucy stood in the doorway, clutching her pillow and a pink blanket. She inched her way toward Sam and Adam. "Adam, do you hate the West that much? Why would you do this? *Lucy*—back to bed, please. This is grown-up talk."

Adam looked at Lucy with her big round eyes. "Your mother is right, Lucy. I'll tell you a bedtime story after we talk. Okay?"

Lucy nodded, went into the bedroom, and closed the door.

Adam waited several seconds, then continued. "Ten years ago, my wife, my two sons, and my mother were all killed by an American airstrike on Rutba, my desert town in Iraq. My mother, Jaide; my sons, Omar and Haris; and Layla, my wife."

Jaide, Omar, Haris, Layla—Johl, the initials of his last name, she thought.

"They were after terrorists and hit the wrong house. None of us were terrorists or harbored terrorists."

"I'm so sorry, Adam."

"Casual collateral damage. That's all we were. They didn't care that we had jobs. Celebrated birthdays, loved, cared. We were just something in a report, a mistake that they probably used correction fluid on."

"And your father?"

"He was consumed by revenge, got us going on it, but he died shortly after it happened. Massive heart attack."

"Wow. You went through some very difficult times."

Adam shrugged. "We said he died of a broken heart. He was so in love with my mother. She was American, working with the Red Cross, helping those ravaged by the Iran-Iraq war when they met in the eighties. He was a prisoner, and she tended to his wounds.

"She never left Iraq after the war ended. She helped so many people, without discrimination. She was a saint and a wonderful mother."

"It sounds like they were all wonderful people."

"Yes, that is why I was blinded by rage. Revenge. I decided I needed to use my expertise to get back at the US, even though my mother was American. I wanted them to feel what I felt: the death of your heart and loss of your soul, the senseless slaughter of a family. For no reason." Adam sighed. "Someone took pictures. Of the bodies. It was in the paper. That was the day we all lived it again, only worse." He wiped his brow. "I bought into everything the jihadists and terrorists were selling. Which all led us to this moment, here."

"What changed? Are you really remorseful for what you've done?"

"Yes, I really am. My mother would be ashamed of what I've done." Sam nodded.

"I have a photo of my family I've hidden on the Cloud. I haven't looked at it since Roxy's. I'm ashamed. I don't feel like I deserve to look at them, like they could see me and what I've done." His eyes teared up.

Sam stared into his eyes. She believed him.

"And you are one of the reasons, too," he said softly. "Why I've changed."

"How did I change you?"

"Your kindness. Your lack of judgment. Your heart. You remind me of her."

Sam smiled.

"And oddly enough, when I delivered the message at Roxy's, I felt elated but confused. I delivered a message of peace and love, but I was consumed with trying to spread violence and chaos. But the moment was so, so powerful. I was in complete control. It was addictive."

Sam nodded.

"Doubt entered. Good and evil battling it out in an already destroyed heart."

"Your true personality won through."

"Maybe. I do feel different. I can't explain it. I still feel pain for my family, but it is more of a missing pain, not entirely a vengeful pain anymore. I need to forgive."

"I truly understand some of your pain, Adam. I lost my husband due to the negligence of a young man. A boy, actually." Sam spoke softly.

"I'm so sorry," Adam said.

"I invited the boy over for dinner, a while after."

"What?"

"I had to. I was dying too. Inside." Sam's eyes filled with tears. "Drunk driver. Seventeen years old, still a child. T-boned my husband at an intersection. Shortly after the accident, the boy tried to commit suicide."

Adam nodded while Sam dabbed her tears. They sat for several moments to the steady sound of traffic and the occasional horn honking.

After a few minutes of silence, Sam continued asking questions to fill in the blanks, and Adam continued on, stringing one incredible word after another. He explained how he was recruited by an al-Qaeda faction following the strike on his town and that the scheme took over seven years of planning.

Al-Qaeda called the project *Megiddo*—a location regarded as the most important biblical period site in Israel—and the word was derived from the Greek word *armageddon*. Through an elaborate non-traceable email network that Adam had created, they conversed freely, crafting the plans to create psychological warfare. No bombs, no virus, just self-destructing paranoia. He revealed that Mansfield was a Muslim and terrorist supporter.

"Paul? Really? He's so—or seems so—Bible-belt and American. Not a terrorist."

"Terrorists don't have a specific look, or color of skin. It's what's in here." He tapped his head. "This is where the similarity is. And it's not visible until they do something awful."

Sam nodded. "So you worked almost entirely by yourself?"

"We all did. Less connect-the-dots for CIA and FBI. Mansfield and I were part of the al-Qaeda connection on this assignment."

"What about the others in the bar? Accomplices?"

"Bar owner paid off; cop paid off. Life-changing amounts of cash for them to help with the magic, coordinating details."

"And what about the two murders the FBI reported as tied in to this whole thing? One in Queens and one in Brooklyn?" She tensed up. She hoped Adam had no part in it, but she had wanted to ask him that question for a while. Was he a killer?

"The Queens fellow owned a fabricating shop that made the famous floating chairs. He made the steel springs. Not sure if the FBI figured that one out yet. I'm sure they found out about his forgery setup though. Created me and Dove."

Sam nodded slowly. "And what about that Brooklyn janitor?"

"He was actually the cameraman for Mansfield."

Sam swallowed. "Who killed them?" she asked quickly.

"Maybe Mark Little, but I wasn't part of any of that, and it wasn't supposed to happen. They were probably all seen as loose ends by my handlers." Adam took a big breath. "And Dove—he's my brother."

"What?"

"We are both blinded by hate. And I didn't pay him, just like I said."

Sam studied Adam differently. "I don't see any resemblance."

He shrugged.

"It all makes sense now... except... What about the earthquakes and tsunami? You could have used this to warn people, help them. You said it was just psychological warfare."

Adam nodded. "I don't expect you to understand. You need to be born into it to fully understand why we did it."

"That's a cop-out; I don't believe it for a second. I've seen people with solid upbringings become mass murderers, and I've seen children of mass murderers become advocates for peace. We all have the free will to choose. After the last few days, I know there is another side to you, a side that wonders if what you are doing is terribly wrong."

"And what if there is? It's too late now. I've done..." Adam stood up. "I'm sorry. I really need to sleep now. I am very tired, and my head's spinning. Sorry, we can finish up tomorrow. I'll tell you anything else you want to know."

"Okay."

They looked at each other in an awkward moment of silence. Sam had just heard a confession story that would win her all of the journalist awards on the planet, yet that didn't matter to her. What was wrong with her?

Adam and Sam took up bunks opposite each other in the sitting room. Sam turned the lights off and tried to turn her mind off.

Patterns of light snuck through the ends of the blinds, moving across the interior of the RV as vehicles passed by. She tried to focus on the hum of traffic to help her sleep. It was oddly comforting.

"Sam?"

Sam rolled over and looked at Adam. She could see a gleam in his dark eyes.

"Sam, I just want to say thank you. For not judging me. What I've told you would make anyone hate me. You've truly opened my eyes to something I've never seen before."

"How'd I open our eyes?"

"You're a very special, selfless, and strong woman."

Sam didn't respond.

"The perfect role model for any child—or adult."

"Thanks. I can see good in you too, Adam. And it's never too late to change. To heal."

"I know."

Sam rolled on to her back and stared at the ceiling.

"God bless you," Adam said, in a soft, sincere tone.

The three words gave Sam goose bumps, like the ones she got when she heard that long-sustained perfect note being hit by an opera singer. "Good night, Adam," she whispered.

20

Friday - Day 7

Sam tossed about on her bunk, trying to get comfortable and trying to clear her mind in order to fall asleep. But she couldn't stop thinking of everything Adam had told her, the chaos in the world, and how to keep her daughter safe. The thoughts brought tears to her eyes.

She got up quietly and drove through the night. Around six thirty a.m., Lucy came to the front of the RV, wearing her jammies and pink bunny slippers. "How close are we, Mommy?" she asked, rubbing her eyes.

"We're almost at the gates. Maybe fifteen minutes?"

Adam sat silently, gazing out at the steady stream of passing traffic. He seemed to be staring off in the distance at nothing.

"Mommy? Are you crying?"

"I'm just happy, Lucy, that we're finally here," she said, wiping her teary red eyes.

"There's a sign! Disney World, t— Ten! Ten minutes, and we're there!"

"That's ten miles, sweetie."

"I'm going to change!" Lucy said, and she bounced back to the bedroom, singing the Mickey Mouse song.

Sam turned on the radio to check the news for the first time since yesterday afternoon.

The announcer sounded morose as he read, "In New York, the death toll of the tsunami topped an estimated eighty thousand and continues to grow despite advance warning. Not one major crime story has made news headlines in the last twenty-four hours. The New York Stock Exchange had been closed for two days—a record—as the markets experience record drops after a week of mayhem and catastrophes.

"And around the globe, stories continued to stream in on events perceived to be marking the last hours. In Europe, the tsunami hammered the coast, flooding all Atlantic coastal cities. Martial law had also been imposed in most European countries in anticipation of riots and looting in the perceived last hours. Around the world, ATMs have been drained, as well as grocery and retail shelves. Borrowing is at an all-time high."

"Turn it off, please," Adam said.

Sam turned it off.

"Let's just enjoy the day."

They nodded at each other.

As Sam drove into the acres of parking lots at Disney World, she was surprised to see them filled almost to capacity. "That's bizarre. Look at all the cars. I guess they all figure it's a great place to spend Friday."

"People want to believe in a perfect world, and Disney World is the closest thing on earth." Adam donned a baggy grey T-shirt, a large floppy straw hat, and wraparound sunglasses.

The three left the safety of the RV to board the parking lot tram. They boarded with several other people. Lucy, seemingly oblivious to the world's woes, bounced up and down in her seat all the way to the main ticket gates.

After Sam bought the tickets, they headed immediately to Main Street to find Mickey, as promised. Sam held Lucy's hand tightly as they maneuvered and pushed their way through the waves of families.

"Adam!" Sam shouted, spinning in a circle, scanning the crowds. She could not see his straw hat. "*Damn*!"

"There he is!" Lucy shouted.

"Where, honey?"

"Right there! Mickey!"

"Not Mickey. Adam. I'm looking for Adam."

"This way, Mommy! I want to meet Mickey!" Lucy tugged on Sam's arm.

Sam spotted Adam under a tree, making a call on a payphone. "Just one minute and we'll see the mouse!" She dragged Lucy to the phones.

"Here you are. Who are you calling?" she asked, catching her breath.

Adam hesitated. "My contact. We were meeting tomorrow morning. And I was trying to reach Dove too; we did have something planned for here today."

"I knew it!" Sam said. "Let's hear it, all of it."

"This was the next step, or show. My grand exit. My contact has a boat that is taking us to Mexico. From there, we are to fly to Europe. I am to go underground, so to speak. And Dove's role changes up for the next stage."

"Who's 'we'? Mexico, Europe? What's the next stage?"

"Slow down, I'll try to answer all of your questions. 'We' is Dove and Paul—we were to meet here. And the contact knows where we are; he's just a travel courier. He only knows his little piece and can be trusted. Mexico is easy to get in to and out of unnoticed."

"And what *show* are you talking about?"

"Something to help me disappear—make a grand exit, if you will."

"Another disappearing act?"

"Sort of. But I'm not going to do it."

"Why didn't you tell me all this?"

"I told you everything that had happened up until this point and why it happened. Why should I involve you any more than I already have?"

"I'm not just involved, Adam. I'm invested, emotionally and personally. You're not just a story... I hope you know that."

"I know. I just thought it best. Sorry." Adam touched her arm. "Take your daughter to see Mickey, have fun, and don't worry about anything. Just enjoy the day." Adam pointed to Mickey Mouse. "I'll hide out. Tomorrow I leave."

Lucy jumped up and down as she held her mom's hand, trying to keep Mickey in her view. "Let's go, already!"

"I'll meet you at the end of the day. Say five? At the main gates," Adam suggested. "I'll go sit under a tree, very low-key. Then we'll have the last supper."

"Did you have to say that?" Sam asked sarcastically.

"Sorry, again. Go have fun, please. It'll mean a lot to me."

Sam nodded and slowly turned away. Lucy pulled her off into the crowd to find the elusive giant rat that she wanted to strangle.

Adam made his way to the lockers. He discreetly removed his money belt, put it in the locker, and hid the key in a planter nearby.

If he was spotted by the gang that was sent there to lynch him, his show would go on, and he would need the cash to help him disappear.

***

Lobato arrived at Arena's apartment with coffee and croissants at eight a.m. Arena answered the door in sweat pants, a Keith Urban concert T-shirt, and a towel on her hair. Arena took her coffee and went back to the bathroom to finish drying her hair while Lobato made himself comfortable at the kitchen table. He drank coffee and read the paper as he waited patiently to the sound of the blow-dryer buzzing from the bathroom.

After fifteen minutes, Arena appeared dressed in slacks, blazer, and blue blouse. She sat down with Lobato.

"I feel guilty," Lobato said.

"About what?"

"Sitting here, having coffee, reading the paper—maybe the last paper—and the world is a mess. People suffering everywhere, and we're not."

"I know." Arena said then sipped her coffee. "But don't. It'll eat you up."

"On the plus side, finally a weekend off." Lobato turned the page of his newspaper.

"Yeah. I read the morning reports. Over forty percent of workers didn't show up yesterday, and today they're predicting an even higher percentage taking a sick day. Essential services could shut down."

"The drive here this morning was eerie, too. Roads are dead."

"So are a lot of people, thanks to the riots in Rome over the death of the Pope."

"And London. Burning, looting," Arena said as she reached over and tapped on the picture in the newspaper.

"Well I guess it doesn't matter what we do today, does it, Cass?"

"Not really. By seven p.m., it will or—probably—won't be over. Then there's the mess to clean up. If that's even possible."

"You think they'd learn. Adam's message was clear, even if it was a hoax."

"The ultimate terrorist attack. True terror through fear, not action. Psychological warfare causing global mayhem." Lobato folded his newspaper.

Arena took another sip and leaned back in her chair. "He's probably in Disney World, according to intel. And Dove has been followed to Florida, as well."

"We know. But what's the point? Let's pick him up on Monday, if he's around. If *we're* around."

"Breno. What else would we do today? Besides, it's our job."

"I think I should cash in some Hilton reward points, get a room, some champagne, and rock your world."

Arena shook her head and smiled, revealing her slightly crooked but perfectly white teeth. "I say we go get Adam in Florida, make him pay for this hell on earth. Besides, you said you felt guilty."

"Why do we need to bring him in? What good would that do?" Lobato sipped his coffee.

"Honestly, I'm not sure what the charges would look like, and if they'd even stick. And with a good lawyer, he'll just—"

"Okay, partner."

"Okay what?" Arena gave him a puzzled look.

"I think you—we—need to do this. Even though his crime is lying, deceiving—we need to haul him in. It shouldn't take long, anyway." Lobato chuckled. "Besides, I've always had a perverted attraction to Minnie. Think she'd join us?"

Arena shook her head. "You need help."

"Mouse costume? Cute little polka dot dress?"

"I'll call for a jet. Let's go get him."

"But we have to wrap this all up by six tonight. You've got to give us at least an hour to say good-bye the right way."

"If we get it all done, Adam caught and bagged by six, deal."

"*Deal*?"

"Don't look surprised; women are the ones to say when. Men are just the ones to say yes." Arena got up. "Besides, it'll take a miracle to wrap this up by six."

21

Sam's wet white blouse clung to her body. She fanned herself with a Disney guide and held Lucy's hand as they moved slowly in the line for It's a Small World.

A man that walked quickly by shouted, "It's the terrorist—they have him!"

Sam turned and caught his arm as he passed their line. "Excuse me. What was that about the terrorist? Who?" She let go.

"Adam Johl." The man took a cautious step away from Sam and straightened his shirt. "A lynch mob has him, and they're dragging him through the park. I hear he's by the Pirates of the Caribbean. I'm going to get some video on this."

Sam looked at Lucy, who stood pouting with her arms crossed. Sam grabbed her hand, and they went off to find Adam.

The crowds were getting thicker as they got closer to the Pirate ride. The mob chanted, "Terrorist! Terrorist!" waving bags, flags, anything they could. Sam picked up Lucy. She pushed and shoved, elbowing her way to the front of the mob. Mothers, fathers, children, grandparents, security guards, cast members—all of them watched. No one helped Adam Johl, and they chanted and shouted in a building frenzy. Sam wept when she saw Adam.

He was on all fours, carrying what appeared to be a fake old wooden post, probably made of fiberglass and from the Pirates of the Caribbean. His head was crowned with Mickey Mouse ears that were tied to his head with wire that cut into his forehead, blood dripping into his eyes. A gang of a dozen men, dressed in red bandanas, NBA sports jerseys, and excessive jewelry, ensured he only got up when they allowed it. One of the gang members whipped Adam with a belt that had a large rhinestone-encrusted skull on the buckle. It sparkled in the sun as it swung around.

"*Adam!*" Sam cried, a few yards from him.

Adam slowly lifted his head, expressionless; his gaze seemed to wander.

"You're gonna pay for the shit you've caused!" the thug with the belt shouted.

"Stop!" Sam yelled as she reached Adam's side, leaving Lucy at the edge of the crowd that threw assorted trash at Adam.

"Get lost, bitch!" the belt-wielding man spat.

"Adam! I'm going to get help! Just hold on!"

The man swung the belt at her. Adam blocked it with his arm, and the belt wrapped around him with a snap. He grabbed the belt with the other hand and tried to pull the man down with it, but he couldn't.

"Go! Please!" Adam said, wincing. "Take care of Sunshine!"

Sam quickly looked back at Lucy, who stood at the edge of the crowd, tears in her eyes. Sam got up and backed into the unruly mob. "Is this the show?" she asked. "Is this part of it?"

Adam nodded slowly. "Take care of Lucy."

"Then stop this! Now!" she shouted as she stepped back, bumping into a security guard who seemed to be enjoying watching Adam get beat down. "Why the hell won't you do something!" she asked him while grabbing his shoulder and giving him a shake.

Lucy grabbed Sam's leg.

The security guard shrugged her off. "Why don't you, lady?"

"Damn you!" She took out her phone and dialed 911, shaking her head in disbelief as tears formed in her eyes.

People were pointing, laughing, throwing things. One boy tossed a red shaved-ice cone at Adam while his parents applauded. Sam cried silently as she witnessed the shavings dripping from Adam's face.

As Sam explained the chaos to the 911 operator, she spotted Paul Mansfield trying to help Adam. She moved closer to them to get a better view while still on the phone and holding Lucy's hand tightly. She wanted to run to Adam's side again, to help him. "Just send someone! Now!" she shouted at the emergency operator then disconnected.

They slowly followed the chaotic procession of Adam's torture. Lucy's view of Adam was thankfully blocked most of the time by someone taller in front of her.

"To your feet, hero!" the man with the belt yelled as he hit Adam again.

"Adam!" Mansfield bellowed. "I'll get you out of here!"

"Paul—just go to the meet and get to the boat! Get out of here!"

The belt *thwacked* hard against Adam's back, drawing blood through his grey T-shirt.

"Adam!" Sam cried.

"They're hurting him, Mommy!" Lucy cried.

"Looks like we need another pole!" one of the gang members yelled. "Get one for his friend here!" He pointed at Mansfield.

Mansfield slowly backed to the edge of the crowd-lined street, next to Sam. Several people pushed him back into the opening, making him fall forward. People pointed at him. "He was the anchor who faked the news broadcast! *Terrorist!*" A couple of the thugs grabbed him.

Sam spotted Dove break through the crowd and run to Mansfield's aid. "Help him, Dove! Hurry!" she shouted and pointed.

"Take your slimy hands off him!" Dove yelled.

The two thugs quickly turned around. One flipped open a switchblade and yelled, "Tough shit, huh? Just another fuckin' spineless terrorist," while the other slipped behind Dove with a club.

"Kick *this*!" Dove's quick roundhouse kick sent the knife flying. Sam cheered. Dove bounced like a boxer, waiting for an opening to jab again.

"I see you bomb huggers know a little girly kick shit," the other thug said from behind Dove as he clubbed him hard over the head, bringing him to his knees. Dove wobbled, and a trickle of blood ran into his eyes as he fell over.

Within minutes, the group of thugs had forced both Dove and Mansfield to carry old-looking wooden poles on their backs along with Adam. Sam stood in the front row of blindly patriotic onlookers, watching helplessly, crying. She looked at her phone as if she expected someone to call her. Maybe 911 calling back. She pocketed her phone.

Disney security staff stood in the background, not interfering. "Help them, you idiots!" she yelled at them.

"Plant them over there!" shouted a thirty-something man in an American-flag Disney T-shirt.

Sam wanted to kick him in the groin. Several times. "Plant you! Pigs!" she screamed.

Two more thugs removed their belts and whipped the new parade members. "Over there, shit-heads!" he said, pointing to the Magic Kingdom's castle.

Dove winced but made his way next to Adam and used his free arm to lift Adam's beam off his back. "Hang in there, brother."

"No problem," Adam said. "Just take care of yourself. I've got this."

"Hang on," Dove said. "Show's still on."

Adam nodded as the belt came down on him again. He looked up at Sam, who was just a few yards away.

Show's still on? What are Adam and Dove up to? Sam thought. *This couldn't be planned.*

"It's almost seven," Dove said quickly, glancing up at the large street clock.

Mansfield stumbled behind them with both his knees badly cut. The belt *cracked* across his back.

"Get up!"

Mansfield tried to get up, and he stumbled again, tripping and falling backward, smashing his head on a concrete curb. Blood quickly poured from his ears and mouth onto the sidewalk around his body. His lifeless eyes stared to the sky. Sam covered Lucy's eyes.

"Oh shit!" Dove shouted.

Mansfield looked dead. Sam and Adam wept.

"Get your ass up on the grass over here!" a thug shouted.

The crowd of people walked over and around the body of Mansfield, chanting, "Death to terrorists!"

Sam was torn. That was no place for a child. It was too dangerous and frightening. But how could she leave Adam? She picked Lucy up and held close to her chest, holding Lucy's head down on her shoulder so she couldn't witness any more brutality.

The two captives slowly dragged their poles up onto the slight knoll, in front of the iconic castle, while being prodded, kicked, and spit at the entire way. The thugs tied the poles to the fence that surrounded the castle, then strung up Adam and Dove by binding their hands to the top of the poles. Their feet dangled a foot above the ground.

"In a few minutes, we're all going to turn to dust!" a man shouted, throwing a partially eaten hamburger at Adam.

"What are we going to do! Oh, my God!" A woman laughed. "Burn them!"

"Burn you, bitch!" Sam screamed. The woman ignored her. Lucy lifted her head off her mom's shoulder, mouth wide open, and looked up at her mom. Sam gently pushed Lucy's head back down, bouncing her up and down a little. "You're going to need therapy when this is all over, sorry!" she said to Lucy.

Low, dark, billowy clouds had quickly snuck in over the park. Adam looked up as ominous clouds swallowed the last patch of dark blue sky. He gazed down at the crowds of average-looking people, all ages, races, ranting and raving.

A cool wind washed over the area, followed by dime-sized, sporadic raindrops that exploded as they hit the hot pavement.

The onlookers paused their harassment of the two captives to look up. The majority quietly withdrew from the open area, seeking cover.

"Is this it, the end? A little *rain*?" one of the punks taunted. He jumped up and stabbed Adam in his side.

Adam looked up in pain. Thunder and a crack of lightening ignited simultaneously in a glass-rattling *kaboom!* Several funnel clouds appeared above the park, then touched ground and commenced their feasting on anything not fastened down. Plants, flags, and garbage swirled up and disappeared.

Sam ran to Adam. "Oh my God! Did you predict this too?" she asked, then ripped her sleeve off at the shoulder and held it to the wound in his side as a collection of more garbage and landscape spun throughout the central courtyard.

The thug stood behind Sam, positioning his knife for another stab. Sam saw Cassia Arena in the corner of her eye. She had her gun drawn and pointed at the man who was about to stab Adam.

"*Freeze!*" Arena shouted.

Sam dropped to the ground.

The thug quickly turned his head, then swung his arm—two gunshots ripped through the heavy rain and howling wind. Arena stood with her arms extended, gripping her pistol that had a small trail of smoke that was quickly extinguished. Rain dripped from her face.

The thug dropped to his knees then fell forward, blood oozing from his chest.

The insignificant remaining crowd scrambled as Agent Lobato ran to Adam with his weapon drawn.

Arena held her ground, weapon ready. Lobato cut Adam and Dove down from the poles.

"I'm going to kill them!" Dove rubbed his wrists.

"There's been enough killing for one week," Adam said, pressing Sam's torn-off sleeve to his wound.

Debris hit them as several mini twisters danced and jogged within a hundred feet of them. They made a shrill train-whistle sound.

Sam held Adam as he tried to sit up. She watched his blood wash down the gutter.

"Go," Adam said.

"Not without you!"

An ambulance managed to maneuver its way to the castle. Two paramedics removed the stretcher; the blankets ripped off the gurney and flapped away in the wind. Lobato helped them load Adam into the ambulance.

"I think he's lost a lot of blood!" Sam cried.

"Wait!" Dove yelled then ran to the ambulance. "Adam!"

On the gurney, Adam turned his head toward Dove.

"Take care, Adam. I'll see you soon."

Adam's eyes closed.

A street vendor's popcorn cart flew overhead and disappeared up into the black clouds.

"We have to get out of here, fast!" the driver shouted then closed the door.

Arena and Lobato took Sam and Lucy into the safety of the Disney World underground until it was safe to surface.

The twisters finished their theme park destruction and seemed to be dissipating as they headed toward the Gulf of Mexico.

As planned—and without incident—Dove vanished from the US, via water then air, leaving no trail of where he was headed.

Adam's heart stopped before they reached the hospital; the attending physician verified time of death as 7:07 p.m.

22

The next morning, Sam rented a car, looked at the map of Florida at the rental kiosk, and picked Key Largo as the destination for her and her daughter. They checked into a beach-front room at the Marriot, and the first thing they did was go for a long stroll along the deserted beach, hand-in-hand. Sam thought it was time to start a little mom-to-daughter love therapy. She also hoped that Adam was still alive, although the blood had looked real and Mansfield really was dead. If this had been planned and Adam had escaped, he was brilliant. She hoped he really was brilliant.

"You've been very quiet, all the way from Orlando. Where's my little Sunshine hiding?"

Lucy looked up at her mom as they splashed through the surf barefoot. "Still here," she said softly.

"Are you sad?"

"Yes."

"So am I," Sam said, squeezing her little hand. What had happened over the past week was tough enough for adults to digest, let alone a child.

She had tried to shelter Lucy from as much as possible of the news of the deaths, destruction, and chaos. But it was everywhere in the media, and everyone talked about it—from the people in the elevator that day to the man at the car rental agency. They couldn't escape it. "It's over now. You don't have to worry."

"I'm not worried, just sad. I miss my friends. And Adam. He was a nice man, and they were so mean to him." Lucy's eyes filled with tears. "I want to go home."

Sam stopped walking, crouched down to Lucy's level, and held both her hands. The waves wet the bottom of her shorts. "You know what we need?"

"Don't say ice cream."

"Really? You love ice cream for every occasion, happy or sad."

Lucy sighed.

"I wasn't going to say ice cream anyway. I was going to say Disney and Mickey Mouse. That's what we need."

"But it's all destroyed and closed," Lucy said, sounding dejected. "It's never going to happen. Ever."

"They're not closed or destroyed in France."

"There's a Disney in France?"

"Yes, and there's a direct flight from Miami."

A large wave rolled in unexpectedly and threw Sam off balance. She fell forward with Lucy, and they rolled in the water, playfully screaming.

They rolled more, laughed, and splashed each other.

After what seemed to Sam like an emotional release, they knelt in the surf, facing each other, and hugged.

"France. Let's go! Thanks, Mom. I really love you!"

Sam picked Lucy up, and Lucy wrapped her legs around her mother's waist. "I love you too, Lucy. We'll always have each other."

Lucy kissed her mom on the cheek. "Does Mickey speak English in France?"

"*Oui*!"

***

Late Friday night, after filing some paperwork with local authorities over what happened at Disney World, Lobato and Arena booked into the first hotel they came upon outside Orlando. Two separate rooms. Lobato didn't try to bed his partner; he felt it wasn't the time or place. Besides, when they did finally sleep together, he wanted it to be special and not forced. And... Cass had a headache—a real one, he convinced himself.

Lobato bought a case of beer and watched a movie alone. *The Notebook*.

***

Marty, Claire, and Daisy's homes in New Hyde Park were spared from any major water damage caused by the tsunami, as their homes sat at around a hundred and twenty feet above sea level. Water had spilled into their streets but retreated just as quickly.

All three of them knew people who had died in the disaster, and all three were trying to mask the pain of that loss—and the pain of the "Adam Johl scam"—with booze.

On Saturday, Marty guzzled vodka and orange juice in his kitchen; Claire drank scotch on her patio. Daisy drank beer at her favorite Caribbean bar.

Marty secretly wished his home had been wiped out so he could start over, start new. Maybe in another city. Maybe stop drinking.

He had hit a new low, if that was possible. He felt as if he was one drink away from losing his job, from losing his family, and from living on the street.

But still, he drank. Only God knew why, he thought. And apparently, God wasn't speaking to him. He didn't at Roxy's, and he wouldn't now.

Claire volunteered at the church to help those who lost their homes. She signed up for tomorrow, Sunday. Today, she was busy drinking and feeling sorry for herself again.

She had been betrayed by another man. Adam. She would never trust another man as long as she lived.

Maybe she should try women, become a lesbian. Maybe they wouldn't betray her? Ellen or Portia looked like people she could trust.

Maybe she should hunt Adam down. Confront him. *Oh wait,* she thought. *He's dead.*

Daisy knew Dove was still out there, hiding, waiting. Probably planning his next evil move. He was up to something; she'd dreamt it and woken up screaming last night.

Today she would take a day to rest, drink, enjoy the handsome bartender, and hopefully forget the awful nightmare. Tomorrow she would find the strength to continue with trying to stop Dove. Maybe kill him

23

Sunday, Day 9

It had been two days since Adam Johl, psychological terrorist who had temporarily convinced thousands that the end of the world was at hand, died at Disney World in Florida. Agent Cassia Arena and Breno Lobato flew directly into Philadelphia Sunday morning and went to work in the downtown FBI office. The office they previously worked out of at 26 Federal Plaza in New York was closed due to water damage from the tsunami. There was fear of structural instability at Federal Plaza, as well as at most office buildings in the area, and the streets were closed.

The south side of New York City looked like Venice, and it was still under up to two feet of water two miles inland. The New York Bight, an indentation in the shoreline, had funneled the tsunami into the heart of the city, and the standing water was slower to retreat than officials predicted. Lobato had told Arena he would paddle a gondola all the way to her apartment, singing the love song "Adagio." She told him he could sing "Heigh-Ho" from *Snow White and the Seven Dwarfs* all the way to the office.

Arena and Lobato were assigned desks that were back to back with a low divider and in the middle of the bullpen. The office was filled with agents and staff. Phones rang. People hurried about, often brushing Arena's chair, which stuck out a little into the aisle. But after the week they'd had, that felt normal to her. Like the world was getting back to what she was used to: organized chaos and paperwork.

They had half-eaten bagels, empty coffee cups, piles of file folders, and national newspapers scattered over their desks.

Lobato teetered back on his chair, strumming his knee with a pen. "I thought we were taking today off? The world's still here, sort of. And we missed date night Friday night—and Saturday night."

"Dream on. After the week from hell, we're behind months' worth of paperwork." Arena stared across her desk at Lobato's antics. "We need to work harder than ever to help get the world back on track. And who knows what's still to come? Wacky weather, earthquakes." She shook her head. "While I remain cautiously optimistic that Johl's death ended this attack, I wonder if it really is over."

Lobato let out a healthy yawn, covering his mouth. "Let's recap again, from the top, and make sure we get this paperwork done right so that it at least looks like it's over." He laughs. "Yeah. We'll fill in the big gaps and get out of here early. I know a great little Philly restaurant. *Puccini's*."

Arena stared through Lobato. *Here we go again. Distractions. Food, wine. Cheesecake.* She sighed.

"They have a Sunday night prime rib dinner special to die for, Cass. And dessert is included. That will help to escape this madness for a short while."

"Focus, Breno." Arena quickly read from her file, "Adam's part of an al-Qaeda sleeper cell. He's called to duty utilizing his specialized skill set and develops a program that can produce false reporting of seismic activity—although I don't see the need for that, when he's calculated the probability of them happening. So the false reports were just an added insurance to get everybody on edge, getting the public to think something big was coming, just in case his predictions were off."

"Add the PhD in geology, and his thesis on seismic interpretation fault analysis and predictions. A real brainiac supreme being."

Arena flipped a page. "Adam then calculates the impossible: the timing of the quake that sends the tsunami to New York. That's the catalyst they need to get the Armageddon fear train in full gear and get people believing in his miracle show."

"That one still bothers me. First off, our research shows it's next to impossible to accurately predict earthquakes, but if he could, he could have saved thousands of lives."

Arena and Lobato locked gazes; Arena was impressed by her partner's concern for the lost lives. "Adam enlists the aid of—"

Arena's desk phone rang. She read the call display; it was Forensics. She held the file while she answered.

Adam's body was missing from the morgue. She shook her head in disbelief.

"What?" Lobato asked.

"No. You're kidding." Arena said into the phone as she scratched her temple. "Secure the room; we're on our way back to Florida." She hung up.

Lobato made the "tell me" nod and raised his eyebrows.

Arena shook her head and laughed. "Adam's corpse has disappeared from the hospital morgue in Orlando."

"Sort of figures. Someone was bound to want to either destroy it or worship it. How'd they steal it? There were guards outside the morgue twenty-four, seven."

"The guards swear no one entered or left the morgue. They have the security tapes. He simply vanished."

Lobato sat up in his chair and leaned forward on his desk. "Who discovered him missing?"

"The medical examiner."

They locked eyes once again, Arena trying to connect the dots in her mind, and by the look on Breno's face, he was trying to do the same.

Arena sighed. "One last thing—and you're not going to believe this."

"He rose into heaven?"

She paused. "There was an image of him burned into the stainless steel storage tray his body was on."

Arena pictured the Shroud of Turin; the image of Jesus burned into the robe that covered his body in the tomb in Jerusalem after his crucifixion. She had been intrigued by all the forensic research done on the cloth and controversy surrounding its authenticity. Maybe even obsessed with it. Was it an ancient magic trick or divine? How could Adam have pulled off his disappearing act? She imagined people a thousand years from now, still examining the steel storage tray that Adam disappeared from.

"Nah," she blurted.

"Nah what?" Lobato looked at her. "Adam's not some Messiah? Dove's not the devil?" He laughed.

"Pass me Dove's file, please," she requested. "All this coincidence is driving me nuts. Could they have planned this far in advance? Could they have known how it would unfold?"

He slid the file across the desk. Arena thumbed through it. She reviewed his gang history from a few years back. Dove had a violent past and nearly beat a young man to death. His lawyer pleaded self-defense; he got off with time served. His record was clean after that. He did a bunch of community service and never even got a traffic violation until his speeding ticket the week before.

Arena flipped through some photos in the file. She stopped at a color photo of the tattoo on Dove's back.

"What are you thinking?"

"This tattoo means something more. That much ink of doves." She slowly turned the picture clockwise, examining it at each quarter turn. The blue shading on each bird made it appear 3D. It was great work. She held it up at an angle, looking for a hidden message or picture.

"Tell me what you are looking for, and I can help."

Arena stared at the photo, looking at it like those pictures that if you concentrated on them long enough, a second image would appear. *Finally.* "Of course," she said, as she laid a piece of paper over the photo. She outlined the subtle numbers that appeared in the curve of the doves' tails. "They're scattered and at different angles, but there are three sixes. And they sort of line up."

"And? Lots of weirdoes have six-six-six or swastikas or born-to-sin inked."

"This weirdo is not your average weirdo. He may think he's someone special. Someone dark." Arena paused. "He's... just not your average weirdo, and that makes him much more dangerous."

"Is *weirdo* a profiler term? Can I quote you on that?"

"Go get me some coffee. Please," she said, lifting her empty cup and shaking it. "And you can sing 'Adagio' on your way. We're going to need more love in this world with this *weirdo* still on the loose."

***

Even though the guards at the morgue swore that no one had passed through the doors other than the medical examiner, Arena and Lobato reviewed the security tapes. They paid close attention to any possible loop or break. Even the best loops had small imperfections: blinks, static, slight changes in color, or repetition of a fluorescent-light flicker. The two agents couldn't detect any signs of tampering. They would send the tape to the lab for proper analysis, and after inspecting the morgue that day, Arena and Lobato would put the guards through the grinder.

The guard punched in a security code and unlocked the heavy metal doors for the agents.

Arena and Lobato entered the sterile pale-green room, shoes squeaking on the polished grey marble floor while the guard waited outside in the hallway.

Three large stainless steel tables were lined up down the middle of the room, with a chain and pulley system hanging on a track above. On the other side of the tables was a wall filled with compartments, three feet by two feet, that were stacked three high. A middle compartment had police tape across the door. Arena walked up to the door and ripped the tape off, then looked at Lobato. Lobato smiled and, without losing eye contact with his partner, opened the door and slid out the seven-foot tray that once held the corpse of Adam Johl.

They paused then looked down. The image of Adam was clearly burned into the steel in a blue-black prism of color. It was as if someone had taken a blowtorch with a pinpoint flame and laid each strand of Adam's hair down in perfect order: his eyes, nose, fingers—it looked holographic.

"Man, he's good. He should have had a magic show on TV; he would have made billions." Lobato bent down and sniffed the tray. "Smells like... burned steel, not flesh."

Arena bent to take a look under the tray. "Oh. Wow. It went right through. This shows the image of the back of his body." She stood up slowly. "He's raised his game. I'm starting to believe that he didn't die. There are drugs out there that he could have taken to give him near-fatal vital signs. There's a new Tetrodotoxin hybrid. But he would need qualified accomplices."

"How elaborate of a hoax is this? He would have needed to stage and preplan his murder in Disney World; would've needed to have the EMT and ambulance driver in on it, as well as the medical examiner and security here."

"All possible. Look at 9/11: years of planning and accomplices, some that didn't even know they were accomplices."

"The coroner? The M.E.? How did he get to those guys?"

"The coroner signed the death certificate Friday night at 9:12 p.m. There was an M.E. there, too. They both confirmed his death, but maybe someone tampered with it. Maybe there was a different body, a double, maybe the drugs—lots of maybes," Arena said, rubbing her chin. There were numerous ways this could be done, she thought. Some ways she probably wasn't even thinking of yet.

"Maybe they were paid off like the cop, Roxy's owner, and all the others. The kind of money this group was throwing around was hard to turn down. They could have flashed a hundred grand, or even a million dollars."

"*Maybe.* Close it up. Let's check the compartments above and below," Arena said, sliding the tray back into its crypt. She opened the door above and slid the tray open and inspected the bottom. "No sign of heat damage here." She closed it, then opened the bottom compartment and slid open the tray. They both looked down at it. It shone like a mirror without a blemish: no heat damage.

"This kind of heat would have left some kind of mark above or below. This tray was probably done somewhere else and placed here. Maybe even before Adam was placed here."

Arena got down onto her knees on the cold floor and crawled halfway into the hollow tomb.

Lobato stood behind her. "Very nice."

"Animal," Arena mumbled. She pulled herself back out with something looped on the end of her pen.

"What'd you find?"

"Toe tag," she said, straightening her blazer.

"You're good with that pen of yours, always finding some kind of tag or something, but this one is not too unusual. We're in a morgue."

"True, but this one belongs to Adam." She swung the tag back and forth on her pen. "It should have burned with him."

"This is just crazy." Lobato closed the bottom drawer and reopened the one that used to hold Adam.

To the hum and occasional flicker from the overhead lights, they stared again at the perfect image emblazoned on the tray.

"This would fetch a ton on eBay, especially if the image of the Virgin Mary on a grilled cheese sandwich could get twenty-eight grand," Lobato said.

"It's all perception."

"What are we supposed to perceive? We're the ones the public have placed their trust in to solve these cases, explain things rationally, and to keep them safe." He ran his fingers along the edge of the smooth image. "How we perceive this will shape our entire investigation. Our interpretation has to be the truth so that we can actually protect the people."

Arena smirked. "You know, I think I like you better when you're staring at my ass; I understand you then." She slid the tray back in, closed the door, and reattached the police tape. "Let's keep this simple. Someone here was paid off to help pull this off. We'll check out everyone that was within a foot of this morgue. That's what the *people* would want us to do with the taxpayers' dollars they pay us with."

Lobato looked at Arena sideways. "Dinner?"

"There's the Breno I understand: ass, food, and booze. Let's grill these guards, then the steaks. If we can find a place open."

They left the room and pulled one guard into the security office at a time. The guards were rent-a-cops hired by the hospital. *If they're lying, they should be as easy to crack as a dollar store combination lock,* Arena thought.

It was a long afternoon of tag-team questioning, but by the end of it, both agents surmised the guards weren't lying or hiding anything. Their stories were too tight to be fabricated. If anything, the guards were all just thinking about one thing: how to sell that burnt tray and retire.

24

The Monday Mediterranean sun cast no shadows as it hung straight overhead at the nearly empty Café Berardo's in Pescara, Italy. The seaside city was swamped from the rising oceans, with fishing boats tossed up on the shore like toys, along with fragments of dock and debris.

The tsunami in the Atlantic had sent ripples all the way to Greece, causing some damage but, thanks to early warnings, no deaths.

Dove was the lone customer at Café Berardo's as he sipped his espresso. He sat at a little round table on the cobblestone patio under the paint-peeling midday sun. Andrea Bocelli played over the patio speakers, and Dove quietly sang along, between sips, and waited for their specialty: *La Spagetatta,* a dish he and his brother had shared and loved when they vacationed with their parents there, years ago.

La Spagetatta was freshly made ice cream fed through what looked like a meat grinder, creating strands of frozen pleasure much like spaghetti that were then gently coiled onto a piece of delicate lemon sponge cake, sprinkled with sherry wine, and topped with perfect whipped cream, more sherry, and a plump, dark, maraschino cherry. Dove had craved that earthly Holy Grail of frozen confections since the first time he and his brother had it a decade before. It reminded him of how close he and Adam used to be, and all the hell they would raise with the local boys there, extorting a percentage of cash from the little mafiaso-in-training who would steal wishing coins from tourist fountains. Adam had actually tossed a ten-year-old boy into the fountain when he refused to pay. But he apologized to him once the dripping wet thief forked over his stash. Dove smiled.

A gentle, moist breeze ruffled the white linen tablecloth as a Vespa sputtered down the lane and pigeons cooed on the other side of the green iron fence. The waiter appeared, wearing white gloves, black suit, and bow tie as if he were ready to serve dinner on the Titanic.

The waiter presented the silver plate, which was adorned with something Michelangelo could have created. Dove's mouth felt as though Pavlov had been ringing the bell for an hour.

He dove into his *La Spagetatta* and finished his first taste.

"You should watch all that cholesterol if you ever want to make it to fifty," Adam said, sneaking up from behind Dove wearing a white straw fedora, large aviator sunglasses, and a seven p.m. shadow.

"You finally made it. I was worried."

"Almost didn't," he answered then sat down at the bistro table for two. "Those idiots you paid to beat us, really beat us." Adam rolled up his sleeve to reveal a bruised arm. "And then there's the stab wound. That was not planned. I lost a lot of blood."

"Yeah, well it all worked out. And it added a lot of realism. We're really set up for stage two."

"It didn't work out for Paul."

"True. He was a good soldier. Real believer."

Adam nodded slowly.

"Hey, nice swan song at the morgue." Dove took another spoonful of the delicacy. "I'll order you our dessert."

"No, thanks. Death suppresses your appetite," Adam said. "I liked it. My exit was flawless."

"I think it had been done before. Two thousand years ago? Definitely not original."

"So you want me to be original like a twenty-eight-year-old construction worker with the tattoo of a bird on his back and arm?"

"It's a dove, and it should have meaning to you, as well."

Adam nodded. "I can't believe, after all the press you've gotten, that nobody picked up on your lame name anagram, 'Nat Fossano.'"

"It will really stir things up once someone plays Scrabble with the letters, especially now that you have risen again. Now comes the death blow."

The waiter came by with a small cup of espresso for Adam, a fresh one for Dove, and two glasses of iced lemon water.

"*Grazie*," Adam said, then watched the waiter leave before speaking. "There will be no death blow. It's over for me, brother."

Dove ignored him as two young women in sundresses and large-brimmed hats tossed flirtatious smiles as they passed by, seemingly oblivious to the woes of the world.

"I've had time to think," Adam said, mouth tight. "I'm out, and we can't go on with it."

"Wow, right to business. Have some ice cream, like old times. Maybe extort a little money from the local fountain thieves?"

Adam smiled slightly then shook his head.

"So why didn't you end it before Disney?"

"I tried. I was hiding when some nutbar spotted me. Started shouting and pointing. I tried running, but when I was caught, there was nothing I could do. They were going to string me up as paid."

"No, no, no. All bullshit. I'll tell you why you didn't really end it and not even go to Disney: Because you know we have to finish this, as planned. In the name of our—your—family. In the name of Allah and honor!" Dove took a deep breath. "On to the next stage!"

"I... I just won't."

Dove took a shaky sip of water. "Know this: You are more than just a loose end."

"Are you threatening me, little brother? *Ali?*"

"Ali died the day the Americans killed your wife, your sons! Our mother! Don't ever use that name again, *Malik!* We swore a blood oath!"

"I knew there would be no convincing you, but I had to meet you and try. But you will never change." Adam pushed back from the table and stood up. "I say it's over for me, and you should stop now, as well. Too many people have died. I'm out, and the fat lady has sung."

"Traitor."

"I can't reason with a blind man. I feel sorry for you." Adam paused, staring at his brother, then walked away.

"Yes, you should feel sorry for me!" Dove shouted, his mouth half full of Spagetatta. "Sorry for being your brother!" He laughed. "You are now a loose end. Take care you don't unravel!"

Adam stopped several feet away and turned toward him. "Threats, Ali?"

"Facts. And it's not me. There are levels above me, powerful men. As you know, they want this all to play out to the end. It's a month-long plan, and you can't bail after a week."

"Why don't you just kill me now, here?" He raised his arms in surrender. "Drown me in a fountain here. Fitting end for me?"

Dove sat back and put on his sunglasses. "Maybe I should."

Adam dropped his arms. "What are you waiting for?"

Dove scanned the bistro and street. "I sense you feel painted into a corner, brother?"

"You're painted into a corner, not me. I'm freer than I've ever been, and I have some mending to do. Undo what we have done."

"Free, huh?" Dove laughed. "Remember when we were young, when I would catch you stealing cake? Or smoking Father's private stash of hookah? I always gave you a way out of me tattling—you liked that game, didn't you? A get-out-of-jail-free card?"

"That was blackmail by a little runt, not a get-out-of-jail card."

"I'll have to put some thought into something good. Good blackmail, as you put it." What could he challenge Adam with? "If you win the challenge I come up with, I will also stop with this plan, and no one will kill you. The ultimate get-out-of-jail card. One last game."

"Childish, as usual," Adam said, shaking his head slowly. He walked away. "You don't get it."

"You say 'childish,' but it got you out of trouble many times when we were kids!"

Adam was almost out of sight down the street.

"And don't forget to pray! Five times a day!" Dove yelled.

Dove resumed eating. "Even if I did give you a way out, you would just fail. The world is destined to fail, and I will deliver it to that destiny!" He laughed, and bits of cake spewed over the table. He held up his empty espresso cup and shook it at the waiter. "Time for the final phase. I hear a fat lady singing in London."

Dove started humming the Bocelli song playing over the patio speakers as he finished his delicacy.

He recalled his Rutba soccer coach, ten years ago, who had secretly led him into a terrorist group and Jihad. His coach made him feel important and inspired him with quotes like: *'Let those fight in the way of Allah who sell the life of this world for the other. Whosoever fights in the way of Allah, be he slain or be he victorious, on him We shall bestow a vast reward.'*

Dove had persuaded Adam that they should join the cause for Jihad the day after the bombing of their home—which had actually not been a US mistake. It had been targeting Dove.

But if Adam had known that, he would have not taken up the cause.

That was why Adam walked away; deep down inside, Adam was soft and would have never joined the fight for Jihad without his blind rage from the bombing.

They were so close to completing the plan. A few more weeks, and it would be fully executed. *I guess I'll be doing it on my own,* he thought. *And Adam better not get in my way.*

He took a large drink of lemon water then raised his glass to the sky. "*Allah Akbar*!" he said with gusto.

The waiter returned with another espresso as Dove held his water glass in the air.

"That took a while," Dove said. "Did you have to go to Colombia for the beans?"

The waiter shrugged, dropped the espresso, and quickly left.

***

As Sam had promised Lucy, they boarded a plane Monday in Miami to go to Euro Disney in France. Most flights were cancelled, and the one they finally got on was nearly empty.

When they landed, they checked into the hotel, barely unpacked, and went to bed. First thing the next morning, they jumped into a cab and went to find Mickey.

The theme park seemed as busy as a grand opening would have been and was so under-staffed that it took an hour to get in through the gate.

Sam spent quality one-on-one time with her daughter, finally slowing down and really listening to Lucy and showing interest by asking questions that showed she really cared.

As far as what was going on in the world, she answered Lucy's questions but left it at that. She didn't want her daughter to worry. She wanted her to be a child, have fun, and enjoy her time with her mom. There was plenty of time to be an adult with adult problems.

Lucy was quieter than normal, almost like when her father passed away. She was calm, not whiney or irritating. Sam really enjoyed her company but worried about her.

Paul dying in front of them. The beatings of Adam, Paul, and Dove. The storm that destroyed the Disney World. The thug that tried to hit her—all of that was probably rolling through Lucy's mind, as well.

And, she suspected, Lucy missed Adam more than she let on. She seemed to look up to him.

Sam missed Adam, too, and felt she had been getting to know him—not as a reporter after a story but as a person. Even a close friend, despite the short amount of time they had spent together. Although she didn't want to admit it to herself, it felt much like it did when she first met her husband. The quick bonding and connection.

It was all too painful to think of right now, and there was nothing she could do about it. *Clear the mind. On to Mickey.*

Arena and Lobato returned to New York and took Monday and Tuesday off. They met for a late lunch on Monday and ended up at Arena's apartment, which had been spared from the flooding and damage, although in the parking garage, water was still being pumped out.

After two bottles of merlot, the lazy afternoon escalated from mutual flirtatious talk to light touching and tickling to ripping each other's clothes off and having sex on the couch, on the floor, and on the bed. Arena made the first, second, and third move, hardly giving Lobato any recovery time between sessions.

After ordering dinner in from the Hunan Chinese Restaurant, they fell asleep entwined on the couch, empty food containers on the coffee table.

Arena awoke after midnight. Her arm had fallen asleep, and Lobato hadn't moved an inch all night. She went to the washroom, came back, and wrapped a blanket over him, then went to her bedroom and crawled into her bed. The next morning, Lobato left, and they spent the day apart.

They arrived at their local office on Wednesday morning. The building ran on auxiliary power and had only what was classified as essential staff working. They spent the day quietly filling out piles of paperwork. At the end of the day, Lobato said good night to Arena. She invited him over for pizza and a nightcap, to which he replied, "I never turn down pizza."

Arena wondered if inviting him over again was the right thing to do. She had been the aggressor the night before. Maybe she should have left it as a one-time sexual romp, and a great romp it had been. But with all that had happened in the world lately—the death, destruction, chaos... She felt as though this was right. Love, passion. She needed the balance.

Lobato had done a good job at wearing her down over the past few months. Well, at least she pretended he had worn her down. She wanted it.

Stock markets remained closed on Monday, Tuesday, and Wednesday, while the price of food and durable goods tripled, making even pet food a delicacy. Batteries traded like gold in disaster areas. No one made fun of Doomsday preppers; they were trying to befriend them. People prepared for the unknown by stocking up on supplies they thought they would need in the event of power failures, store closures, and maybe even war.

China imposed martial law and food rationing, which triggered rioting, violence, and numerous public canings—and that information was just what was known from what people could smuggle out using their cell phone cameras. People were arrested for breaking any of the restrictions on Internet and social media, and anyone leaving the country was thoroughly searched for any form of smuggled media.

Adam Johl the Prophet was the second hottest topic of discussion. Global disarray was the first. The connections between the prophecies and global events were also still widely debated, with the majority of people believing biblical prophecy still seemed to be unfolding.

Wednesday afternoon, one of the morgue security guards from where Adam's body vanished went to the press with stolen video, photos, and a story of how he thought Adam had vanished into thin air, possibly rising from the dead. It sent a ripple throughout the world at warp speed, reviving hope in believers, fear and skepticism in agnostics, and a media frenzy not seen since the end of World War II.

Headlines in major newspapers played on the "Adam has risen from the dead" theme. That was enough to push those on the edge of doomsday prepping to quietly stocking up on water, beans, batteries, generators, and whatever weapons they could garner.

25

Thursday - Day 13

Adam shaved his hair using a No. 2 trimmer, creating a stubbly appearance, and now sported a mustache. He got dressed in loose white cotton clothing, a straw fedora hat, and wraparound golfer sunglasses. He hoped no one would recognize him.

He paid cash for a used laptop from a small local dealer and booked into the modest, three-star Le Chateau hotel in Paris. Adam sat on a black cast-iron chair on a tight balcony patio overlooking the street, drinking peach-flavored iced tea from a can while he blogged using the handle 'I Miss Sunshine.' His goal was to try and undo what he felt he was responsible for starting: mayhem and chaos.

He created countless blogs and joined multiple chat threads, stirring up as much support as possible from believers, support to calm the people and stop the violence. Adam tried to connect with readers on an inspirational level. As he thought of his wife, sons, parents, brother, Sam, and Lucy, their inspiration helped his words flow. Words he hoped would help him atone for his monumental guilt:

"The real war between good and evil has never been fought on a battlefield. It is first fought in the mind and heart. The one who can inspire and open the minds and hearts of the masses will control the world, its destiny, and win the war. Kill evil, the enemy, in the mind and heart, where it hides."

***

Sam surfed the net from her contemporary room at the Hotel de Sers in Paris. She cracked open another cola can, took a sip, and placed it next to the two empty cola cans on her desk.

"Mom, you look so sad." Lucy gave her mother a squeeze. "It's okay. I miss Adam, too."

"You do?"

"He was very nice. I felt safe with him, and he made you smile. You don't smile much."

Sam forced a smile then dropped it.

"That was not a good one."

Sam smiled again, trying to make it believable.

"Better."

"Time for bed. It's been a long day."

"I had bad dreams last night. About Adam at Disney World. I was scared." She hugged her mom. "It was so real."

"I know," Sam said, stroking her hair. "I felt you tossing and mumbling. I woke you gently, and the bad dreams went away."

"Stop them again tonight, if they come."

Sam nodded and kissed Lucy's forehead. "Goodnight, Sunshine."

She didn't argue and let her mother tuck her in with butterfly kisses. Within minutes, Lucy was out, and Sam went back to her computer, frowning.

She checked her email. There were four hundred thirty-five new ones. "Now, there's a dose of reality," she said quietly. She scrolled through the pages of subject lines. Many said, *"Call me!"* and *"Where are you?"* She kept running through them, opening the occasional one. Then she spotted the subject line on a chain email: "Kill evil in the mind and heart, where it hides."

"Adam?" she shouted, then covered her mouth and looked over at Lucy, who snored lightly. "Adam's alive," she said softly.

She'd heard the reports about his supposed resurrection and wondered if someone had stolen the body or if maybe, just maybe, he performed an incredible magic act again, escaping death. When he was being beaten in Disney and she had asked him if it was part of the show, he nodded yes. She was sure of it. And she hung on to that hope.

Adam had spoken those exact words, "Kill evil in the mind and heart, where it hides," in the email thread to her when they were driving to Florida in the RV. She had asked where he heard that, and he said he made it up at that moment and that she had inspired him.

Sam frantically searched the original thread with the quote. Surfing the net for that exact phrase, she finally found the source at one a.m. The author called himself "I miss Sunshine." *It is Adam!*

"Okay, Adam. Where are you?" Sam said then took a sip of cola.

She searched for forums and blogs that "I miss Sunshine" frequented. There was one common site that showed up in a string of search results. She clicked on it, and it took her to a major political discussion website. She signed up and entered the forum. She posted a message: *"Hi, 'I miss Sunshine'! My Sunshine finally got her picture with Mickey as we promised her. She said she wishes you were there too."*

While she waited for a reply, she searched and read every piece written on Adam's "rising from the dead" and watched the video the morgue attendant had smuggled out. At three thirty a.m., with her eyes burning, she set the alarm for six forty-five and crashed on the king-sized bed next to Lucy, who had been swallowed up by the blankets.

***

Lucy rolled on top of her mom, giving her a spread-eagle squeeze.

Sam looked at the clock; it was six thirty a.m.

"Let's go, Mommy! It'll take us forever to get there on the train and stuff. We have to be the first ones to see Mickey again."

Sam rolled onto her back. "Let Mommy sleep for another half hour, please. I haven't really fallen asleep yet."

"Okay," Lucy whispered as she bounced off the bed and into her pink bunny slippers. She sat on the swivel chair at the desk, legs dangling, and fired up the laptop.

Lucy checked her email, Facebook, and a few forums for messages. Most of her friends were missing after the tsunami in New York, but every day she hoped she would see a message from one. Instead, there were dozens of messages from people she didn't recognize.

Lucy then went to her YouTube videos and read new viewer comments. She scrolled down the list and stopped on one from someone who seemed to send several comments in a row. From @I_miss_Sunshine, she read out loud, "Sweetest Sunshine, keep up the great work on spreading the good news. Your videos are helping to make people think and change. Please say hi to your mom."

Sam sat up. "Who sent that to you?" She jumped out of bed and read the message over Lucy's shoulder. "It's got to be Adam! I know it!"

"He's alive?"

"Has to be!"

"How? I saw the news," Lucy asked, swinging her legs at a quicker pace.

"Magic. Let me check something please, Lucy."

"Why would he do that?" Lucy said then slid off the chair and onto the bed. She curled up with her doll as she watched her mother.

Her mother did not answer.

After ten minutes of checking the forums, Sam found him online, conversing with people, trying to inspire them. She frantically typed, "It's me. Mother of all Sunshines." Then she waited, watching her cursor blink teasingly, painfully.

Within thirty seconds, the reply came. "Miss you and Sunshine. Sorry if I caused you grief. It was not my intent. Let's PM?"

"Grief?" Sam said out loud as she typed a private message to send Adam. "That's an understatement. What number can I reach you at, and why didn't you answer me?" She hit send and stared at the reply box, not blinking.

"So sorry. What number can I reach *you* at?" he responded promptly.

"Sorry? You'd better be," Sam said as she typed in the hotel number and room number, as well as her cell number; Adam called her on the landline immediately.

"Adam! You're alive? How? Where are you?" Sam fired off. "Why?"

"Slow down, Sam. I'm fine, I'm... relaxing. Letting the bruises heal."

"How did you do it? The morgue? That was the disappearing act, wasn't it? The final show?" Sam attempted to put on her *Hotel de Sers* housecoat and slippers, jockeying the phone from shoulder to shoulder. "I saw the news reports. You burned up?"

"That was quite something, huh?" Adam asked.

"Quite something?" Sam took her cordless phone out onto the partial balcony, while Lucy watched her with her wide brown eyes. "You rose from the dead!"

"It was good, wasn't it? And it was my last one."

"Good," Sam said softly, staring off into the Parisian skyline. The cool moist air gave her tolerable chills as she focused in on the Eiffel Tower. *It's so romantic.* "I'm not sure if I'm mad at you or hate you or what but you need to tell me in person what happened and why." She paused. "I want to see you. Lucy would love to see you too."

Adam did not respond.

"*Hello*? Adam?"

No answer.

"Adam! Answer me, please! Are you there?"

Lucy came to the patio and slid the door open. "Mom, there's someone at the door."

Sam listened to her phone. "I'm going to hang up if you don't say something..."

"Answer your door," Adam finally responded.

Sam stood a moment, wondering how he knew, then she walked quickly to the door and swung it open without using the peephole.

"Adam?" She dropped the phone. "How the..."

"It's me. Just changed my look a little."

"Are you really Adam?" She grabbed him by the shoulders momentarily. She wondered if she should hug him. "You look younger—and tanned? And almost bald. I don't understand. How did you get here so fast?" Sam rambled. She noticed a laptop he held under his arm.

"Slow down. Had to have a miracle makeover so I can walk around freely. And I was just waiting for you to find me online. I'm real good with the computer, remember. Your flight and hotel booking were easy to find; I just checked in. My room is just down the hall."

Lucy shouted, "Adam!" and hugged his waist.

"My, my. That's quite a welcome."

"Come in!" Lucy squeaked.

Adam finally entered the room and looked around as if he expected someone else to be there. He put his laptop on the desk.

"You're supposed to be, um, deceased."

"I was, wasn't I?"

Sam finally hugged him. He hugged her back tightly. "I'll order breakfast for three. We have lots to talk about. Can't wait to hear how you pulled it off."

"Yes, pulled it off," he responded. "Lots to tell you... and lots left to undo."

***

Lobato took Arena breakfast on a wooden tray, adorned with three silk daisies in a slender vase.

She sat up in bed, dressed in a black T-shirt that read *Bomb and Booby Trap Camp* and smiled as though she was on a honeymoon. "Waffles, strawberries, whipped cream. You are good."

"Actually, breakfast is the waffles with real Canadian maple syrup. The whipped cream and strawberries are for extracurricular activities."

"*Rrreally.*" She grabbed one of the two glasses of orange juice.

"Really." Lobato dipped his finger into the bowl of whipped cream and brushed it over her tiny nose. He sat next to her on the bed then leaned over and licked it off.

"I prefer the whipped cream on my waffles," Arena said, laughing. "That was so awkward. And lame."

"But points for trying," Lobato said quickly.

She dove into her breakfast while Lobato read the *New Jersey Herald* and drank his coffee.

They sat in contented silence, with only the sound of newspapers rustling and cutlery occasionally tinkling the plate. The morning sun streamed in through the bedroom window, warming their faces.

Lobato looked at Arena, who inhaled carbs at breakneck speed. "This is definitely a moment."

She swallowed. "What do you mean?"

"It feels like this all sort of fits. We fit."

"It was just sex—and waffles. The waffles are great."

"Let it down, hard ass."

"Thank you. I work hard on it."

"Ever let your guard down?"

"I keep telling you, you Portuguese are too emotional." She put the last bite in her mouth. "You should learn to enjoy the moment, and don't read anything more into it."

"It's against our nature. Love is more than just a feeling, it's—"

Their cell phones vibrated on the nightstands and pinged three times, indicating an urgent message from their director.

"Saved by the bell." Arena reached for her phone.

Lobato sat, waiting for Arena to read him the message.

"We're off to Israel," she said as if it was an everyday occurrence.

"What's up? That's way outside our playground."

"Read your mail, and you'll find out."

"Read my mail?" Lobato lifted the tray, placed it on the floor, then jumped on Arena, pinning her down to the navy blue sheets. "I prefer torture to get my answers." He licked her cheek.

Arena twisted to the side, grabbing hold of Lobato's wrists, and flipped him over onto his back, straddling him—all in one fluid movement. Lobato smiled, willingly yielding to Arena as the sunlight filtered through her tousled red hair that tickled his chest.

"Agent Lobato, we have exactly ninety minutes to get to the airport."

"Perfect. Enough time for you to fall in love with me—if you haven't already—get married in the Baptist church of your choice, then we can buy a house and *plant* a family."

"My father would have not approved of you getting married in a Baptist church, or to me... If he was alive, I'd have to hide you from him. Forever."

"We elope. Whatever."

"What am I going to do with you?" She licked his nose. "We'll only have time for the planting part."

"I'm going to change you." He kissed her. "Deep down inside there, somewhere, there's a sensitive tender female yearning for motherhood and romance."

"I like guns and fast cars, not baby bottles and minivans with stick people."

Their phones seemed to vibrate again on the nightstand—along with the lamp and anything else not nailed down.

"Earthquake!" Arena said.

"I tend to have that affect on women!" Lobato smiled.

The subsonic rumbling intensified, shifting to a slight sway and shaking books off the bookshelf. A glass-framed Matisse print dropped from the wall, smashing against the back of a chair. The plates and glasses on the tray on the floor tinkled.

"Shit!" Arena held Lobato, pulling blankets over her head as their bed moved across the hardwood floor. It stopped when it hit the dresser.

"That'll save you." Lobato laughed at Arena's antics as the movement stopped as abruptly as it started, having lasted only six seconds. "The floor in here must be on a slant."

"Damn, that was big for New Jersey. Probably five-point-oh."

"People tend to forget there's a fault that runs along the Hudson. Not like San Andreas, but a fault."

Arena turned and locked eyes with Lobato. "Things almost seemed normal for a little while. Sort of forgot the mess we're in."

Lobato held her tightly, stroked her hair.

"This isn't over, is it?" Arena asked.

"You're asking me? Nice twist. But as long as it keeps going, we'll still have a job."

Their phones vibrated again. They braced, but it was just a message that time.

Arena reached for her phone and read it out loud. "Adam Johl is really Malik Al-Lami. And Nat Fossano is... Ali Al-Lami. Both born in Rutba, Iraq. Father Iraqi, his name was Adam. Mother *American*, her name Jaide, sons Omar and Haris, wife Layla."

"Wow. Adam and Dove—brothers?"

Arena nodded and kept reading. "A missile strike wiped out their family in Rutba, Iraq."

"And there's the motive for revenge."

"I almost feel sorry for Johl." Arena put her phone back on the nightstand.

"See. You're a sensitive person."

Arena punched Lobato on the shoulder, hard.

"Ouch."

"I said 'almost.'"

Arena grabbed her phone from the nightstand and stared at the names of his family on the screen.

"What do you see?" Lobato asked.

"I see how Adam chose his alias. His first name was the same as his father's; his last name is made up of the initials of his mother, sons, and wife. All who died when the bomb hit their house. He carried them with him in his name. Every day. Every minute." She placed the phone back on the nightstand once again. "That's sad."

They lay on their backs, staring at the ceiling. Lobato inched his hand over to touch Arena's hand. They locked fingers.

"I wonder if we're going to get any aftershocks?" Arena asked.

"There usually are, right?"

"Yes, there are." She sighed.

26

Breakfast was delivered with linen and silverware on an ornate wooden cart. They feasted on eggs Benedict, crêpes with whipped crème, and pastries. The berries and fresh-squeezed orange juice they ordered were not available, due to food shortages.

"The sun's out, Mommy!" Lucy planted both of her sticky hands on the glass patio doors. "We have to get going, it's..."—she looked at the clock radio—"nine twelve; we have to catch the train by nine thirty!"

"We have a guest, Lucy. Please be patient."

"Not *that* word again." She sighed, grabbed her doll, and dropped facedown on the bed as if she had been shot in the back with a Magnum.

"Adam, we need to talk," Sam insisted.

Adam cleared his throat then sipped his tea.

"What really happened in Florida? Who are you, really?"

"There's the reporter in you."

"And why are you here, with me?"

"Why don't we go for a stroll? We can talk."

Sam hesitated. "Sure."

"We are in beautiful Paris. We can stroll down the Champs-Elysées and talk."

"I think I should get a sitter."

"Nooo!" The muffled cry came from Lucy, still facedown on the bed.

Sam arranged for the concierge, whom she had befriended, to come to the room. Lucy filed a formal protest and threatened to start a blog on parents who break promises and little girls' hearts.

Sam and Adam strolled the avenue like enamored tourists, arms entwined. Adam wore his fedora and sunglasses; Sam wore a large-brimmed white hat and sunglasses as well. They kept their hats and heads tilted down and avoided crowds.

Adam looked at her. "Smoke and mirrors," he said, explaining how he'd resurrected from the dead.

"How?"

"Maybe there was a foil coating on the slab tray, which had been prepared days ahead of my arrival and planted ahead of time."

"Coroner signing you were dead? Getting out of there undetected?"

"There is always someone who can be bought, and electronics that can be tampered with. This was all exquisitely planned."

"But you said you planned to leave Florida by boat... to Mexico? Not a trip to the morgue to be resurrected."

"Yes, but there were two boats. The first one was for Dove and Mansfield. I was scheduled for another, after the morgue."

"How did you plan getting caught by those criminals in Disney? And all the other little details?"

"Dove arranged that. Everything was thought out and planned, Sam."

"How far ahead have you planned?"

"Over seven years to architect this, from beginning to end."

"Is this the end? Is it over?"

"This is not the end of the plan, but it is for me." Adam quickly glanced at two young people sitting on a bench they passed. "They still have unfinished work, a few weeks maybe."

Sam stopped and pulled him back under a tree. "Who's 'they'?"

"Dove, mostly—he did a lot of the coordinating. And there were some unnamed contacts. We never met most. All was arranged by encrypted communication."

"He had me fooled. He seemed like such a nice guy, so likable."

"He is. He could charm a herd of snakes into a basket of fire."

"Snakes herd?"

Adam laughed. "Actually, I think it's 'nest'?"

Sam leaned back against the tree and looked up at the shimmering leaves rustling, the pillowy clouds rolling by, and a few seagulls circling high above. Nature seemed okay, oblivious to what was happening. "What made you stop now?"

"That's a great question. I was consumed with hate for so many years. The goal of revenge was a distraction from the grief." Adam swallowed. "And you and Lucy helped me realize that. I found my true self again. I was never the hateful person Dove tried to form me into."

"We helped? Really?"

"There's something about you that helped open my eyes like no one has been able to. Like I've had them welded shut with hate, and you used a nuclear blast to open them." Adam sighed. "It's just not right, none of it. Forcing destiny was—is—wrong."

"Destiny?"

"The fate of mankind, as it is written. We were trying to force the fulfillment of biblical prophecy."

Sam examined his eyes then his mouth. "And Dove still is trying."

"Yes. He will never stop." Adam gently grabbed her hand and pulled her off the tree, and they resumed walking. "Dove is delusional and has a dangerous, vengeful obsession."

"Where is he?"

Adam turned to her. "He's in Italy, getting the next stage fired up. Then he's off for a public appearance at the University of London."

Sam stopped walking, jerking Adam back slightly. "Let's sit down somewhere. There." She pointed at a street-side café that had a dozen round bistro tables and no customers "I can't focus."

They took a table on the patio, in the corner, and Sam ordered a carafe of chardonnay while her mind built up a slew of questions. She took a sip. "I still find it hard to believe you two are brothers. Same father?"

"Yes. His real name was Ali. Mine was Malik, but we don't use them anymore. Our names died with our family."

"Malik?" Sam asked quietly. "What do you mean your names died?"

"When my wife, daughter, and parents were killed during that American assault on our town"—Adam's eyes glassed over—"Dove and I made a blood oath. To abandon our names, create new ones—American ones—and we started to plan revenge. He tattooed one dove for each of the dead members of the family on his arms. The large tattoo on his back has the doves carrying hand grenades with their beaks, a constant reminder that he wanted vengeance for their deaths."

"I'm sorry." Sam's eyes teared.

"So am I."

"I know how you feel. You're never whole again."

Adam nodded.

Sam looked up at the small wisps of clouds set against a brilliant blue sky. "My change happened when I had the boy over for dinner. And it was extremely difficult to sit across the table from him. Someone who decided to party, drink and drive, and kill my husband. Lucy's father."

"That must have been incredibly hard."

"What I didn't tell you last time was that I actually thought of poisoning him. Something slow, painful. Maybe lead. I replayed how I would do it."

"Really?"

"I was never going to do it, but it felt good imagining it. So I did invite him for dinner, but I didn't give him my best cooking effort. My shrink told me I had to get over it and forgive. It was either that or die inside myself, and I couldn't do that to Lucy." Sam used her napkin to dab the corner of her eyes.

"You're such a special person."

Sam forced a smile. "Lucy and I visit my husband's spirit on the lake in Central Park. We rent a rowboat from Loeb's Boathouse. Sometimes when we're paddling on the pond, we look up and we see his face in the clouds. We talk to him there. It was his favorite place to take Lucy and me on Sunday afternoons in the summer."

"He hears you." Adam moved his wine glass and reached over to grab her hands.

She leaned forward, looked up at him, and nodded. They held hands momentarily, then she sat back, straightened herself, and took a large sip of her wine. "Aren't we a sad pair? What now?"

"I'm a sad pair, not you. And I need to stop Dove. He's filled with enough hate to fill hell all by himself."

"What can you do? What can we do?"

"Interfere with the plan, get in his face—and fast."

"I want to help, in my own unique way."

"Of course you would." Adam sipped his wine.

The air was painted with anticipation, Sam wondering if Adam already had a brilliant idea of what to do next. She thought of Lucy's online school video project. "Kony 2012!" Sam blurted out, slamming her hand on the table.

"What about it?"

"The first real massive social network attempt to mobilize the world for a good cause. Not everyone heard of it, but it had excellent traction and was ranked the most viral video of all time by *TIME*. In just a few days, they had a hundred million hits. And people acted on it, although it never really worked to catch Kony... but maybe it can for our cause."

"You want to run an online campaign?"

"Not just a campaign, a mind-altering campaign," Sam said excitedly. "Raise the bar on the meaning of viral to the moon."

"Propaganda machine?"

"Yes and no. What I have in mind is like the hundredth monkey effect."

"That sounds like your own unique way, all right." Adam sipped his wine.

"It's just a theory, but there have been studies. Actually mostly discredited, but I like the idea of it—and think it could work!"

Adam looked puzzled. "So it didn't work, but you think you can make it work? Go on."

"When people believe in something strongly, anything is possible. In the fifties, Japanese scientists were studying monkeys on islands," Sam said in a quick burst, then continued. "There were two islands in the Pacific. Monkeys on both islands found sweet potatoes that grew in bushes, but the potatoes fell to the sand. On one island, the monkeys tried eating them as they were, covered in gritty sand, and stopped eating them because they were nasty. On the other island, the sweet potatoes fell in the sand as well, but a monkey accidentally dropped it in the salty sea, washing off the sand. He ate it, and other monkeys started dropping them in the sea, as well, before eating them; they loved them clean and salty."

"Me, too."

Sam smiled then continued. "When it reached a critical mass of monkeys performing this same behavior, they say the hundredth monkey, the monkeys on the other island started dipping sweet potatoes in the sea as well, eating them, and loving them. It was as if the feelings of good thoughts transcended metaphysical boundaries."

"I see where you are going with this. I like it."

"We just need to implement the theory with mankind. What if, let's say, ten percent of all people started having thoughts of peace. Would the rest of the world feel it? A universal consciousness?" Sam played with her wine glass.

"I doubt it. And you believe you can get at least seven hundred million people to have these good thoughts? At the same time?"

"What option do we have? You say we need to act fast."

"Talk about your Hail Mary on steroids."

"I—we—can do it! Especially you and all your magic. Make people think they are feeling it? It could work. Open their eyes to what's happening."

Adam smiled and shook his head. "I can see the headlines now... 'Reporter saves the world from Armageddon with a barrel of monkeys.'"

"Amen."

"Yeah, amen."

They sipped their wine, staring through each other.

"We need a name, something catchy to launch this campaign," Sam said.

"Universal consciousness for peace? U-C-F-P."

"Nice. So catchy. Just leave it to a computer programmer to be creative."

"So that's a no?" Adam asked.

"I said catchy. Something Monkey."

"Project Monkey Peace-Wave-Thoughts—"

"Love!" Sam interrupted. "Project Monkey Love. Fun, simple."

"Nice."

"Thanks."

"So, how does one start a Monkey Love party?" Adam asked.

"Send out invites, chain emails." Sam paused. "Billons of them. But we have one small problem."

Adam raised his eyebrows.

"You. You're dead. If this is going to work, you'll need to be alive and come clean on your exit stage left at the morgue. Just explain like you did to me."

"Maybe it would be easier to change my appearance. Drastically. Maybe a nose job."

"I'm the one that could use the nose job, but no, we need to start fresh, clean. You need to be honest, open. Completely transparent."

"Your nose is so perfectly wonderful."

She stared at him. That was what her husband used to say, verbatim.

"Coming clean would be very hard and unbelievable, despite being true. You could have asked for a simpler task."

"Like what?"

"Getting men to leave the toilet seat down?"

"That's not easier."

"It's ironic. Dove has already gone down the road to redemption, and he is lying about it but everyone buys in. Why will they believe me? They think I've just betrayed them again, with the morgue disappearance."

"They will. Just be your sincere self. It stripped away any doubt I may have had."

"You're one in a billion, Cott."

"Okay, do the math. There are seven billion people on the planet, so that means six other people will immediately believe—that's a great start."

"You are an extreme optimist. With a perfect nose."

She rubbed her nose. "Quit your whining, holy one. Let's plan your re-appearance, and I know the perfect spot."

"I know what you're thinking."

Sam looked at Adam as she digested the meaning of that reply. "Dove's speech, at the University in London. You can start undermining him at the same time. Maybe sneak in some live TV airtime to tell your story."

"I was right."

"Kay. What am I thinking now?"

"Not sure, but I'm sure you're right, whatever it is."

"See, you know what to say. It'll be a piece of cake."

Adam nodded. "I think I should have stayed dead."

27

Friday - Day 14

Lobato and Arena were following a SIGNIT-originated operation. Signals Intelligence, or SIGNIT, was run and controlled by the NSA. Lobato got his first insight into the power of this supercomputer collaborative endeavor between the CIA, FBI, and other agencies. Arena had worked several operations driven by it in the past and told him that it was freakishly accurate.

During his initial FBI training, he had visited SIGNIT's location in NSA's headquarters in Fort Meade, Maryland. He watched as it primarily mined specific phrases, words, inflections, and languages like Arab, Persian, Urdo, etc... It ran all day, every day.

SIGNIT's newest program also pulled every piece of available information on the Web, combined it with every piece of literature, news reports, blog, tweet, and social media entry ever published, then surmised future scenarios. Combined with its primary purpose, the new program continually spit out predictions regarding terrorists, trends, markets, governments, weather, and the unknown. Lobato witnessed firsthand the rooms filled with analysts, glued to their monitors with dark circles around their bloodshot eyes, deciphering a continuous flow of Nostradamus-type information. They were the new spies.

During his studies there, he viewed some predictions that made no sense, like the one that said the President of the United States would win an Oscar within ten years. Those predictions were lunchtime laughter. But when something was clear, concise, and measurable, it was run up the mast for further analysis. SIGNIT's latest prediction was run to the top of the mast and triggered a terrorist red alert, issued for the second time in US history, and a DEFCON 2 alert, the state of preparedness prior to imminent nuclear war. The epicenter of the threat was the Middle East. Nat Fossano and Adam Johl were identified as major threats to global security.

That SIGNIT prediction created orders that sent Arena and Lobato to Haifa, Israel. They were just two of hundreds of special agents dispatched around the globe after the US president signed the actions then went into secure hiding with his family and key staff. As

Arena and Lobato had been on Johl's case since day one, it had been decided by the director of the FBI to send them to investigate.

The hot sticky air of Haifa, painted with the smell of airline diesel and cigarette smoke, hit Arena and Lobato as they entered the gangway at the airport. For Arena, it triggered the memory of her first visit to Haifa on assignment, years before. She'd been a field office contact and liaison with the local Israeli government—a boring post filled with doing paperwork and digging up dirt on locals, but it had earned her a promotion and respect because she performed her tasks as if they were the most important duties in the FBI. She felt as if the current visit would be the complete opposite of boring.

Their contact picked them up at post seven and handed them encrypted data chip stickers, no larger than postage stamps, that Arena and Lobato stuck on their smartphones. They watched and listened with their ear buds, getting detailed instructions on where they were to meet their next contact. They peeled the stickers off and melted them with a lighter.

They were dropped off at Hotel Prince Harry, where they transformed into Canadian tourists wearing shorts, carrying cameras, and wearing straw hats. Lobato wore a T-shirt with the Toronto Bluejays logo while Arena wore a plain white tank top with a faded Canadian flag across the chest. Lobato had to tell her how hot she looked in it. Arena said thank you.

They grabbed bottles of water from the hotel and headed to Haifa's Talpiot Market.

The marketplace was filled with locals shopping for produce, nuts, spices, and local fare. The smells of root vegetables, incense, and musty rugs wafted in waves as they milled through the crowd. Arena looked for their next contact. The contact had a scarf booth called Fashionette.

"Yip-skip-a dee-yap... Smile, Cass," Lobato said, taking a picture of her.

"No pictures of us—delete it. I thought I went over that."

"It wasn't a picture of your face," he mumbled.

She ignored him and looked up. The sign above the booth read *Fashionette*. She stopped to handle a silk turquoise scarf meshed with lines of gold thread. "It's beautiful," she said to the short, dark-skinned middle-aged woman merchant.

Lobato zoomed in on the fabric as Arena ran it over her shoulder and across her cheek.

"Look good on you—special price today!" said the woman selling the scarves.

"I'm looking for a blood-red scarf with three blue camels?" Arena asked.

The woman squinted, looked left then right, then reached down below the table to retrieve a tightly rolled scarf. "I do not have one with three camels; I have one with four." She handed the scarf to Arena.

"Four is one better than three," Arena answered. She paid the woman, smiled, and left with Lobato trailing her.

They walked a short while, threading their way through the bazaar, then made a left down a narrow, quiet alley. Arena carefully unrolled the scarf as Lobato kept watch.

She felt the outline of the encrypted mini memory card stitched to the center of the scarf. "It's here." She ripped the thread holding it in place then inserted the encrypted card into her smartphone. She motioned for Lobato to come and look at the screen. He came over and stood next to her.

She accessed the drive. Small green letters that read "Joshua Tree" flashed three times on the black screen, then disappeared.

"Why they pick these names..." Lobato said softly.

"Joshua led the Israelites to the promised land." Arena gave Lobato a wireless earpiece, inserted hers, and hit play.

"But the actual tree was in the US," Lobato said. "U2."

Arena made a shush motion, and they listened intently.

They both stood silently in the alley, like frozen ghosts, for a few minutes while the computer-generated voice told them that Armageddon was happening. It explained the battleground and that nukes would be exchanged between Israel and Iran or Iraq. It identified Johl and Fossano as major threats to world peace and explained the agents' roles.

The memory card shot from the side of the device and dropped to the ground with a small pop sound and white puff of smoke. "I wonder where they got that idea," Arena said, watching the card fizzle out.

Lobato removed his earpiece. "Are they serious? Is SIGNIT advising on this? Has it been signed off on by the big boss in the White House?"

"Probably. SIGNIT has been collecting chatter, events, intelligence from all over the world. This supercomputer is smarter than Einstein, Newton, and Oprah combined. It's calculated every probability, combination, and scenario, and it believes this is Armageddon, and so does our boss, and his boss's boss. And the big boss that has probably gone underground."

"And at the city of Megiddo. It always seemed like... fiction or prophecy from soothsayers and magicians."

Arena removed her earpiece and walked down the cobblestone alley toward the open market. "'Do what it takes to stop these men' is the part that is open to interpretation."

"Well, if the world's going to end *again*, we should enjoy ourselves *again*. One last romp," Lobato said, catching up to Arena.

They looked at each other as they walked. Arena wondered if Lobato was up to the task at hand. "You need to work on your timing. Really," she said.

"I am."

She kept walking. "Let's stay serious while we're on the clock, okay?"

"Fine. Just trying to bring some levity to the situation."

They turned a corner and were back into the bazaar and shoulder-to-shoulder people. Lobato reached for Arena's hand; she pulled away. He grabbed it and squeezed it; she held on, that time.

"Let's get a beer and talk. On-the-clock shop talk." Lobato pointed over to a street-side café and bar.

Arena nodded.

They sat at a wobbly table that Lobato balanced with a folded beer coaster. He was preoccupied with securing the area visually, while Arena just watched him.

"Stop that," Lobato said. "I know you're staring at me."

"You really have a great smile."

"Feeling a little more not on-the-clock? You thoroughly confuse me."

"Do you think it's really going to end?"

"SIGNIT's just a bunch of motherboards, solder, and loose wire. Look how Adam twisted computers. Hell, maybe he hacked his way into SIGNIT and made it spit this prediction out."

"But it's seldom wrong when it's coherent, from what I have heard and seen."

"Seldom leaves room for error."

A middle-aged waiter approached the table.

"Two beers please," Lobato said quickly.

The waiter nodded and left.

"If the big final battle is upon us, then technically we should have a Messiah and the Antichrist," Arena said.

"SIGNIT said that Johl and Fossano were terrorist threats. Maybe they are playing those roles. You can't believe they are actually them?"

"Of course not; I'm not crazy."

The waiter returned with semi-cool beers and glasses. They grabbed their beers, tinked the bottles, and drank.

"Besides, how would I cuff the Antichrist?" Arena smiled then chugged her beer.

"We could ask him to surrender himself, for the good of mankind," Lobato said, laughed, then emptied a third of his bottle down his throat. He wiped his mouth with his short sleeve.

Sensing a shadow behind her, Arena glanced over her shoulder.

There was no one there.

"Spooked?" Lobato asked, poking her shoulder.

"*Spooked?* Are you kidding? We're FBI, not spooks." Arena felt a cold breeze brush her face. "Did you feel that?"

"You playing footsy?"

"Never mind. Let's get out of here, find a top-notch theologian. There's one in particular that I know of in this holy land." She stood up quickly and threw down thirty shekels. "We need some human religious intel before we start chasing a computer-fabricated supreme being."

"You're right." Lobato followed Arena to the street, where she hailed a cab to a mosque synagogue where they would find a specific English-speaking rabbi up on his Armageddon—a rabbi that Arena had studied during her theology degree. Saul Appel.

The synagogue's white marble floors had smooth paths worn in them from hundreds of years of worshippers shuffling across them in search of giving praise, asking for forgiveness, and seeking answers.

Saul Appel was six foot two and looked as if he could play linebacker for the Packers. They met in his quarters, which were lined with exotic hardwoods and adorned with photographs dating back to probably the first camera.

On one full wall was a library of books that went to the ceiling ten feet above; a wooden rolling ladder was angled against a rail.

"Tea?" Saul asked.

"No thank—" Lobato started.

"Yes, please. We'll have tea," Arena said.

Saul smiled then poured dark tea into three delicate ornamental china teacups that were so fine, holding them too tightly could shatter them.

"So, what is so urgent that two FBI agents must speak to me on such short notice? Changing faith? Looking for another explanation on this holy war?" He tapped his desk pad with his fingers. "Not to mention, what is the FBI doing working here? A little far from home?"

"Yes, we are. Special mission, I guess you could say. And the CIA is short staffed?"

Saul laughed.

"Rabbi Saul, we really appreciate your time. I have read some of your articles and hoped that you could help us." She cleared her throat. Her voice tightened. "We are investigating rumors that Armageddon is underway," Arena said.

"You need to be employed as a rabbi to be called a rabbi. Just Saul will do." Saul raised one bushy eyebrow. "And, yes, it has been underway since day one. What you really want to ask is when will it end. When will it escalate to Judgment Day?"

"Yes. When will it end, and are those days close at hand?"

"You ask me? Not even Jesus himself is supposed to have known the answer. Only the Father in heaven truly knows. I am flattered you would think I would know." Appel smirked.

"But the signs. Adam Johl."

"I've been watching that closely. Very peculiar."

"Peculiar?" Arena asked.

Lobato took a sip of tea and sat back. He and Arena had decided before entering the synagogue that Arena would do the questioning.

"Peculiar because it didn't happen like it has been told. There was no foretelling of these kinds of events at Roxy's and Disney World prior to the end." He sipped his tea.

"Please, explain your thoughts a little more."

"It is said that people of the world will fall in love with the Antichrist and follow him to the ends of the world. We didn't see that last week. Not at all. We saw a possible terrorist hunted, killed, and someone steal his body."

"Maybe it was the start? Dove is very charismatic. He is developing a following."

"The start was the day Jesus sacrificed himself on the Cross. That was the beginning of the end."

Arena took a big breath. "We have good information that the end of days are finally here. Happening all around us."

"Jesus doesn't know, but the U.S. people do?" Appel laughed. "You Americans have egos bigger than Lucifer. But I do agree things are happening all around us. Earthquakes, the tension, wars. Anyone can see it, but it is too late to stop—no one can stop it, if it is underway. It is written, and so it shall be. The Bible simply tells us how the game plays out. Just like TiVo."

"TiVo? Then why can't we rewind it? Pause it."

"Not possible. When you find the Antichrist, call me, though. I would guess he's out there as we speak." He sipped. "So are the messiahs."

"Messiahs? Plural?"

"Yes. The Essenes believed that there would be two messiahs—one priestly, one political. And they believed there was one God." He looked around then whispered, "I think they're right."

"Two messiahs? You mean two good guys?"

"Supposedly. The priest and the politician team up to take on the demon. Great combination."

"That's in the war scrolls, isn't it?" Arena asked.

"You are learned, aren't you? Yes, it was found with the Dead Sea Scrolls."

"The priest could be Adam, but who would his politician be? He's been on his own, more or less." Arena squinted, looking up at the wall of worn leather-bound books mixed with contemporary titles. "Do you have any books we can read on the final days?"

"The Bible. The Koran. Oh yes, the Torah, too." Appel smiled.

"I've sort of studied them. Something more specific to the final days. Something that explains things a little clearer why God would create such a wonderful world then destroy it?"

"Religious sarcasm. Splendid. The Bible says no finite mind can fully comprehend all of God's reasons for creating—or destroying—the world." Appel scratched his dark beard. "But..." He went to his ladder and rolled it to the middle of the wall. He carefully climbed three rungs and fingered along his books, stopping on one. "Uh-huh, this is the best one. Unbiased, unabridged, and first edition." He came down the ladder and handed the book to Arena. "Very valuable and rare."

She read the cover out loud. "*A Twentieth-Century Interpretation of the Torah.*" Then she flipped it over. "You wrote it."

"I did? Yes, I guess I did. It's still the best reference for you. Keep it. No one bought them. That's why it's rare."

Lobato looked at the book jacket. It was covered in ancient scribe and symbols.

"I deciphered straight from the original Aramaic writings, no bias." He chuckled.

"I have a degree in theology, and that is what I tried to do with several passages. Very difficult."

"Good for you, Ms. Arena. So you know that Christian eschatology is the study of its religious beliefs..."

"Yes, and of future and final events, as well as the ultimate purpose of life on earth, humankind, and the Church."

"Good. So which view do you believe in? Historicist? *No*, you are an idealist."

"Actually a bit of a futurist and preterist."

Lobato sat there, looking like a schoolboy who had skipped a week of classes on what they were talking about.

"I believe most of the signs have already passed," Arena said, nodding. "Torn between the different millennialism views."

"Aren't we all?" Lobato asked. "Mille-nia...ums?"

"I buy that we are in an era of postmillennialism. The Antichrist is gradually being squeezed out by the expansion of the Kingdom of God, all leading to the second coming."

"What about your faith? You're Jewish, a rabbi?" Arena asked.

"Remember an unemployed rabbi is not really a rabbi. I am also a theologian. I study religion from every angle, just like you do a crime."

Arena raised her eyebrows.

"No one will hire me as a rabbi after I published this book." He tapped the cover of the book Arena was holding. "But they let me stay here, in the attached residence. Pity, I take it."

"What was so wrong?"

Saul removed his round spectacles and dabbed the corners of his eyes with a hanky. "I guessed the time. That's sacrilegious, to think you would know as much as God. And show-boating, I guess."

"What time?" Arena sat up.

"The time of the second coming and Armageddon."

"Let me guess: the hyped-up 2022 prophecy?" Lobato asked. "Since 2012 fizzled out."

"Close."

"*How* close?" Arena asked.

"It's a guess—a really good guess." Saul looked at his cream-colored watch with a worn, black, oily leather strap. He slowly wiped his forehead with his hanky, looked at the agents—obviously building tension in his own way. "Within two weeks. It's in there." He tapped the book with his glasses again. "I did a little mathematical calculation."

The words clung to the air like cold, wet noodles on a fridge.

Arena had chills.

Lobato gave her a look as if to say, "Yeah, right."

28

Dove became a global celebrity after his confession and was requested to appear on talk and TV shows daily. His honesty, vulnerability, and likability drove the "Love Dove" fest. People said he was like an orphaned puppy, left in a garbage bag on a hot day. They felt sorry for him, then adored his strength, charm, and ability to bounce back. He was seen helping the poor, donating everything he owned to charity, and any money he made from his appearances or endorsements was also all given away. *Saint Dove*, many called him.

He enjoyed a faster rise to popularity than the Beatles, Elvis, or Susan Boyle. With every appearance, his following and support grew. He leveraged all of the positive press to persuade the United Nations to allow him to address them via teleconference, citing that his complete reform and his denouncement of terrorism had fueled his desire to try to influence world peace. It would be fed to the networks and broadcast live around the world.

Dove's appearance at the UN created international controversy. However, the Secretary General was able to convince the members that allowing a converted terrorist to address them would show understanding, compassion, and forgiveness in a world that needed a lot of each of those traits.

From the US Consulate General's office in Naples, Italy, Dove wore a royal blue silk suit and a tie of twenty-four karat gold thread, spellbinding the public as he evolved into the perfect young gentlemen from the former terrorist, former gang member, and rough-cut blue-collar worker. Dove watched the UN assembly live on a monitor.

"In 1950, William Faulkner said," Dove started with a soul-piercing smile, "'I believe that man will not merely endure: He will prevail. He is immortal, not because he alone among creatures has an inexhaustible voice, but because he has a soul, a spirit capable of compassion and sacrifice and endurance.'" He paused. "We are at a precarious crossroad where we must awaken that soul without hesitation and call on it to guide history onto the correct path." He paused again. "I am the luckiest man on the earth, because people have forgiven me, accepted me. And I don't feel like I deserve any of that. Correction: I know I don't deserve it. But thank you. Thank you for saving me," he said, shaking his head and tearing up.

Dove purposely inflected sincerity and calmness in his voice, like a father consoling his daughter after her first heartbreak. The inflection on his words and the way he spoke from the heart had UN members tearing up.

"To start on this correct path, those that are wrong must admit it. Awaken." He paused. "I was wrong. Blinded by hate, raised in hate, bred to hate, trained to hate and kill. I lost a lot of family and close friends in this war in the shadows." Dove cleared his throat; he didn't want to tell the whole story. "I don't want to be forgiven; I do not deserve it. I just want to be heard. A voice for those who are lost, confused, and wrong, as I was. I am so ashamed."

On the monitor, Dove noticed the camera shot zooming in on his face showing his glassy eyes. He turned on his tears.

"I will spend every waking moment stopping terrorism and terrorists and helping them understand and see the truth. If I can break the chain, I know many more can. This is the only way we will finally put an end to thousands of years of inbred hate, inherited racial bias, and twisted perception."

The UN members applauded. Some stood. Dove forced a quiver from his lip and smiled as he let the last tear drop silently to the floor. He bowed his head and clasped his hands out in front of his face in a symbolic gesture of world peace.

"I also realize my choice to cooperate with the authorities will make many of my old acquaintances unhappy, you could say. So I will endeavor to continue my quest until they catch up with me, and maybe at that moment, I can convince them they are wrong as well before they put a bullet in my head."

The cameraman in the consulate's office gave Dove the closing signal.

Dove smiled. "So please join me in creating a better and safer world. It's time. Thank you very much for allowing me to speak and be heard today. I know it was not an easy decision for you to let me address this council, and you will never regret this day and will be recognized as true humanitarians and concerned global citizens." Dove then made a peace sign, and the cameraman turned off the feed.

Dove took off his jacket and loosened his tie. "So, Mr. Cameraman, do you think I'll be top story today on *Entertainment Tonight*?"

The cameraman looked puzzled.

"Did you get my good side?" Dove asked, turning his head slightly to the left. "That's okay; they're both my good side." He laughed. "Time for me to get to work."

The cameraman quickly and quietly rolled up his cables, dismantled his camera stand, and packed everything in boxes.

But before getting on with his "work," Dove would head off to Pescara for some more Spagetatta as a reward for a job well done, then back to work in London for a special royal date—a date that would propel his popularity through the roof enough to take him to the next step of his month-long plan: an "in" with the Royal Family and key political influence.

29

Saturday - Day 15

Adam waited for Sam and Lucy in the lobby of the Hotel de Sers, sitting on an antique red leather, curved wingback sofa. He sipped on English Breakfast tea while admiring the craftsmanship of the hand-carved paneling that framed colorful frescos on the ceiling. The painting of the sky was trimmed by tree branches that looked so real, they appeared to be swaying in the wind. *Long gone are the days a person would spend months, even years, finishing a piece of work like this,* he thought.

The grey-haired concierge approached Adam. "Mr. Evans," he said, interrupting Adam's thoughts, "I have ordered you a cab for the airport. It will be a few minutes, however. Sorry."

Adam, wearing his disguise, nodded and smiled. The concierge went back to his desk in the lobby.

Familiar laughter came from a child coming out of an elevator. He looked down the hall and saw Lucy running toward him with the purest smile on earth; Sam followed behind with a newborn calm and confidence.

"*Bonjour*!" Lucy shouted.

"*Bonjour*! I'm impressed. Only a few days in France, and you are pretty much fluent."

"I'm not really *floont*, I'm 'merican." Lucy laughed hysterically.

Adam and Sam smiled as Lucy plunked herself on Adam's lap.

"And you seem to be very comfortable with Mr. Johl, too," Sam said, taking Lucy's hand and leading her off Adam's lap.

"That's fine; it's nice," Adam said.

"See!" Lucy said then jumped back on Adam's knee.

Sam sat on the sofa next to them. "So, Adam. I need to start counting monkeys."

"And I need to start combating wits with Dove. Not that I think it will do much good."

"I saw his speech last night on CNN from the UN. Why don't you just do the same: mesmerize the world with your words."

"He's beat me to it; he has the world's attention in a time of need, and he's so good at it."

"I'll go to the press with my story on the so-called reformed Dove. I'm going to cast doubt and try to wake up the public to what is really going on. Then I'm going to implement Project Monkey Love."

"You can try, but he's got his target locked on his flock, and they won't listen to you. He's going to lead them straight to hell, and I don't think even God can stop that," Adam said, scratching his head.

Sam searched Adam's eyes for something, or someone. "We'll win, won't we? The good guys always win, in the end-end?"

"I guess it's written that way. In the end-end." He laughed.

"Dove is a strong believer in prophecy, right, Adam?"

"Understatement. The similarities in what's happening and his role are amazing. He must believe it is unraveling as written in the Bible and that he has something to do with it."

"So why then does Dove keep trying? I mean, if he believes it is following biblical prophecies, then he would believe that the bad guys lose in the end. So shouldn't he just give up?"

"The age-old question." Adam looked at Lucy and pulled her chin up slightly with his finger. "Lucy, dear. If your mom told you that the hot chocolate drink was too hot and that you would burn your tongue if you drank it too soon, would you still try to drink it right away?"

Lucy giggled. "That already happened. The little marshmallows looked so tasty floating on the top, I had to try. But it left little bumps on my tongue. That hurt." She stuck out the tip of her tongue.

"Dove is sort of like a little child in that way. He knows what is written and believes in it, but thinks he can change destiny—destroy the world and become whoever it is he thinks he's going to become."

"Is there any chance that he could actually pull off the master plan you guys started with, right to the end?"

Adam shook his head. "I'd say he has a snowball's chance in hell."

Lucy put her little hand over Adam's mouth. "*Another* swear!"

"Sorry. You're right, but if hell is a place, then snowballs can't live there."

A middle-aged concierge dressed in a red blazer and tie came over to them. "Mr. Evans, the cab you ordered for the airport is finally here. So sorry for the long delay."

"Thanks," he said, as he handed the concierge the baggage claim tickets and a tip.

The chandelier in the grand foyer shook and tinkled while a solid deep rumbling could be heard and felt.

The concierge dropped to his knees and covered his head. "They were warning us this could happen!" he shouted.

Lucy closed her eyes and held onto Adam. Sam wrapped her arms around Lucy and Adam for eight seconds of tremors.

Then they stopped. The hotel was eerily quiet.

Someone screamed in the distance. A small piece of plaster dropped from the ceiling fresco onto Adam's pants; the plaster had the tip of a branch painted on it.

"Just another warning of bigger things to come," Adam said.

"Can't wait," Sam said.

"I can! I don't like that, Mommy, it scares me!" Lucy said.

As they held each other, Adam stroked Lucy's hair.

***

Arena and Lobato sat at a table at a side-walk café drinking Goldstar beer, eating falafel, and sharing the English version of the daily Israeli newspaper, *Ha'aretz.* Their table was next to a blue-painted low concrete wall that separated them from the sidewalk. Lobato was on his second beer; Arena still nursed her first.

Arena and Lobato had finished reading Saul Appel's controversial book and reviewed several of his published papers before taking this needed break. A lot of what they read, Arena knew, but several revelations that were new to her jumped out. Appel had predicted that the Antichrist would not only influence the masses as Hitler did, but would influence the world religions and churches, and that they would turn against their gods to embrace the new leader and his idyllic thinking. Fossano was doing exactly that.

"Look," Arena said, turning the section of newspaper she was reading around to Lobato. She tapped on the photo on the front page.

"Unreal. Dove turning the shovel on the site of the new Jerusalem Temple. How the hell did he pull that off? Why pick him of all people for such an important event?" Lobato shook his head.

"This is one of the final signs. Image of the Antichrist at the Jerusalem Temple."

"But it's not the Temple; it's just dirt."

"Semantics. Dove probably paid someone so he could do this. So the leader is in place, now, if we're playing by prophecy." Arena shook her head then drank her beer, washing down the last bite of her falafel.

"Only in Dove's mind. He may think he is the Antichrist, but it's not reality." Lobato shook his finger. He took a drink then looked at his watch. "We've been here for an hour."

Arena's smartphone vibrated on the table. It was a message about SIGNIT's latest prediction.

"What is it?" Lobato asked, checking his smartphone, which was silent.

"And we now have one hundred percent confirmation of who the mastermind of the 'destroy the world' plan is," Arena said. "Well

SIGNIT *thinks* it knows who it is. It must have digested today's newspapers."

"I'm jumping out of my pants here. Who is it?"

"Come on. You know: Dove, Ali, aka Nat Fossano—anagram: son of Satan."

"Must have been Dove's speech and the shovel of dirt that made him the front-runner."

"Shovel of something... SIGNIT tabulates all current events as they happen, mashes them with all the probabilities and combinations it has already collected, including religious prophecies, and spits out Dove as the Antichrist." Arena tapped her phone on the table. "But SIGNIT does add a rider that says, 'given that the supernatural has never been proven, this is hypothetical and more than likely impossible in that realm.'"

"Makes sense. But it doesn't matter, because if Dove actually believes he's Satan, he'll act like him."

"I think you're right."

Lobato looked around as if Satan had found them and listened to their every word. "I think SIGNIT got this one wrong."

"What? SIGNIT's usually never—"

"It's Homer Simpson. That's who the Antichrist is."

Arena laughed loudly. People at the table next to them stared at them.

"Think about it. He has been on the air for over twenty years, molding the minds of the young and old to follow him. All he has to do is air an episode that says 'Pick up your guns, pitchforks, and Twinkies—and revolt!'"

"Funny, Lobato. You're real funny." Arena looked up at the clear blue sky and squinted. "Do we arrest Homer or the artist who creates him?"

Lobato stopped smiling. "Unfortunately, my gut tells me that SIGNIT's right, as bizarre and unrealistic as it sounds. Not that Dove has any super-powers; he's just our next Hitler but worse. That kind of Antichrist."

Arena played with her beer bottle. "Hitler believed in the occult and weird things, too. Who knows, maybe somewhere in that dark mind of his, he may have secretly thought he was the Antichrist."

"Yeah. I really think Dove thinks he is, too."

"If you really stop to think about it, it makes sense. He's had his foot in the door since the beginning of this entire mess, and he tried to discredit Adam's message."

"That would mean that Adam Johl could think he's—"

"Don't say it. Just think it."

"Why?" Lobato said, looking over his shoulder again.

"I don't know. We just need to stay grounded in reality. These guys are all delusional."

"Then there's the side of me that says if I really believe in God—which I do—then I need to believe in Satan and hell and heaven and everything else written in the Bible." He sighed. "And if it's true—the Bible, that is—and the prophecies are referring to the actual events happening now, then it really is over."

"I'm having a tough time believing this is the end. And that this is the actual unfolding of thousands-of-years-old prophecy." Arena dabbed her forehead with a napkin. "I've had religion rammed down my throat by the spoonful when I was a little girl, and... I just don't know."

"I'm just a little confused. Reality is fuzzy right now."

"I'm confused, too. Don't feel bad, and I've studied this stuff because it really interests me in an effort to get to the truth. A little girl always wants to believe in her father." Arena sighed. "Maybe because I want so much to believe in something bigger than me, us, man." Arena finally finished her beer; Lobato tried to catch up by guzzling the rest of his. "Are you up to the challenge, Breno? Want to battle the beast? Lock horns with Beelzebub?" She laughed.

Lobato put his empty Goldstar bottle on the table and belched politely. "Yeah, let's blow this pop stand."

"Don't say that too loudly." Arena picked up Rabbi Saul's book then scanned the restaurant.

Lobato threw down two hundred shekels, and they made their way to the street to catch a cab.

Several white cabs were lined up, with cabbies leaning against their cars, smoking and having heated discussions about probably everything. They went to the one in front of the lineup.

Lobato opened the back door for Arena. She piled in, and Lobato followed her. An older white panel van crept forward and stopped abreast to them. A young male driver with dark olive-colored skin and sweat beading on his forehead made quick shifty eye contact with Arena.

Arena blinked then pushed Lobato out of the cab, grabbed him by the collar, and pulled him over the low concrete wall as an explosion rocked the block.

Glass, brick, metal, and wood rained down on them while flames licked over them and black smoke that tasted like hot metal and burning rubber filled their lungs.

People continued to scream as the echo of the explosion subsided. Car alarms wailed.

Lobato slid Arena off him and rolled on top of her.

"A bit late for that now," Arena said.

"You never know."

They stayed still for several seconds then crawled away from the inferno of the car along the wall that used to surround the patio restaurant. Smoke and dust filled the air.

"Was that for us?" Lobato drew his weapon then took a quick peek over the wall.

"Yes. The driver of the van confirmed his target when he looked into my eyes; I could tell. He looked anxious."

Arena took a quick peek, as well. "He tried to disguise killing us with just another suicide bomber blowing up a marketplace."

Lobato grabbed Arena's hand and squeezed it. "Are we that much of a threat that they'd try to kill us?" he asked, with a new heightened awareness of his surroundings.

"We're getting close to something or some-one." She squeezed his hand back. "Dove has connections everywhere. And he would have them here too."

They got up and scrambled away from the marketplace to tend to their minor cuts and bruises.

Arena was quiet all the way back to their hotel. They watched everyone and everything, looking for signs of threats. Their cover was blown, and they were concerned that more than just Dove knew FBI agents were in that country.

"Someone doesn't like us digging. Do you think maybe the rabbi had something to do with it? Maybe he let Dove know we were there asking questions?" Lobato asked as they packed their bags.

"Just tried calling him, and the staff there said he's disappeared from the synagogue and no one knows where he is, so I guess we can't ask him. We need to keep moving," Arena said.

"Where do we go from here?"

"One of two places." She closed her eyes and rubbed them. "London, if we think we can stop this, as Dove is booked at the University there for another speaking engagement in less than two days. Or Megiddo, if we want to watch the end play out."

"London. We can stop this," Lobato said. "Let's blow this pop—"

Arena winced. "Do you ever learn?"

Lobato motioned zipping his lips shut.

Arena poked her head out of their hotel room and checked the hallway. All clear.

They made their way to the stairwell instead of using the elevator. They walked down seven flights of stairs and exited into a narrow back alley from where they would make their way to the airport.

Arena's heart rate had not been normal for what seemed like days. She definitely didn't need cardio. *There's always a silver lining,* she thought.

30

Arena and Lobato flew on a US government jet and arrived at Heathrow by dinnertime. Their first stop was Timothy's restaurant in Westminster. They were to receive a drop from their London contact there.

Arena ordered the spiced lamb skewers with peas and carrots, and Lobato had the mixed grill with fries. They ate quickly and quietly, both feeling guilty about enjoying a good meal when they knew time was of the essence and so many people around the world were still without food altogether. They would wait at their table until their operative made contact.

The waiter returned with the *Daily Telegraph* newspaper, which neither Arena nor Lobato had asked for.

They scanned the restaurant again, reviewing all the faces they had already committed to memory. Their contact was invisible, just as trained.

Arena pushed her plate aside and thumbed through the thick paper. Stuck in the middle was a small white envelope sealed with FBI hologram privacy tape. She discreetly opened it and reviewed the file, masking her actions with the newspaper.

Lobato picked through the leftovers from Arena's plate. "Something big?" he asked.

"Huge. Are you enjoying that?"

"It's great. *Huge*?"

"The Saudis, who have hidden the amount of their oil reserves for over fifty years and disputed the fact that they overstated their reserves by forty percent, finally confessed to having less than what they have been saying. Which means proof was leaked, and they want to make a statement before the documents are made public. No numbers have been given yet."

"Wow."

"That means that Iraq, Iran, and the United Arab Emirates are all probably scraping the bottom of their barrels, too. Which means we'll be pulling all troops from the Middle East. No reason to keep the balance of peace when there is nothing worth protecting."

"I guess we'll be putting our troops in Alberta next. Hell, maybe Saskatchewan or Manitoba."

Arena smiled. "This is no joke. This is life-changing stuff, depending on the numbers. Global power-shifting change, as if the continental shelf just broke away and a continent slipped into the ocean." She looked at her plate. "Are you done with that?"

Lobato stopped picking food off of Arena's plate, as there were only a few peas left. "What about Dove? Anything on him?"

"He's been busy. They have hourly updates on CNN, on 'Where's the Dove of Peace?' His latest rant calls for the US to increase troops in the Middle East to stabilize peace."

"Why?"

Arena ran her finger along the article, speed-reading. "Says here that Dove is asking the British Prime Minister to increase troop presence as well, to protect Israel. Figures the news of the oil will spark another war with a nothing-to-lose attitude."

"Russia has one of the next biggest reserves on that continent."

The waiter cleared the plates and asked if they would like dessert or coffee. They declined on the sweets but both requested coffee.

"The sticker?" Lobato asked.

Arena glanced around the restaurant then peeled a small sticker off a wax square from inside the envelope. She stuck the sticker on her smartphone. She donned her earpiece and listened as she slid the paper across the table to Lobato, who also scrutinized it. When she was done, she handed the ear bud to Lobato. He seemed to hold his breath as he listened.

They had received instructions to kill Nat Fossano.

Lobato slowly pulled out the earpiece. "This makes no sense."

"I know."

"This is not something our department does, ever. This is usually something other agencies would do, agencies we don't even know about," Lobato whispered.

"They've probably called them, too."

"So they've sent the task out to multiple agents—all agencies?"

"Correct. This way—"

"They won't miss the target," Lobato finished then put the document back in the envelope. "They really want him dead. Now."

"Yeah, but it'll be like the Cannonball Rally. Very messy and desperate. And if we have any leaks, anyone Dove or his contacts have bought off, he will know we're coming."

They sipped their coffee. Arena tapped her fingers on the table, and Lobato tapped his foot noticeably while they gazed into each other's eyes. The restaurant was noisier than when they first arrived, but Arena liked it. She thought the noise was like a security blanket for their conversation.

"Talk about baptism by fire," Lobato said.

"Honeymoon's over, Romeo. I suspect you'll see it all in the next couple weeks."

"I expect it, and they trained us for the unexpected, but when it happens... Well."

"You'll soon become your environment. It'll all seem sickeningly normal, and that's when shopping at Wal-Mart or cutting your lawn will seem abnormal." She paused. "You will look at a shopper and know that they have no idea what goes on behind the scenes so that they can push that cart, safely, down the aisles and buy their toilet paper."

"Have you done this kind of thing before?" Lobato tapped twice on the document envelope.

"I can't answer that. Even if I haven't done it."

"Sorry for asking."

"No problem. We should get going. We have a long night of planning ahead of us."

Lobato nodded and finished his coffee.

"You haven't been this quiet since... ever," Arena said.

"Just getting in touch with my dark side."

Arena reached over and touched his arm. He looked back at her with innocent eyes, eyes that Arena knew would soon change. And she knew exactly how he felt.

Across the street from Timothy's restaurant was the five-star restaurant Ten. Someone dining at Ten was worthy of the dozens of paparazzi perched on the sidewalk, in pecking order of stature.

"I wonder who's over there?" Lobato asked as he held Timothy's restaurant door open for Arena.

They stood on the curb, gazing across the busy street. A black Rolls Royce limousine with fully tinted windows slowly rolled up in front of Ten. Three men in dark suits exited the vehicle and took position at the front door of the restaurant. They had earpieces and dark glasses.

Arena and Lobato stood there, watching the circus of activity. "Maybe Bono or Elton John," Lobato said then addressed the valet standing by the parking sign. "Excuse me. Who's at Ten tonight?"

"Princess Anne, and rumor is that Nat Fossano is a guest of hers."

"Thank you," Lobato said as he and Arena stepped away, locking eyes with each other.

"What the hell? How come we didn't get this intel? Do we have to be the freakin' press to get tips?" Lobato said quietly.

"Yes, our intel *should* be tied into the paparazzi's connections."

"What do we do?" Lobato asked.

"Nothing now, but let's try to get a closer look," Arena said, heading toward the crowd. Lobato trailed a few steps behind her.

The two agents crossed the street and stood behind the pile of reporters about eight deep. A few minutes later, Dove, Princess Anne, and two bodyguards exited Ten.

As they stood on the red carpet, Dove smiled and seemed to be preparing to say something while the flashes roared like white fire. Princess Anne had her head tilted down slightly, trying to hide an infectious smile. They made an adorable couple.

Arena and Lobato bounced up and down on their toes to get a glimpse of Dove as he spoke to the crowd.

Dove suddenly pushed the princess to the ground and huddled over her body.

Bodyguards jumped on top of them, shielding them from what seemed like shots, although none were heard.

People screamed.

A few of the paparazzi fell to the ground, prone position, covering their heads; others dropped to their knees but kept the film rolling.

"Up there! The shooter!" someone yelled. "The Haworth building, fourth floor window! Second window from the end!"

Security guards whisked the princess and a bleeding Dove into the waiting limo, and it sped off.

"It could be one of ours trying to kill Dove," Arena said. "We should get up there, protect them if possible."

Arena and Lobato bolted across the street toward the shooter's supposed location.

Arena and Lobato entered the Haworth building and dashed for the elevator; they took it directly to the fourth floor.

"Do you think it was one of ours?" Lobato asked, drawing his weapon as the elevator stopped at the fourth floor.

"Not sure," Arena said as the door opened. "But how did everyone know Dove was here except us?"

They did a standard exit check and made their way down the hall to the second suite from the end.

The door was ajar—kicked open, with the frame cracked. Lobato entered the suite and inched his way forward, back against the wall. He could hear a man talking into a phone. He stepped it up, turned the corner into the living room, and aimed his weapon at the two men standing over a corpse on the floor. The men wore dark suits and had earpieces with cords dangling into their jackets.

"Easy. Point that thing away. We got the bad guy," said the taller of the two men in dark suits. "I'm Agent Smith. This is Agent Harris," he added, pointing to his partner. "MI5."

Lobato kept his weapon trained on the two men as Arena entered the room, striking a similar pose.

"Lower your weapons," Harris said, holding his weapon to his side. "Who are you?"

Lobato looked at Arena. She nodded, and they holstered their handguns.

She doubted that they were MI5. What would they be doing there? Waiting for someone to shoot the princess? It didn't feel right but she wasn't about to ask for proof from them. "FBI," she said slowly. "We're operating out of our London legat... legal attaché office." She quickly flashed her badge.

"We know what that is," Smith said abruptly. "What are you doing here?"

"Chasing terrorists. We're cleared with Interpol and your government on this."

Smith sneered. "No terrorist here. Just probably some royal stalker."

Arena walked over to the corpse, budging her way through the two MI5 agents who didn't seem to want her near the body. The attacker's gun was still on a tripod, positioned at the window. His rifle case was open and empty.

"Pretty sophisticated weapon for a stalker... How did you get to him so fast?" Arena asked as she checked for a pulse. "He didn't even have time to dismantle his weapon."

"My guess is that he wasn't going anywhere. He was probably preparing for more shooting. He also felt fairly certain no one identified his location," Smith said.

"I don't think so," Lobato said as he pulled out his phone and snapped a picture of the shooter's face.

Arena looked at him.

Smith raised an eyebrow. "Do you see his rifle packed up?" he asked as he and his partner slowly separated.

Arena knew from experience that it wasn't the place to argue. "Looks like you chaps have everything under control. We're going to go check on Dove." She backed nonchalantly toward the door. "Let's go, Breno."

There was a distinct moment of tension, like trying to back out of a den filled with lions that had just awakened and hadn't been fed.

Lobato bravely turned his back on the two supposed MI5 agents as Arena continued to shuffle sideways to the door. The agents slowly followed them then stopped when some laughter sounded in the hallway.

"You take care. It's a dangerous world outside," Harris said.

"You take care, too," Arena said. "It's also a dangerous world inside."

Arena and Lobato walked calmly to the elevator, passing a young couple flirting at the doorway of a suite.

The elevator door quickly opened, and they got in and jabbed the lobby button. "Dove's covering all his tracks," Arena said, as the elevator door closed and they descended. "Not sure how or why he did this."

"Yeah. Why try to kill the princess? Or was it one of ours trying to take Dove out?" Lobato pulled out his phone. "I'll send this picture into head office now and get it checked out." He sent the photo.

"My guess? He saved her by taking a bullet for her. He's now not just a hero—he's a super-hero," Arena said as the elevator door opened. "One that the Royals owe a favor to."

Two police officers were standing guard outside the door. Arena and Lobato flashed their credentials with the Interpol passes. The officers nodded and let them through.

They exited the building through revolving doors and entered the street that was shoulder-to-shoulder people and emergency vehicles.

"We need divine intervention," she let out, as if she'd been holding the reply since the elevator. "This is the part where the Antichrist really gets the world to love him."

They stood there for a moment and watched the crowd. People were sobbing, shouting, congregating in small groups.

"What do we do now?" Lobato asked.

"More than ever, our job."

***

Claire Nadeau thought of the night at Roxy's that Adam Johl spoke to her and the crowd. It had changed her life and now brought her back to London where she had been only once before. It was with her husband four years before, just before she found him cheating.

That trip had been cold and uninteresting. London seemed ugly. Dirty. And she hated the people. Rude and unfriendly.

This time was sublimely different. It was beautiful, romantic—culturally stimulating and exciting. And the sun was shining, and the people smiled.

She looked up at a map of London in the Waterloo Train Station. As people hurried by, bags and children in tow, she took in the moment. If someone would have told her a few weeks ago that she'd be travelling halfway around the world, chasing the possible savior of the world and doing it on her own, she would have laughed hysterically. Even if she didn't find Dove, she felt satisfied like she had accomplished something. She was proud of her newfound independence.

She smiled, looked at the map once more, then continued on her journey with purpose.

***

Marty came out of the gas station store and bumped into a short skinny teenage boy in a plain white T-shirt and faded jeans at the doorway. "Sorry," Marty said, head half hung as he clutched the white plastic bag that held his just-purchased bottle of vodka.

"Hey, man. You're one of the disciples. I seen you on TV," the boy said.

"I was."

"What'd you mean, 'was'?"

"It's all a big joke. Get over it." Marty lit up a cigarette.

"Joke? You seen the news lately, what's going on in this messed-up world? How could you say that?"

Marty exhaled and looked at the boy. "Do all you young kids feel the same way?"

"Hell, yeah. The school's all about this. We're pushing hard for some change and peace. You guys inspired us."

"Keep pushing then, 'cuz us old guys don't give a shit." Marty walked away toward his car at the gas pumps. "And I don't recycle either."

"I forgive you!" the boy shouted. "For being so fucking stupid! Asswipe!"

Marty waved his hand backward and got into his van. He sat down, pulled down his visor, and looked into the vanity mirror. His eyes were bloodshot. He had a day and a half of beard growth, and he looked pale. "Nice," he said to himself.

His cell phone rang. He looked at the call display; it was his wife. He tossed the phone on the seat next to the bottle he just bought, started the van, and drove off. "Why doesn't everyone just leave me alone! What did I do to deserve this?"

***

"Kenny, I told you last week that Dove is the Antichrist—I've seen it with my own eyes! Felt it in my bones!" Daisy said to the deejay of a

Caribbean radio station on a live broadcast. "And his name? If you unscramble the letters in Nat Fossano, it spells *Son of Satan*."

"Easy, Granny Daisy. Chill. I remember the anagram for William Shakespeare from my school days. His name spells *I am a weakish speller*." Kenny laughed. "Dove's a saint, mon. He saved the princess! Troo' his body on the woman. Sacrificed himself. Would the Son of Satan do that?"

"He's as slippery as an oiled snake, and I'll chill when someone takes that evil man out. Toss him in a sulfur lake—that's what the good book says."

"And who's gonna do it?"

"Hell, if you or no one will, I'll take care of business!"

"I don't doubt that for one second." Kenny laughed, spewing smoke from his mouth.

"Know where there's a lake of burning sulfur? Somewhere close?"

He laughed again.

"I know you guys think I'm just some crazy old woman, but remember this one thing: In the Bible, it says the Antichrist is a charismatic, charming man who fools the masses. And that's Dove—the Dove of death. The master of deception."

"Ooh, Daisy, you are going to make a lot of people mad. Maybe they'll try to lynch you!"

"That's fine. I'd rather die fighting for what is right than compromise my beliefs."

"You are one gutsy woman, Daisy. I'll give you that."

"And right. I'm one *right* gutsy woman!"

"That you are!"

"Kenny, you married?"

"No, why?"

"You want to be?"

Kenny laughed. "Back to some music. Thanks for comin' today, Daisy!" and he put on "Runnin' with the Devil" by Van Halen.

31

Sunday - Day 16

When Adam, Sam, and Lucy landed in Heathrow, news of the attempt on Princess Anne's life was all over the airport monitors. They had identified the dead shooter as Essa Salo, a Norwegian right-wing extremist who hated monarchy. Travelers stared at the TVs as if mesmerized, looking disbelieving as they watched the event replay. With the plethora of media on hand at the restaurant Ten, photos and video had been shot from every conceivable angle, and they were all being shown.

The question everyone asked was why Essa Salo had tried to kill the princess. The answer was given in a tidy police statement that seemed contradictory: Essa Salo acted alone, as a stalker with a deadly fixation on Princess Anne and a hate for monarchy. His apartment had a shrine of photos and newspaper articles, with candles and incense in front of the creepy shrine.

Witnesses said that Dove luckily pointed out a window on the Haworth Building where he spotted the glint of the rifle barrel or scope. He was quoted as saying he was just looking up to the night sky to look at the stars. He then threw himself on the princess, taking a bullet for her. Dove was at an undisclosed hospital where he was being treated for a non-life threatening wound to his upper arm.

The news that followed the headline story was filled with riots in Greece, looting in Mumbai, and more earthquakes—smaller ones with magnitudes from four to five—scattered around the globe. News of the earthquakes was now tagged onto the end of the news instead of leading.

Sam pulled herself and Lucy from the monitors and headed to the baggage claim area. The less Lucy knew, the better, although Lucy had seen most of the news.

"What's the rush, Mommy? You're going to tear my arm off."

"We need to get going, places to see."

"Are you trying to make it so I don't see all the bad news? And the princess being shot? *Mom?*" Lucy blurted in short gasps.

"No," Sam replied as she slowed their pace.

"Yes, you are."

Sam nodded. Why lie about it? *Lucy has witnessed so much already.*

"Why does someone want to kill the princess? She is so beautiful and nice. We learned about her in school. She helps starving children all over the world."

"Well, Sunshine, it—"

"And why do all the good people have to die! Adam, do you think my dad will meet her in heaven if someone kills her?"

They had arrived at the baggage carousel, and Adam grabbed a baggage cart.

"If she dies—which I'm sure she won't anytime soon—yes, she will meet your dad," Adam said, pushing the baggage cart closer to the carousel. "They are both saints."

Sam could see Lucy's mind churning—imagining, by the way she scrunched her face and crinkled her forehead.

All three of them waited in silence for their suitcases. After only a five-minute wait, they had their bags and were off to the car rental kiosk.

Adam rented a small Toyota Hybrid, punched into the GPS the address of the Hamilton Hotel that Sam booked, and they left the parking lot.

"I need to finish Project Monkey Love," Sam said as Adam maneuvered through congested London traffic. "The world needs peace and hope more than ever."

"How about I drop you off at the Hamilton, I run my errands, and we'll meet for dinner?"

Sam looked at Adam sternly.

"What?" Adam asked.

"You think you're going to run around saving the world without me?"

"Just some errands. Need to get a new laptop."

"Errands, right. I'm coming."

Adam laughed. "You amaze me."

"Why?" Sam smiled.

"You just do." He paused. "How about you fire up that laptop while we drive? Just try to get things done while I run my errands."

Sam reached around to her satchel, retrieved her laptop, and connected to the Internet via her broadband card. "Where's our first stop?" she asked.

"Look at all the pigeons and the beautiful fountain!" Lucy shouted from the back seat.

"This is Trafalgar Square," Sam said.

"Can we stop and take pictures?"

"No, sweetie... We can take pictures while we drive."

"Why not? A short break would be nice," Adam said.

"Yay! I can feed the pigeons from my hand like that boy!" Lucy pointed, jabbing her finger—which had been in her mouth—onto the window.

Adam wheeled around to a side street, where a parking spot seemed to be waiting for him outside the café. "Our lucky day."

They got a table by the street with a view of the square. Sam and Adam ordered coffees with scones, and Lucy ordered a bowl of three-flavor ice cream.

Adam hacked into servers, gaining access to numerous mailing lists. Sam was stunned at how effortless Adam made it seem, and she felt guilty about breaking international laws of unsolicited email.

"We're breaking some big laws here," Sam said, dipping her scone into her coffee.

Adam stopped typing and looked up. "Yes. But, as you know, it is for a great cause. We're not trying to use the email addresses to sell Viagra or run a marketing scheme. And I've made it untraceable, so don't worry."

Sam shrugged.

"Jesus broke laws too, if that makes you feel any better."

"You're saying we're like Jesus?"

"No, not at all. Just saying that he sort of set a precedent, in my mind. He touched a leper. Worked on a Sabbath. Let an adulterous woman walk away without being stoned... and a few other things. But it's the reasons he broke those laws that was most important, and it is the reason we are here, as well. It is the right thing to do."

"You should be a salesman. Used cars," Sam said, shaking her head.

"Your turn to break the law—you lawless wreck," he said, turning the laptop toward her. "We'll go to jail together." He took a sip of coffee.

Sam's job was to set up massive distribution lists from the top Internet sites like Facebook, LinkedIn, Twitter, and others that Adam had hacked. She would also hit everyone she ever met, all the media and news organizations in the world, different governments, the UN. Then on to purchasing every available legal mailing list from the largest mass-marketing companies on the Internet.

Adam's unrivaled computer prowess enhanced Sam's plan, with solid tips and advice to supercharge the campaign through powerful search engines. Through programming, he would make her entries pop to the top of searches and popular social media sites. They estimated that they could reach over three hundred million people, and those people would hopefully spread the word of Project Monkey Love and the YouTube messages that she would create. Sam would also piggyback on Lucy's YouTube videos that had gotten incredible viral traction.

Reaching people was no longer a problem.

The most difficult piece was yet to come: Creating a message that would go viral, setting a new benchmark for hits in the shortest amount of time. Having those three hundred million people repost, retweet, and forward the email message.

Her words had to motivate, inspire, and in essence, save the world. They had to relate to every class, race, and religious persuasion. Sam needed to get buy-in on her plan to unite the world in a moment of peace and consciousness—a global sit-in for peace, so to speak.

She opened a Word document and stared at the blank page with the cursor blinking while Lucy continued to enjoy her ice cream.

Adam sipped his coffee and breathed in the surroundings.

"Give me the opening line, Adam. Please."

He shook his head and smiled.

"Why won't you help me out here?"

"Then they wouldn't be your words."

A waiter approached the table to refill the coffee cups. "Can I get anything else for you?" He stared at Adam as if he recognized him.

"No thanks, I'm fine." Adam adjusted his hat downward a little.

"And you, miss?"

"A pocket full of prose, please," Sam said.

The waiter looked puzzled.

"I'm fine, thanks. My cup is half full." Her mind suddenly cleared as if she'd walked out of a misty forest into a sun-filled meadow.

Adam still smiled.

"Why do you seem so happy?" Sam asked.

"Because you look happy, all of a sudden."

Lucy took her spoon and scraped the watery ice cream from the bottom of the bowl. "You look happier now, Mom."

"Just had an inspiration, out of nowhere."

"I think from somewhere," Adam said.

Sam pounded away at the keyboard to nail down her thoughts as they flooded her mind.

***

The Benjamin Hotel was a mile from the University of London. Not that it was necessary, but Lobato and Arena registered as Tom Smith and Barbara Brown, freelance reporters. They would use those identities to get closer to Fossano when he spoke at the university. Their mission: to assassinate Fossano.

Internationally, the FBI usually interacted in joint efforts with local policing agencies and US foreign agencies, but sometimes they acted solo in special clandestine operations. Where US assets or citizens were involved in a crime or a terrorist incident, FBI agents could travel abroad and do what was necessary to maintain the safety of the US and its citizens. And SIGNIT was strongly advising that Nat Fossano was the most major threat to the US and its citizens since Imad Mughniyah.

One of the ten most wanted terrorists by the FBI, Imad Mughniyah, had been killed in 2008 by a car bomb planted inside the driver's headrest. He was thought to have killed more United States citizens than any other militant before the 2001 US attack. Although the general population, via media, assumed the Israelis carried out the assassination, the American National Whistleblowers watchdog group had called for an investigation into FBI involvement based on leaked intel.

Rumor within the agency was that Mughniyah's death was a proud unspoken moment in FBI history. Fossano was planned to be the second FBI assassination outside American soil in the past two decades, unspoken and privately celebrated.

Sitting on the sofa in their shared hotel room, Lobato cleaned his weapon, his tools strewn on the coffee table, while Arena jotted notes on a map of London at the desk. She worked in a focused silence that he respected.

Arena had used their London intelligence affiliates and put together Dove's itinerary for the next few days. That afternoon, he was to be at the University of London to give a speech on stability in the Middle East and required global intervention. That would be their best chance at taking him down.

Arena had two sets of fake ID. One was for their press credentials, which would give them unrestricted travel throughout the campus when Dove spoke. The other set was for an air conditioner repair company, which would gain them access to set up some equipment before Dove was to speak.

Lobato reassembled his weapon and asked Arena if she wanted him to do hers. She refused. Having someone else clean and check your weapon was just plain old bad luck in her mind, something they didn't need. Instead,

Lobato ordered some food and reviewed the plan while Arena prepped her piece. They continued to work in ubiquitous silence, focused on what could end up being Lobato's first kill.

After only sampling some of the hotel food that had been delivered to the room, they commenced their walk to the university to finalize preparations in what could be an unwritten historic FBI event. The plan was solid but rushed. Rushed always left gaping room for error.

They had a Univac heating repair van parked half a block from the university waiting for them. In it were uniforms, ID, tools, and schematics for the university's heating and cooling systems.

The entire mission had been out of the normal realm for an FBI agent, but neither questioned the commands they were given. They worked in extraordinary times, which called for equally extraordinary measures.

As they strolled past a patisserie, Lobato yanked on Arena's arm, bringing her to an abrupt stop.

"What now, Breno?"

"Lunch was not enough, and we didn't finish it. How about a quick cheesecake?" He pointed at the window display of artistically placed baked goods. "A moment of reprieve in culinary heaven?"

Arena looked at her watch as people passed them on the sidewalk. "I've had more diversions with you in the past few weeks than my entire FBI career."

"That's not what I asked. Cake or no cake?"

She looked at Lobato, dressed in traditional cameraman khaki, looking like a young boy asking his mother for candy. She needed to start acting like the senior partner again. Immediately. It would be a sign of hope, as if they still had a long future and career ahead of them. They needed to stop acting as if those were the last days on earth. "No cake, Breno. We have a job to do. Final answer."

"Oh, come on. It's just a little cocoa and some—"

"Let's go!" She continued on.

Lobato watched Arena walk away. He looked back at the window. "I'll be back for you," he said, pointing at a man-sized slab of chocolate cheesecake.

"Wait up, partner!" He caught up to Arena, who had picked up the pace. "Come on, Arena. Chill."

Arena looked into his eyes as they walked. "We really need to focus, and I don't know how many times I have to remind you. I'm letting you down by indulging your whims."

"Sorry, but cake is a whim? We have tons of time, honestly."

Arena lowered her voice. "Cake is another interruption and diversion from the task at hand. Do you think the men in Iraq or Afghanistan stop for cake or coffee or anything when on duty? No. They're at war. So are we, and until the battle is over, I have decided... It's all business."

"*All* business?"

She nodded.

They waited for a green light to cross the street, scoping the area out three hundred sixty degrees. A small group of people had collected next to them, also waiting for the light to change. Some were dressed in suits, some in dresses, and three people looked like tourists with cameras and duffle bags.

"Sorry," Lobato said. "I was just hungry again. I get grumpy when I'm hungry."

"No need. It's my doing."

The light turned green, and they crossed the street with the small crowd of people.

"I'm letting my partner down by indulging his distractions," Arena said quietly.

Lobato laughed.

"What's funny?"

"You."

"Why?"

"You're my biggest distraction, Cass, not food. If you could see you from where I stand, you'd understand."

"Maybe I should ask for a new partner for you." They were a mere block from the university, and she slowed their pace. "Maybe a master baker."

Lobato grabbed her shoulders, stopped her in the middle of the sidewalk, and turned her toward him.

She looked at him. She didn't fight it by shaking his hands off her. She let him hold her and waited, as she wanted to see where this would lead. Did he get her message? They stood in an awkward moment of choice; did she force the issue of being all-business, or just go with it?

Lobato let his hands slowly slide from her shoulders as people brushed by them. "The reason I'm acting this way is that," he said softly, "love makes me think of food, for some reason, and act stupid."

"Please don't say that. Not now. Not here."

Lobato pulled her aside, up against an office building. "I just want you to know. I can't hold it in anymore."

"I already know."

"How? When I said it in the past, it was sort of joking, me being funny. But now, now it's so real."

"The way you made love. The way you touched me, looked at me. That's how I know."

Lobato smiled. "And you? Do you love me?"

"You Portuguese are so emotional. It was just sex for me."

"I don't believe it for a second. I'm going to crack you yet, Cass."

She laughed and walked away. Lobato followed.

You already have, she thought. *Damn.* What was she going to do about their relationship? How did you douse love, or hit the pause button even? It was so complicated, especially given the circumstances.

They found the van and changed into Univac uniforms. Arena put her hair in a ponytail, put on fake eyeglasses, and donned the bright blue Univac cap to match the overalls. Lobato put on a believable fake mustache, glasses, and the same uniform as Arena. After clearing security with their servicemen credentials, they made their way to the hall where Dove was to speak. Lobato gained access to the grid of walkways above the theatre room for HVAC reasons and secretly positioned a six-inch black box armed with a .22 caliber barrel with silencer. The box was disguised as an electrical conduit. They tested the remote functions, closed up the grille it hid behind, and left the university.

Dove's little reign would be over soon. Everything had been triple checked, and barring both of them getting run over by a bus between now and the hit, by tomorrow night they would be back home.

But Arena had one task left. She had to mentally prepare herself and Lobato for the execution of Dove. Not that she could wave a wand and they would both be fine with it—it was more of an exercise of distancing themselves. Dove was a hard target. A threat. They could not see him as a person with feelings and personality. If they did, it would be hard to do. There should be no hesitation for Lobato, who would be the one to pull the trigger. Aim, breathe, shoot. One, two, *bang*. Mission complete, and no paperwork on this one.

Then go for a strong drink, just like she had done the first time she killed someone, although the drinks didn't help with her post-shooting trauma. She had been with her previous partner, working out of the Austin office. They found a suspect in a bombing that killed a dozen people in Grapevine, Texas. The order was dead or alive. Her partner knew someone that was killed in the bombing, a roommate from his college days. Her partner wanted the suspect dead. They questioned him, then each shot him. Arena put three bullets in him; her partner unloaded four, including one to the head. The report said the suspect came at them with a sword. The coroner's report was never released to the public.

When they went for the drink after that shooting, they stayed in the bar until three a.m. The next day, she asked for time off and a transfer to one of the New York offices.

Arena hoped that this time, it would be different. No guilt or trauma. Just a clean, warranted hit. She liked where she lived. And... she liked Lobato.

32

Monday - Day 17

Adam and Sam headed to Beveridge Hall at the University of London, where Dove was to speak. Sam left Lucy with the hotel babysitting service that Adam reassured her was safe. Sam felt guilty, again—for dragging Lucy around the world, for putting her in danger, and for peddling her off to yet another sitter.

As they drove through London, Sam continued to scribe her most important piece of work—words that she hoped were worthy of re-tweets, forwarding, liking, sharing, and posting. *The new way to create gospel,* she thought. Wouldn't it be something if she could pen an inspiration that would be quoted for decades to come? *"The Gospel according to Samantha Cott." Sounds stupid and arrogant!* She shook her head and continued trying to create words that would hopefully inspire.

When politicians, royalty, or celebrities spoke at the university, there was usually some degree of protest outside—placard-waving students bent on speaking their minds and letting the world know what travesties were unfolding. The groups ranged from five or ten to hundreds, even thousands. That day, for the first time, there were none. Not one placard, sign, bullhorn, person on a soapbox—nothing. There were only people milling about asking how they could get in to see Dove speak.

Dove could do no wrong in the eyes of the vast majority of the public, who expressed support for the ex-terrorist blue-collar worker.

The renovated hall, built in 1936, still maintained its classic era with a modern edge. It was jammed beyond the occupancy permit of five hundred eighty. The last time the University had allowed that level of overcrowding was for an appearance and celebration of the British Olympians, twenty-nine gold medal winners in 2012.

Adam gently pushed their way to the front of the crowd and found standing room by the side of the stage. The buzz in the air was intellectual and reserved. Mostly young faces, searching for something to believe in, kept watch on the empty podium, which was perched in the middle of the large stage that was framed by floor-to-ceiling black curtains.
"Does he know we're here?" Sam asked Adam.

"I think he'll be expecting me, after our last conversation. He'll expect me to interfere."

"Will it do any good?"

"You're asking me now? Wasn't this sort of your idea to come here? So, it should work perfectly. Get some live TV airtime. Sell the truth. Everyone will believe me, Dove is exposed, then we go for ice cream with Lucy before bedtime."

"So, you have no plan then," Sam responded.

"Everything is planned."

"Riddles again."

A young girl cradling some books, raised a finger to her lips and looked at Adam and Sam.

There was an instant hush over the crowd as two spotlights lit the podium and the house lights dimmed. It had all the feeling of a big show about to commence.

The shiny hardwood floors gleamed as another spotlight followed the short and heavyset dean across the stage, who stopped just to the right of the podium. He put one hand on the podium and spoke with the aid of a lapel microphone. "Ladies and gentlemen," he said in a short burst, as if he had difficulty breathing. "We are pleased, today, to have Mr. Nat Fossano, a former terrorist who has converted into a global humanitarian, speak to us about his amazing transformation and his appeal to the world for change and peace. As he said to me a few minutes ago backstage, he wants to the slap the world so hard in the face that it wakes up and realizes what it's doing is wrong and that it has the power to change." The dean paused for a moment as people applauded. "He will also speak about challenges facing the Middle East, as he perceives them. And how he believes we can fix them."

The dean looked to his left, where he made eye contact with Dove, who waited in the wings, flanked by bodyguards. "I have been truly inspired by this young man's ability to touch on the essence of critical issues, and at the maturity in his approach for solutions. Not sure where he has been hiding his entire young life, maybe a compound in India"—no one laughed—"but I, like many others, am ecstatic at his own incredible awakening, his transformation, sincerity, and how he is inspiring millions of people around the globe. And those changes he has gone through, we wish and pray that every terrorist would embrace."

Applause rippled through the crowd. A few people whistled.

"And of course, we can now add 'hero' to his résumé after he selflessly threw himself on top of the princess to save her life." Another round of applause broke out. "Without further ado, I give you Mr. Nat Fossano, aka Dove, our dove of peace!" The dean clapped, triggering a thundering standing ovation from the audience.

Dove's entrance was marked by the blaring of the song "Instant Karma" by John Lennon. The image of a large blue dove lit up on a large screen behind him. The dove slowly flapped its wings, circling on the screen then veered off onto the ceiling and around the room.

The applause built as the dove, which appeared to be 3D, was joined by a several more doves, which then all joined to form a peace sign above the crowd on the ceiling. Whistles and cheering erupted.

Dove glanced up at the glowing blue, peace sign made of the delicately drawn birds. These students were creative, inspired and mislead, he thought.

The doves reminded him of the day the missile destroyed his home and family. He was in the cellar getting wine for the family dinner when it hit. It took half a day to remove the rubble and rescue him. He was the only survivor. His brother was at the University of Baghdad that night, working on a seismic project. The US intelligence agency knew Dove was in the house that night and knew he was a leader in his cell. They must have had drones or other sophisticated devices he was not even aware of yet, monitoring him. *That is why we must crush them and their allies—they are too powerful and think they're God! Deciding who lives and dies!*

Dove took a deep breath and whistled it out as he adjusted his jacket. He forced a smile, peeked out at the audience, and then thought to himself; *follow me to the slaughter, dumb bastards.*

Adam stared up at the images of the Doves. He thought of his family as the image faded and a spotlight went to the corner of the stage where he anticipated his brother's entrance. *I'm going to end this here, now.*

Lobato was ready. Target locked on. Just another day at the office, he convinced himself.

MARCH 2015

Contact the author:

Email: mario@mariomolinari.com

Website: mariomolinari.com

Thank you for buying this book!

Grazie!